D1409698

BROKEN little RICH girls

2

K MADDISON PUBLICATIONS

Copyright © 2018 by Dominique Thomas All Rights Reserved.

No part of this publication may be reproduced, distributed, or transmitted in any form or by any means, including photocopying, recording, or other electronic or mechanical methods, without prior written permission of the publisher, except in the case of brief quotations embodied in reviews and certain other noncommercial uses permitted by copyright law.

This book is a work of fiction. All names, characters, locations, and incidents are products of the author's imagination. Any resemblance to actual person's, things, living or dead, locales, or events is entirely coincidental.

Hey ladies! Let's first give glory to God. This year is coming to an end and while it was hectic for me and a lot of other people lets be thankful, we made it. We're still standing and it's by His grace. After writing part one, I was drained. The women took a lot out of me on top of my everyday life but that's what a good story is all about. For part two I felt they needed redeeming. Heck, we all do at some point in our life.

Psalms 26:11 But as for me, I will walk in mine integrity: redeem me, and be merciful unto me.

Ladies you all showed up and showed out for this series! The messages I received warmed my heart. There were so many women that could relate to these broken women. I pray that if you are dealing with any of these issues you find your peace. I really do.

I love these characters. I have to admit it felt good to write about real women dealing with pain. Enjoy the story and let me know how you like part two.

Remind yourself, nobody's built like you, you design yourself...

-Jay-Z-

Prologue
Present Day

—···⟨♡⟩···—

Anger, worry, and fear clung heavy to the inside of the sedan. As the sun began to peek through the clouds the day was alive with energy. Many people had already started their day while two individuals struggled to understand what was happening to them.

"Miko what the fuck you saying!" Zyir barked so loudly it caused her to jump.

Miko glanced over at Zyir and noticed her window was shattered with pieces beginning to fall onto the street. Her heart pumped faster as she saw the rage filling his eyes.

"Zyir, please she needs us," she said nervously.

Zyir shook his head. A deep scowl sat on his handsome face.

"Nah, don't do that. You hid this from me, Miko. From me? Why!"

Miko stared straight ahead as she drove at an alarming rate. Cop cars tailed her vehicle making other drivers pull to the side not wanting to get caught in the car chase.

"Because I was scared! I was only a kid Zyir!" Miko cried.

Her tears fell in gallops down her cheeks. One cop car quickly turned into three as Miko turned onto the street closest to her parents' home. She caught sight of Enika struggling with a burly, Caucasian man and she gasped.

"Oh, fuck nah!" Zyir griped and jumped out of the vehicle.

Miko rushed to place the car in park and was out before she could blink chasing after him. The police officers parked behind Miko's vehicle and followed suit with their guns drawn.

Zyir reached the abductor first and hit him with a lethal two-piece. Some shit the heavy man had never seen before that immediately dazed him. Miko cried as she ran up on Enika and pulled her into her arms tightly.

"Who the fuck you thought you was gone take my nigga!" Zyir growled and kicked the man in his face.

Before Zyir could deliver another lethal blow, he was tasered by a tall, dark male officer. Miko's eyes widened as Zyir's body seized up and he began to shake.

"He was protecting our daughter! That motherfucka was trying to rape her! Why the fuck are you doing that!" she yelled.

Another officer walked up with his gun out. His chest heaved up and down as he assessed the situation. Muffled yelling caught his attention and he walked over to the white van. He opened the back door and his eyes doubled in size. Six underage girls lay tied up by the hands and the feet with scarfs around their mouths. He pulled out his phone and mumbled something into the receiving in while shaking his head.

"Enika please stay right here," Miko mumbled as she let her go.

Miko stood up and when she headed for Zyir the male officer that tasered him held his hand up.

"Wait! Let us get this situation under control. If that's your daughter, then stay by her. You still broke several laws and will be attained," he replied curtly before pulling the cords from Zyir.

Miko went back to Enika's side as Zyir's cousin pulled up. He jumped out of his police car and ran over to Zyir. Miko was able to exhale as she watched him explain the situation. Miko grabbed Enika and pulled her back into her arms. Miko held her tightly as thoughts of her being taken away flashed through her mind.

"I'm so happy you're okay," she whispered into her hair.

"Its other girls in the truck Miko," Enika said as the cops helped the girls out of the back of the van.

Miko glanced back at the van and her tears fell as she watched the young girls cry and hug the police officers.

This was real. Enika was *that* close to being taken away from her. Never did she want to feel that fear again. That shit was frightening. Something she would wish on no one.

"Thank you, God," she whispered.

Although she wasn't a churchgoer she believed in the Most High and new it was only because of him that her daughter was okay.

"Yes, thank God. We gotta call momma," Enika said and hugged Miko back tightly.

Miko's body went stiff at Enika's words. Miko eyed Zyir as he came towards her with a scary glare on his handsome face. It was all out, and this was a truth that she couldn't sweep under the rug. She had to face it head on whether she wanted to or not.

In Philly...

With each squeeze of the trigger, her heart pumped faster. The gunshots were loud, almost ear-splitting. The spark from the bullet leaving the chamber lit up the vast bedroom. Immediately Snowden ducked for cover. The bedroom door opened, and Jeremiah stepped in with a sneaky grin on his handsome face. He glanced down at the shell casings and chuckled.

The pistol in his hand seemed colossal to Jerzey as she worriedly stared at it.

"You know life got a way of being funny as fuck sometimes. Let's not get shit twisted, I never been a friendly nigga, but I show love. If I see you and you hungry and I can help, I will. My thing is don't bite the hand that feeds you and if I need a favor later on you bets make sure you can return that shit. I 'ont do all that fake shit. Gnash was cool until he wasn't. Nah, mean? He started dipping in the pack and he owed up. I let that nigga slide for a month off love, but business is always business ma. It's never personal," Jeremiah replied, and his words caused anxiety to course through Jerzey's veins like lava.

Jerzey staggered back and her eyes shot to Snowden who was now standing with his own weapon back out.

"Jeremiah, fuck youse saying?" Snowden asked breathing hard.

Jeremiah shrugged. The nonchalant demeanor he carried with his large frame only angered Jerzey. She swallowed hard as he aimed his pistol her way.

"I'm saying I shot this bitch once and she ain't die. I can't have nobody having nothing over me. She a liability and you know what that means. She gotta fucking—"

The blast from the gun made her scream out in shock. The bullet tore through the side of Jeremiah's head and flew into Snowden's wall. His body fell immediately and Jerzey screamed again as her body shook violently. Snowden moved around the bedroom silently as he picked up the shell casings. Jerzey watched him as her heart thundered in her chest. She was in complete shock at him killing his brother.

His own flesh and blood.

"*Snowden,*" she whispered scared out of her mind.

Snowden shook his head. His face was tight with anger. He briefly glanced Jerzey's way before clearing his throat.

"Leave the gun and go. Act like this shit never happened," he said in a gritty tone.

Jerzey's body grew tense at his words. She stood up and placed the gun on his bed. She watched Snowden lay a blanket over his brother and her stomach knotted up. She didn't wanna leave. She wanted to thank him for saving her life. Even help clean up the mess they'd made.

"Snowden I'm sorry. I'm so sorry—"

"Aye! I said get the fuck out! On some real shit youse this fucking close to getting clipped in this bitch, get the fuck out Jerzey! Go!" he roared with watery lenses.

Jerzey rushed to exit the bedroom. She tripped as she ran down the stairs and her tears fell rapidly down her face. She held her hand over her mouth and cried harder.

Her eyes ventured up the steps towards the bedroom and almost like he could feel her lurking, his body emerged in the doorway. He was now in his boxers with gloves on. With his alluring eyes hard as flint he glared down at her.

"Jerzey, go," he muttered in a pained tone.

His pain collided with her's and all she wanted to do was make it easier for him. She used the little strength she had to stand up. Jerzey walked out of the townhome on depletion. She was shoeless as well as heartless as she walked down the sidewalk aimlessly.

Her heart was in the possession of the man that had just killed his own brother to protect her. Jerzey was in a state of shock at what had gone down.

One

The wedding was one for the books. It had not only made the local news station and a few local magazines it was also featured in a national religious magazine that her mother was extremely proud of. However, the mention of her being solely his wife and not a doctor had her heated. Her new husband might not have picked up on the anger, but her daughter surely did.

Nelly walked around on eggshells hoping not to set her off. Her bedroom stayed clean. She spoke and said all of the right things and had gone days without taking an actual bath simply, so her hair would be intact. She'd resorted to washing up in the sink so that she wouldn't wreak of foul odor.

Thomas smiled as Nelly entered into the kitchen. She was famished and looking to eat an actual meal while her mother was napping.

"Good afternoon Arnelle. How are you?" he asked with a big smile covering his face.

Thomas was always gone and when he was home, he was in his study, reading the bible or talking with an associate. Nelly liked him but couldn't understand how someone as kind as him could fall for her mother?

Jacklyn was the devil in her eyes.

"I'm fine Thomas. How are you?"

"Thomas? Is he not my husband?" Jacklyn asked stepping into the large kitchen.

Even at five in the evening, she wore pleated pants with a silk blouse and four-inch heels. She looked outlandishly beautiful with her soft, flowy curls and freshly done up face.

Thomas stood up from the island and greeted her with a smile. Jacklyn walked into his embrace and as she hugged him, she ice grilled Nelly. Nelly could feel the hairs stand up on her back as she stared at her mother helplessly.

"I'm not her biological father baby. Be nice to the girl and relax. She's scared to fully be herself because of you. Even some of the sisters at the church noticed how hard you are on her. Kids rebel when they're being pushed too far. Let her be a child. Trust me she's perfect," Thomas said and placed a kiss to Jacklyn's forehead before grabbing his car keys.

"I have some work to do at my father's church. I'll be back in a few. Have a good night Arnelle," he said before walking away.

Nelly swallowed hard as she watched him exit the kitchen. Her mother leaned against the island as Nelly stood nervously at the refrigerator.

"I know you're happy now. Not only am I just his wife. I'm also a bad mother that doesn't allow for her screw up of a daughter to be herself. Congratulations! You've successfully made a fool of me. What do you have to say for yourself?" she asked.

Nelly closed her eyes as her heart thundered in her chest. She could hear the anger in her mother's sophisticated tone. She was fucking livid with her and she would pay. Nelly knew that this beating would be painful. She was tired, so tired of it all.

For once she wanted Jacklyn to be a mother to her. A normal mother that loved you, flaws, and all.

"Mom, I'm sorry. I didn't do anyth—"

Slap!

After the strike to her face, Nelly was shoved into the stainless-steel refrigerator. Nelly's small body winced in pain as Jacklyn unleashed a barrage of anger out on her. The hits came quickly and were placed all over her body. It was as if Jacklyn didn't care who saw her battered appearance. She was out for blood.

Nelly's blood to be exact.

"This is the last time you will embarrass me! You're just like your fucking no good father! A fucking disgrace! A mistake I should have flushed out of me!" she yelled angrily.

Nelly cried as she held her hands over her head.

"What.... what are you doing Jacklyn?" Thomas asked in shock.

In his hands were the flowers he'd run out to grab her from the corner store. They fell as he took in the scene before him. He rushed over to Nelly and her mother and pulled Jacklyn off of Nelly. His brown eyes narrowed in anger as he looked down at the battered-up Nelly. Her lip was busted, her right eye was swelling up and her fair skin was covered with dark bruises.

That quickly her appearance had morphed into something horrible.

Thomas shook Jacklyn as he glared into her eyes.

"What the hell are you in here doing to her!" he yelled angrily.

Jacklyn's stunned eyes peered up at her husband. Her lip trembled before she began to cry.

"I'm...I'm...sick baby. I need God to fix me," she cried out.

Nelly's small feet moved on their own accord at her mother's words. Nelly could see by the look in Thomas's angry eyes that he would give in. Already he'd gone from shaking Jacklyn to holding her loosely.

Nelly raced out of the large home and her feet hit the pavement in determination. In her two-piece pajama set with her skin burning from the beating of her mother she ran.

Nelly ran for her life.

Nelly ran for her sanity.

Nelly ran for a chance at life.

A real one because if she had to live one more day in her mothers' home, she would take her own life without giving it a second thought.

Harsh breathing filled the room. By the window, AC blew cooling off the already chilled space. With every turn of her sore limbs, her head would ache. The kind of pain that made you wince and scrunch up your nose in pain. In her sleep, she was with him. Together they rested in the bed while smiling and it made her happy. It felt so real that she didn't want to wake up still that irritating ass headache wouldn't let up.

Nelly groaned and slowly opened one eye at a time. Her vision gradually cleared and landed on her fiancé. Long cat-like scratches marred his handsome face. His head was bandaged at the top while his left eye was red with his blood vessel busted in the eye. Nelly swallowed hard as he sat up in the seat.

Despite his battered face, his clothing was immaculate. Jannero wore blue jeans with butter Timberlands and a crisp white V-neck. His favorite chain hung from his neck as he scowled her way. The anger brewing in his eyes was enough to make Nelly close her own eyes in shame.

She'd done this to him. Actually, harmed him to the point that his head was bandaged up. It was unnerving and sad. Real fucking sad that she'd lost control of herself in such a way.

"I'm sorry," she whispered sincerely.

Jannero cleared his throat.

"Arnelle..."

Her name angrily spilling from his lips made her stomach queasy. The growl of his voice wasn't lost on her. He was mad as fuck and she could feel it. If only she could go back and change what she'd done to him then she would. Nelly would take it all back.

"Is the baby okay?" she asked quietly with closed lids.

Jannero stood up and walked over to Nelly. Her eyes remained shut as he grabbed her hand. As he began to pull off her engagement ring, they sprung open. Nelly stared worriedly up at Jannero as he gently tugged off the ring.

Jannero placed the diamond in his pocket and leaned down. His Bond. No 9 cologne, intoxicating even in the hectic moment wafted over the bed Nelly was lying in. Jannero grabbed her face and as Nelly's eyes watered his grip tightened.

"When you get out, call me and I'll let you see him," he spoke glaring down at her.

"...What? Jannero, I'm sorry. I'm so fucking sorry baby! I thought you were cheating on me. You had that hoe all up on you and she grabbed your dick!"

Jannero shook his head. He let go of Nelly's face and closed his eyes. His tall, toned body swayed for a moment before he looked back at Nelly. Nelly could see that besides anger, pain also covered his face. She watched him take a few deep calming breaths and rub his red eye gently.

"Fuck this bitch Nero. Let's go and the doctor said you need rest. Jasir is already with Snowden," his sister said stepping into the hospital room.

Nelly went from worried to angry in a matter of seconds as her eyes darted over to Taya. She'd known his sister for years and *never* had she spoken to her in such a way.

"Taya this is between me and my fiancé. You need to leave, and you might wanna watch how you speak to me," Nelly warned her.

Taya's head cocked to the side and Jannero quickly went over to his sister.

"Speak to you? Bitch, I'm not Nero. I'll beat your ass and smile while doing it. You could have fucking killed my brother and I'm supposed to let that ride? Shit, I wish he was with his ex, at least she wasn't abusive to him. He should have fucked you up the first time you slapped him! Old dumb ass hoe that can't do shit right. Hell, yeah he's done with you, we all are!"

Nelly's eyes welled with tears and she began to cry. Many emotions swept through her body as she laid in the bed. Anger, shame, and confusion were just a few. She'd fucked up, but they were family. Jannero couldn't be done with her because she wasn't done with him. Nelly loved him too much to ever give up on him and she thought he loved her the same way.

Her eyes connected with Jannero's and she noticed he was teary-eyed as well. He cleared his throat before swiping his left hand over his hair that was in need of a cut.

"You have a blood clot on your uterus that caused you to bleed. They said it was a threatened miscarriage, but the baby is good. Don't even let that miscarriage shit run through your head, ma. We having this baby, safe and healthy. You can see to it that it happens by relaxing and getting some rest," he replied.

Taya shook her head with her nose flaring.

"Fuck rest somebody needs to lock this crazy hoe up! Trust we gone see to it that you stay far away from my nephew," she said angrily.

Jannero glared down at his sister and relaxed her with one firm look. He subtly shook his head before turning back to Nelly.

"Shits not even going down like that. Regardless we still family and we not bout to do this shit. Arnelle get some rest. Jerzey's coming up here to get you. You can go to the apartment downtown. I'll hit you up later to check on you."

Nelly shook her fuzzy head. He couldn't leave. He was supposed to stay with her. Yes, they had problems, but they could work through them. The issues they had wasn't enough for them to break-up. None of this was making sense to her.

"Nero wait. What's going on? What do you mean you'll hit me up later? Baby, please don't go."

Jannero glanced up at the ceiling and sucked in a deep breath. He exhaled as he peered back down at Nelly.

"Just get better. We'll discuss all that other shit later. Jerzey is headed here now and she'll fly home with youse," he replied tiredly.

Very seldom did Jannero speak like a Philly native so when he did Nelly knew he was upset. She rested back on the bed and stared up at the ceiling as Jannero and his sister exited the room.

The second the door closed Nelly's lip trembled and her eyes watered. Silently she cried again as she ignored the pounding headache she had.

"I'm sorry," she whispered with a heavy tongue.

Two days ghosted by and Nelly found herself being discharged from the hospital. A quiet unlively Jerzey stood by her side. Nelly glanced over at her unmade up, all-natural girl and frowned. No colorful units, lashes or cute attire covered her chocolate friend.

"What's going on Jerzey, you good?"

Jerzey's eyes found Nelly and she smiled. It was tight-lipped and fake. Plastic as hell that Nelly immediately saw through.

"I'm good, just happy you're okay. Nero's sending us home on the jet and everything, so you can be comfortable. Are you ready?"

Nelly pursed her lips. Her fair skin was lifeless, and void of the pregnancy glow she had been sporting. She too looked like hell in her navy leggings and logo tee that Jerzey brought up to the hospital for her. Her curly hair was a tangled-up mess while dry patches decorated her skin but none of it mattered. The only thing on her agenda was getting to her family.

"Yep, I'm feeling much better. Let's go," she replied before walking off.

Jerzey quietly followed after her friend. They exited the hospital and Jerzey passed Nelly a set of car keys. Nelly stared down at the fob with the capital *L* on it and she frowned.

"This is mine?"

Jerzey nodded. She pointed to the black GX 460 and cleared her throat.

"He got it yesterday for you. He said he didn't want you to see the car and have flashbacks of what happened.

Even with so much going on he's still thinking of you. It shows that the love he has for you isn't conditional," Jerzey replied and walked over to the shiny new truck.

Nelly took a deep breath and sighed. She absentmindedly rubbed her bare ring finger.

"Nero," she whispered before walking off. Nelly got into the truck and glanced over at her girl.

"Now will you really tell me why you're so quiet?" she asked her friend.

Jerzey quickly shook her head.

"I'm just tired. Will *you* really tell me why you assaulted that man? Nelly this is crazy, and you could have killed him. I saw his hospital papers. He has a fucking concussion."

Nelly drove off and glanced over at her friend.

"And I told him I was sorry. I get angry Jerzey and I become someone that I don't like but I can't stop it. I kind of blackout."

Nelly shrugged while Jerzey frowned at her.

"Nelly that's fucking crazy. Do you think you're becoming your mom?"

Nelly's truck slowed up. She peered over at Jerzey questioningly. Her chest heaved up and down as she stared Jerzey's way.

"Miko told you my business?"

Jerzey sighed and her eyes dropped down to her lap. She shook her head as she looked back up at Nelly.

"No, I read your diary years ago. We'd just gotten in from the club and you had it on your nightstand. I know it was wrong and I'm sorry for violating your privacy, but I was curious. You never speak about your family and well I now see why. The same way men can sometimes become their father after witnessing abuse women can too. I think you should do counseling, so Nero can see that you're trying to change," Jerzey suggested.

Nelly's hand tightened on the wheel.

"Jerzey I regret what I did, and he knows I'm sorry. However, I'm not becoming my fucking mother. You have no idea how heartless that bitch was to me. I'm nothing like her."

Jerzey nodded.

"And you would never hit Jasir? What about when he gets older and becomes disrespectful, then what? If you have this inside of you, you're liable to beat him up as well," Jerzey replied.

Nelly turned onto the street of Jannero's sister home and pulled up behind a black Range Rover. The same truck she knew belonged to her fiancé.

"Jerzey I'ma ask for you to never repeat that bullshit again. I would never beat on my kid. Ever. I'll be right back," Nelly replied and exited her truck.

Jerzey quickly followed after her and Nelly frowned while glancing back at her.

"I said I would be right back, Jerzey! Damn, stop acting like that," she fussed.

Jerzey ignored her rant as Snowden stepped outside with Taya in tow. Taya held a large butcher knife in her hand as she glared at Nelly.

"Aye, put that shit up, this Nelly," Snowden reprimanded Taya.

Taya shook her head as she looked at Nelly. Nelly began to walk up the steps and Jerzey grabbed her arm attempting to hold her back.

"We just want Jasir," Jerzey said speaking shyly.

Nelly's face fell into a frown.

"No, where is Nero? Now he can't talk to me? I'm his fiancé and he has my son. The same son I brought into this fucking world. I'm leaving with both of them," Nelly said and balled up her fist.

"Nelly please let's just go," Jerzey whispered eyeing Snowden.

Snowden took a step back and shook his head.

"I know youse see his truck but he's really not here Nelly. Jasir is but we can't let him go with youse," Snowden replied.

Nelly's head whipped back in shock at Snowden's words.

"Who the fuck gone stop me? That's my son Snowden and I'm taking him with me. I fucking wish you all would try to keep me from getting my son!"

Nelly pulled away from Jerzey and dashed up the steps. Jerzey ran after her as Snowden grabbed an angry Taya up into his arms. Taya swung her arms wildly with rage brewing in her slanted brown eyes. In the process, she slashed the top of Nelly's shoulder.

Nelly ran up on Taya and hit her with a left hook that made her immediately drop the knife. Taya's eyes closed, and her body went limp in Snowden's arms.

"What the fuck is going on!" Jannero shouted running up on the porch.

Nelly halted from running in the house and glanced back at her man. Her heart raced as she stared up into his eyes. Just weeks ago, they were discussing their upcoming wedding. Enjoying her pregnancy and trying to beat a case together. Overnight they'd become opponents instead of lovers and that saddened her. Her shoulders slumped, and she sighed. She gave Jannero a dampened smile and his nose flared. Nelly watched Jannero take in the chaotic scene before his eyes shot back her way. Angrily he snatched her up and led her off the porch. Jannero pulled Nelly down the steps and over to her vehicle.

"Do you love me?" he asked leaning into her. His warm minty breath brushed against her skin as his body pinned her to the truck.

Nelly nodded while breathing hard.

"You know I do."

Jannero grabbed her face and pulled her head up towards him.

"You gotta stop Nelly. Just cause you say sorry don't mean shit alright. You fucked up and you almost killed our baby in the process. I want you to go back to the apartment and get some rest. In the morning take the jet and go home."

Nelly closed her eyes as she processed his words. This was really happening. In the hospital, she'd convinced herself that it was a dream. That he was upset and needed to calm down. However, days had passed, and they were still apart. Her heart couldn't take the things he was saying to her.

"And what about you two? I can't leave without my family. Nero that's my son," she said sadly with tears filling her eyes.

Jannero nodded. Pain covered his handsome peanut butter toned face as he stared down at Nelly. Even in the midst of the storm Nelly still found herself admiring her man. Images of all the happy moments they'd shared flashed through her mind like a movie. Nelly then remembered there not so jovial moments and she swallowed hard. Sadly, she'd had a hand in creating those times. The scars covering his skin pained her deeply and as she watched him lick his thick lips she sighed. There was no way in hell she was leaving without him and her son.

The shit wasn't happening.

"And he's my son too. It's my job to protect him and that's even from you if I feel you a threat. Nelly go to Detroit and we'll see you in a few days. Okay?" he asked calmly.

Nelly swallowed hard and Jannero let her face go. He wiped away her tears and kissed her forehead.

"You fucked me up with this one here and I need some time. Go home," he said and walked away.

Nelly hugged herself as she watched Jannero trudge up his sister's steps. Jerzey rushed over to Nelly and hugged her tightly. Nelly watched Jannero enter into the home and she closed her eyes. She felt as if the ground was moving beneath her feet.

"That's my family. The only family I have besides you guys. I can't lose them."

Jerzey nodded still hugging her.

"And you won't. He loves you so much. Just give him time to get over it," she replied.

Nelly cried harder at her friends' words. She wanted to believe her but wasn't so sure if time away would be enough for him to forget and forgive the things she'd done.

Two

The sanctuary was at capacity. Black attire, soft cries, and heavy breathing occupied the large church space. In the front row sat his family. His wife, her son, and his daughter.

His sorrowing, beautiful *still* recovering daughter. Her dress was black as well. Fitted, with a sweetheart neckline. Oval black Chloe shades covered her eyes while black six-inch pumps sat on her feet. Kritt held her hand and every time she attempted to pull away, he'd hold it tighter.

Rumer swallowed hard as her flow of tears never let up.

"Now is the time for us to let the family speak. His daughter has some words to share," the reverend announced.

All eyes went to Rumer as Kritt pulled her to his side.

"You don't have to do this," he whispered.

Rumer snatched away from him and closed her eyes.

God, why? How much could one person take? She pondered solemnly. Rumer sighed and rose to her feet. She held her head high and walked with fake confidence up to the podium. She gave the reverend a tight-lipped smile before taking off her shades.

The funeral goers stared at her with empathetic gazes as she blinked a few times to clear her vision. Her lashes were laid holding up despite the heavy crying. Her unit was so nice that once it had been glued on, she'd even thought it was her real hair. It hung in soft onyx waves down her back while framing her face as red lipstick stained her lips.

Rumer cleared her throat as she felt her stomach tighten. She was hungry. Hadn't eaten in days and was close to passing the fuck out from starvation. Between recovering from a heart attack and planning her father's funeral food had been the last thing on her list of shit to do.

"I can say I'm shocked to be here," she said feebly. Rumer glanced over at her father in his white and gold casket and swallowed hard. "That man is my life. He showed me what real love is and loved me even when I didn't love myself. To learn that on the day that I suffered from a heart attack that he did as well saddens me. It makes me angry. Very *fucking* angry," she replied, and the funeral goers gasped at her choice of language.

Kritt, Rumer's mother and her girls jumped up and headed for the podium. Rumer scowled as she stared at the sea of faces crying over the loss of her father. How dare they try to mourn his death as if they loved him like she did? She scoffed as she rolled her watery eyes.

"I don't get it. He was a good man. He was good to people and he's dead. Like how, you know? Why? Why not the person that's out there doing bad things? Why not me? *God*, why didn't you just take me instead?" she asked hysterically and Kritt pulled her into his arms.

Rumer broke down as Jerzey walked over to the podium with Miko and Nelly by her side. Jerzey smiled weakly at the funeral goers that stared her way. Miko hugged Jerzey's arm as Nelly held onto Miko's hand as Kritt carried Rumer out of the sanctuary.

"Mr. Matigo was a great man. I remember the first time I met him I was so impressed. You couldn't be around him and not notice how strong he was. It was in everything that he did. To watch him and Rumer together was always a treat for us. They were very close, and Rumer is incredibly saddened by his death. The family appreciates all of you for coming out and we ask that you keep Rumer and his wife in your prayers," Jerzey said and flashed the crowd a small smile.

Rumer cried hysterically on Kritt's shoulder until Jerzey, Nelly, and Miko stepped into the fellowship hall that was hosting the repass. Rumer's friends pulled her into a circle and together they embraced Rumer. She cried for the loss of her father as her friends rallied around her. Rumer's knees gave out and she dropped down to the ground. Her friends dropped down with her and Jerzey rubbed her back lovingly.

"God, we ask for understanding. We ask for peace for Rumer and comfort for her family," Jerzey swallowed back her own tears before continuing. "Please comfort our friend, Lord," Jerzey prayed and when she opened her eyes her own tears fell freely down her face.

"Can I see her?" Kritt's mother asked walking up.

Her cheeks were wet as well but she was more composed than everyone else in the fellowship hall.

"That's my daughter Kristen. If she needs anything, *I'll* get it for her," Rumer's mom spoke rushing over with her church sisters.

Kritt shook his head as he looked Rumer's mother's way.

"This not about old stuff," he griped with a frown.

Rumer's mother nodded.

"Exactly, this is about my daughter losing her father," she replied emphatically, and Rumer's bloodshot red eyes shot to her mother.

"Mom, can you please go sit down? I'm okay," she said in a raspy tone.

Rumer's mom Rachel reluctantly nodded and walked away with her church sisters. Rumer stood on shaky legs and grabbed Kritt's mother's hand. She led her over to the largest table in the room and they sat down. It was intended for the family and as Rumer took a seat another tear fell from her eye.

"Your father really loved you, Rumer. You must know that and while he was honest about needing rest, he did embellish the truth about his health. He's been suffering from high blood pressure and stress for years. He's always pushed himself to do more. That was just him," she told her.

Rumer sighed giving Kristen a weak smile. She wasn't ready to speak of her father in the past tense. Rumer wouldn't dare say she loved him, it was still "*loves*" to her because the emotions were very much present.

"I know, I guess I get that from him."

Kritt's mother nodded staring Rumer's way.

"You do and that's why he wrote you a letter. Actually, he wrote you and Kritt one, but I have it with me. It was a *what if* letter and I swear he had no inkling that something such as this would occur, but he was prepared.

Please read the letter and process what it's saying. His words were, of course, coming from the heart," she replied.

Kritt's mother went into her bag and pulled out the letter. She passed it to Rumer and Rumer glanced down at the white envelope. It felt weighty for it to only be two sheets of paper as she held it in her small hand. Her worried eyes glanced back up at Kritt's mother.

"Was he happy before he died?" she asked quietly.

Kritt's mother sniffled. Her lenses watered, and her tears then fell.

"The happiest he'd been in years. We got to sit on a yacht and just be us. He was at peace out there Rumer and that's what he wants for you. Real happiness."

Rumer nodded. Her tongue felt heavy as she processed her step mother's words.

"But does that exist?" she wanted to know.

Kritt's mother leaned towards Rumer and caressed her wet cheeks.

"We create the life we want to live. Don't wait for happiness to find you, you create it yourself. I'm going to miss my husband dearly and right now I just feel like crawling into a grave beside him, but I find peace in knowing he was okay. I find peace in knowing that he didn't suffer when he passed, and he was happy. And he would want us to be that way as well," she replied before pulling Rumer into her arms.

Hours later Rumer stood in the middle of her bedroom with Kritt by her side. The day had been a nightmare. Torturous even and she was drained. Slowly she stepped out of her heels as Kritt rubbed her back.

He'd been with her every step of the way still she was upset with him. His lies mixed with deceit and possible baby on the way changed her feelings towards him. He was no longer viewed as her rock but just another fuck nigga in her eyes. He'd done her the same as Takim.

"Let's take a shower," he suggested and grabbed her hand.

Rumer followed quietly after Kritt allowing him to lead her into the bathroom. Although he was on her shit list, she was grateful to have him there at the moment. Her girls wanted to stay back but Rumer didn't want to be up under everyone also she could sense they were all dealing with their own share of problems.

"Come on ma," Kritt said after taking off her dress.

Naked Rumer followed him into the shower and he picked her up. Kritt carried Rumer under the largest shower head and she closed her eyes. Her heart pounded in her chest as the hot water beat down against her soft skin.

"Let it out," Kritt whispered and kissed her lips.

Rumer began to cry as he pulled her away from the water. Kritt sensually kissed her lips as his member without direction found her center. Slowly he thrust up into Rumer making her moan out in pleasure.

"I'm sorry baby. I'm so fucking sorry," he apologized driving his penis in and out of her slowly.

Rumer whimpered as it stretched her walls. His dick felt so good it made her body tremble with pleasure. Rumer hugged him tighter wanting to forget her pain, shit *needing* to forget it.

"Please don't stop," she begged.

Kritt's teeth chattered together and he groaned. He grabbed a handful of Rumer's wet extensions and yanked them back. With one hand on her hip and the other one holding her head, he fucked her aggressively until her body fell apart for him.

From the mahogany desk that held a pristine shine to it down to the butter soft leather chocolate chairs, the office screamed luxury. The building was in a pricey part of the Northville suburbs and while the office was satisfying to look at the occasion made everyone in attendance uneasy.

Rumer sat at the middle of the table next to Kritt and her mother.

Her mother.

Yes, even she was shocked to learn her mom had been placed in her father's last Will and Testament. Rumer also wondered how his wife felt about that?

"Sorry about my impromptu call. As you all know this is the reading of Sheldon's Will. He actually sent me over this copy two months prior to his passing. Again, I'm very sorry for your loss," the prestigious widely known lawyer Goldstein said taking his seat.

Rumer nodded as she swallowed hard. She'd eaten a bowl of grapes with cottage cheese and was fatigued. Her body was literally running on fumes.

"Can we hurry this along?" she asked in a slurred voice.

The attention in the room shifted to Rumer and Kritt raised his brows. He grabbed her hand and kissed the back of it.

"You good? You look sick?"

Rumer's mother stared at Kritt with disdain and rolled her eyes.

"That's not appropriate behavior and she is far from good. On top of her father passing away Rumer has a lot of issues that she needs to fix," her mom replied.

Rumer glared at her mother and the lawyer cleared his throat.

"Let's proceed. I Sheldon Matigo leave in my departure half a million dollars to the American Heart Association. I also leave half a million dollars to the Boys and Girls Club of Detroit. To Kritt who is my son even when his stubborn ass didn't want to be, I leave $1,000,000. Take the money and follow your dreams son. I believe in you. To my wife, the one true love of my life I leave $5,000,000. I love you always and forever baby, you made life worth living."

The lawyer's words emanated snorts from Rumer's mother Rachel. Rumer shook her head as the lawyer continued.

"To Rachel, we haven't been friends in a long time but because you gave me Rumer, that makes you someone of importance to me. I leave you $100,000. Take the money and get back on your feet so my baby girl can get her peace of mind back. That should be enough to do so and if not, Rumer can give you more."

"That's it? I had his daughter and raised her and that's what the hell he leaves me? I planned on donating most of the money to my church so I'm going to need more," Rumer's mother argued angrily.

Kritt's mother glared Rachel's way and shook her head.

"He didn't have to leave you a damn thing honey. You took his daughter and hid her for years from him all because he no longer loved you. You then bad mouthed him whenever you could, and you believe he owes you something? You are out of your damn mind. I have to go," she snapped and stood up.

Rachel frowned as Kritt's mother briskly exited the room. Rumer glanced over at Kritt with tired eyes.

"Can you go check on her?"

Kritt nodded and followed after his mom. Rumer looked at the lawyer and smiled.

"I apologize about that. You can finish now."

The lawyer nodded. He went to another page and cleared his throat.

"To my Rumer. The sunshine of my life I leave you my company. You are to do with it what you please. I leave you the home in the Hampton's because you love it so much. I leave you my yacht and also $30,000,000. My only goal in life was for you to be happy my beautiful daughter. Take the money and wipe your ass with it for all I care. All I ask is that you do something to make yourself smile. Papa loves you and while I'm not here with you in the physical form I will always be with you in spirit. I promise."

Rumer's mother gasped as Rumer stared straight ahead. Her chest heaved up and down as she mulled over the words the lawyer had just spoken to her. While many families prayed for the moment they received their parent's money she detested it. Instead of relief or hope, she felt anger. All of the things the lawyer called off paled in comparison to her having her father alive. Nothing no matter the price tag could replace him.

"Wow," her mom whispered.

The lawyer nodded with raised brows.

"Yes, he also left stocks and bonds to you as well Rumer. It's all here. You are a very wealthy young woman right now," he said and smiled.

Rumer grabbed the papers as he slid them over and glanced down at them. Money or her father? She'd always choose the latter without having to give it a second thought.

"But I don't have him," she whispered almost inaudible and when she dropped her head more tears cascaded down her face. "What the fuck is the point of being wealthy if you're unhappy? My life is in shambles right now. This money just won't make that pain go away. It won't!" she declared, and her mother pulled her into a hug as she cried into her chest.

—···〈♡〉···—

Loud ruckus was the normal setting for the biker club. On the first floor, the prospects flooded the bar with their regular banter while the four friends sat on the second floor. Rumer sat on the sofa with a bottle of tequila in her hand. Her regal look did nothing for the mood she was in. The black tattered boyfriend jeans that she'd paired with a black bodysuit and long ankle length cardigan showed off her small frame. She was thinning away and had noticed all of her friends stare at her body but was thankful no one pressed the issue. Huge Mui Mui shades covered her eyes as her hair sat in soft waves down her back.

"Remember when we took your pops car in high school? That fucking Ferrari. He was pissed!" Miko said with a glum smile.

Rumer nodded solemnly. She took another swig of the tequila and shook off the burn. The crazy thing was she welcomed the sting. Praying it would kick in and take her away from the pain plaguing her heart.

"Yeah, we took our dumb asses downtown. Hit that fucking cop car and shit. I think he only let us go because we were crying so hard," she mumbled.

Jerzey rubbed her leg and Rumer rested her head on Jerzey's shoulder. She blinked and when she opened her eyes her tears fell again. They slid beneath her shades as Nelly rubbed her arm.

"He loved you so much. He was an amazing father. Even in his death, he ensured that you would be okay. If only everyone could do that," Nelly told her.

Miko nodded with a sad smile gracing her face.

"Yeah, well take it from me. People can only do what they can. Everyone doesn't have the means to leave their kids millions of dollars. Rumer is one of the lucky few and I'm sure she doesn't wanna discuss this right now," Miko replied staring at Rumer.

Rumer nodded. The tequila running through her system made her eyes lower and her body grow warm. *Finally,* she was feeling the effects of it.

"Please not now. You guys know how much I loved him. To not have him here really hurts me. It's like who am I supposed to lean on now?"

Jerzey cleared her throat.

"God, then us and your mom. In time it will get easier to deal with. Still, the pain will be there. Pray for comfort and remember that we will always be here for you. No matter what," Jerzey replied staring at her.

Rumer removed her shades and rubbed her eyes.

"Rumer, we need to talk!" Kritt's pregnant friend yelled running up the steps.

Rumer slowly sat up as she watched Kritt appear out of nowhere and stop the beauty. Kritt spoke aggressively in her ear and yanked her down the steps.

"Let me go, she deserves to know!" the pregnant woman yelled making Miko stand up.

"Kritt you can let her go. What she gotta say to our friend?" Miko asked.

Kritt stopped mid-step and glared down at the pregnant woman. The woman cowered under his heated gaze and her shoulders slumped. She shoved his chest before storming down the steps. Kritt went after her and Miko sat down.

"What the fuck was that about?" she asked looking Rumer's way.

Rumer looked at her girls and noticed they were all staring at her. She shrugged as she gazed at all of them.

"Can we not do this right now?" she asked.

Miko nodded. She licked her lips and grabbed her own bottle of tequila.

"You're hurting, and I get it. We all have shit going on, so I won't pressure you to talk. Just know that if we let them, these niggas will drive us crazy," Miko told her.

Kritt snorted as he walked up.

"Good thing I'm a man, and not a nigga. The only thing I intend to do is bring Rumer happiness," Kritt stated.

Miko smirked as she popped the cork on the tequila.

"Kritt please, the road to hell was paved with good intentions," she replied making Rumer give her a small smile.

Three

The room was dimly lit by the flimsy table lamp that sat on the nightstand. The warm hues of brown and orange bounced at you however as the bullets from the pistol drone into Melvin's tall, burly frame none of that mattered.

Like a frightened cat, Miko jumped back and covered up her frail, underdeveloped thirteen-year-old body. She cried tears of joy as she watched her abuser fall back onto the ground. Her aunt didn't stop shooting until her gun was empty. Then her red, teary eyes flew to Miko. She grabbed a blanket off the bed and wrapped it around her crying niece as all three women in the room began to wail.

"I'm so sorry baby," she apologized hugging Miko tightly.

Miko continued to cry as she stared down at an unconscious Melvin. With blood seeping from his gunshot wounds she was praying that he was dead however with his chest heaving slowly up and down she wasn't so sure.

The building was huge with floor to ceiling windows that were always good for displays and the location was perfect. It sat on Livernois close to Eight Mile Road. The area over the years had undergone gentrification and was thriving with black-owned businesses.

Miko's heels clicked with every step that she took as she scanned the vacant renovated space. While her mind and body was tired, she looked beautiful as ever. In her slim fit jeans that were cuffed at her ankles, she wore a black top and Fendi pumps. The matching belt bag sat on her small waist as she sported her freshly done hair. Miko sighed and licked her plump lips.

"I like it. I really do this is—"

"Aye, I'ma need to speak to her alone."

The rumbling of Zyir's voice made Miko swallow hard. For the last two weeks, she'd been dodging the shit out of him. He'd cornered her at Rumer's father's funeral and only because of Rumer did he let her make it but Miko could tell he had time today.

She looked at the building owner and smiled sweetly at him. He was cute as shit and kind of reminded Rumer of the rapper *Fabolous* but with Zyir around she knew better then to flirt. She knew his patience with her had run out.

"I'm going to take this spot. Can you give us a minute please?"

The owner nodded coolly and rubbed his hands together which in turn made the diamonds on his watch sparkle.

"You want me to grab them papers beautiful?" he asked.

Zyir snarled and Miko walked over to him. She attempted to grab Zyir's hand and he snatched away from her like she had the plague. Despite him being angry he still looked sexy. He wore faded blue jeans with high top multi-colored Nike Dunks and a black hoodie that showed his own logo. Hanging from his neck was a rose gold chain with his business name spelled out in diamonds. No more was Zyir's dreads that he was known for rocking instead he donned a low-cut fade with an immaculate line-up. Miko was shocked to see the dreads gone but had to admit the fade suited him better. Made him look manlier if that were possible and only added to his sexiness. Miko admired his looks until his hand grabbing her neck snapped her from her reverie. It wasn't abusive, hell she liked it rough, but the quick move had caught her off guard.

"Fuck this building. Take a ride with me," he demanded and let her go.

Zyir walked off before she could respond, and the building owner stared at Miko questioningly.

"You good miss lady?" he asked pulling out his cell phone.

Miko nodded with her eyes on the door Zyir walked out of. Was she good? Hell no, she was far from it but what could the real-estate nigga do to help her? Shit, she surmised.

"Yes, I'm good. You can email me the contract."

Miko exited the building and found Zyir leaning against his truck smoking a blunt. Her eyes skated up and down the block hoping no law enforcement was around.

"Zyir you shouldn't smoke that out here."

Zyir's angry gaze shifted Miko's way and his jaw tensed.

"You just Enika's momma not mine. Chill the fuck out," he replied bitterly.

Miko cleared her throat and hugged her body tightly as he finished off his blunt as if it were a cigarette. Zyir then opened his truck door and looked down at Miko.

"Ride with me and before you say you drove on some real shit fuck your car. You been hiding out for too fucking long," he said before getting into his truck.

Miko watched the realtor slide into his own SUV before she looked back at Zyir. Zyir's nose flared as he glared her way.

"Fuck you staring at that nigga so hard for?"

Miko shook her head as she slid into his truck. It was clear to her that everything she did was now getting under Zyir's skin.

"Zyir please," she mumbled putting on her seatbelt.

Zyir sat back and placed his phone on his lap. His cinnamon shaded eyes peered at Miko intently as she pretended to be engrossed by the people walking down the sidewalk.

"Where you been staying at Nanmiko?"

Miko licked her dry lips. She closed her eyes and her heart pumped faster when Zyir's rough hand slid into her hair. His fingers grazed over her shaved side before sliding to the back of her head. He leaned towards her and Miko held her breath.

"I really wanna beat the fuck out of you. Do you know that? Do you understand how fucking hurt and angry I am at you? How I had to tell my fucking mama and family about a kid that I didn't know I had only to have them look at me crazy as fuck. On my life you gone make this shit right, now where the fuck y'all staying at?" he asked again.

Miko swallowed hard as he held the back of her neck firmly. She knew he wouldn't harm her, however, to know she'd hurt him like this made her feel guilt beyond measure.

"A hotel in Novi. The one you used to take me to," she whispered.

Zyir chuckled as he let her go. He drove off and glanced over at her.

"I need you to tell me how this shit happened. Start talking now," he said and grabbed her hand.

With anger radiating off his frame Zyir still managed to caress Miko's small hand. Miko stared down at their joined hands before looking at his handsome umber-toned face.

"After my aunt shot him, I was rushed to the hospital. It was there that my family learned about the baby. It was like Melvin didn't matter anymore as everyone tried to process that I was having a child. I was five months pregnant and didn't know it. I didn't even look pregnant, but they said it was because I was so small...." Miko stopped talking and Zyir squeezed her hand gently.

"Keep going," he murmured.

Miko slouched in her seat.

"I was the only person really checking for him. I even had a detective on my side," Miko smiled at the thought of the one man she felt was determined as her to get Melvin in a jail cell. "He tried Zyir, but Melvin hid out and my family eventually stopped talking about him. They all wanted to know what I would do with Enika? I tried to raise her, but it was hard. I was young, and she was something clearly, I wasn't used to. My mom offered to take her, and I eventually agreed to it. Then the question came up if she was his daughter? I knew she wasn't and so did my aunt. From the minute I saw her Zyir I knew she was your kid. Outside of Melvin, you were the only person I had ever been with. Melvin rarely ended his rape inside of me and you know we never pulled out. My aunt also told us that after they had my cousin that she tried for years to have another baby and it wouldn't happen. They went to the doctor and they learned he was infertile. It was due to something in his scrotum being twisted. I can't remember what it was called but she said he couldn't have any more kids and he just didn't like to admit it."

Zyir sighed, his body relaxed more in his seat at Miko's words.

"And why didn't you tell me?"

Miko frowned at him.

"For what Zyir? You was a kid like me. I didn't want to do that to you or your family, but I kept you around. For everything I made sure you was there," she replied.

Zyir shook his head and Miko squeezed his hand tighter.

"I'm sorry Zyir. From the bottom of my heart, I'm sorry for keeping it a secret."

Zyir glanced over at Miko and licked his lips.

"On some real shit, was you ever gone tell me?"

Miko broke Zyir's gaze and he let her hand go. He nodded before clearing his throat.

"Damn I see how much you really love my black ass," he grumbled.

Miko opened her mouth to reply and clamped it shut. She leaned against the window as he turned on his stereo. Thirty minutes later Miko and Zyir sat across from Enika inside of the plush hotel suite. Enika wore silk pink pajamas with her hair in a high ponytail looking like a younger version of Miko. Zyir stared at her nervously as Miko fidgeted beside him.

"All this time and I just thought y'all looked alike cause she was your sister," he mumbled before shaking his head.

Miko swallowed hard and rubbed at the back of her neck. Her eyes connected with Enika's and she quickly looked away from her.

"I can't do this," Miko breathed out and stood up.

Zyir cleared his throat.

"Enika we need to speak with you about something real serious," he said calmly.

Miko glanced up towards the ceiling and Zyir rubbed her leg in slow circular motions. The move caught her off guard, but it was also appreciated. She reluctantly sat back down and Zyir pulled Miko to his side. Miko tried to hide her face in his hoodie and he shook his head.

"Don't do that. Just relax," he whispered with all anger gone from his voice.

Miko stared up into his cinnamon peepers and swallowed hard.

"I'm scared Zyir. I can't. I can't do it," she revealed and bit down hard on her bottom lip.

Enika watched them closely while frowning.

"Is this because of mom? I'm sure she's mad that I'm here with you but being almost abducted is traumatizing as heck. I'm scared to go to school!"

Zyir looked at Enika.

"You shouldn't be. We won't let anything happen to you. Matter of fact I can start dropping you off and picking you up," he replied.

Enika smiled for a moment before her brows pulled together.

"Why? My momma won't like that either. She already thinks Miko spoils me too much. Is us being here bad, Miko?" she asked.

Miko's eyes watered and Zyir kissed her forehead.

"You want me to tell her?" he asked quietly.

Miko nodded then suddenly shook her head. She was a lot of things but weak was no longer one of them.

"Enika this is very serious baby," she said and Zyir rubbed her arm. Miko licked her dry lips and sighed. "When I was younger, I was raped by my cousin Peyton's father. That's why I don't like her or her mother. Although it wasn't their fault, I can't be around them. It brings back horrible memories that I want to forget. It went on for three years but in between that time I also started to um...see Zyir. We were young. Too young to be engaging in sexual activity but we did. You know how I always explain sex to you?"

Enika nodded with eager eyes.

"Yes, and I swear I listen! I won't give up anything to no nasty boy," she replied.

Zyir smirked and Miko looked around the room slowly. Her words felt heavy as fuck and she was struggling with getting them out. She looked back to Enika and exhaled.

"I got pregnant and everyone in the family found out about me being molested. I was only a child and the guy that raped me had disappeared before his court date. My family chose to focus on me having a baby instead of finding him. It was like the rape no longer mattered. Only thing they cared about was that I was carrying a girl..." Miko's eyes watered as she stared at Enika.

"A girl that I delivered on my birthday and I named her Enika Hana. She was *and* still is the most beautiful thing I have ever laid eyes on. She's also a baby I made with Zyir, not the man that molested me. My parents took her away from me because I was a child and I was happy. I wasn't ready to be a mom, so she became my sister, but I always loved her. I still do. I still love you very much Enika," Miko replied sincerely.

Enika stared at Miko and Zyir with a blank expression on her face. Zyir let Miko go and he sat up.

"You okay?" he asked Enika.

Enika gave him a wry smile.

"I don't understand what's going on? Can you all please take me home? I wanna see my momma."

Miko hugged Zyir's side as he looked at Enika.

"Enika do you understand what we're saying to you?" he asked.

Enika stood up and swallowed hard. Her chinky eyes watered as she looked at Miko and Zyir.

"I don't. I wanna go home right now. Take me home!" she yelled and stomped her foot.

Miko closed her eyes as Zyir stared at Enika. Enika began to cry and Zyir nodded.

"Cool, get dressed and we got you. We're not trying to upset you," he replied.

Enika walked away and once she was out of the room Zyir let Miko go. He stood up and pulled his keys from his pocket. He made a call on his cell and began to talk as Miko watched Enika step into the room with her bag packed.

"Miko I think the kidnapping has you confused. I was scared too but you're not thinking properly. My mom is at home. You are my sister," Enika told her now fully dressed.

Miko shook her head. Her mind was swirling with thoughts of her daughter and her horrid childhood.

"Enika I carried you and I gave birth to you. You are my child, sweetie. I wouldn't lie about that."

Enika took a step back and licked her lips.

"You've been lying to me all of this time? Why?"

Miko stood up as Zyir put his phone away.

"Because I was scared to admit the truth! I had lied for so long that I felt like I couldn't fess up and you were happy. I didn't wanna ruin that Enika," she replied.

Enika rolled her eyes. She blinked and glanced around the vast room.

"I wanna go home," she said lowly.

Zyir walked up and grabbed Enika's bag.

"Let's take her to your mom's place. My mom is gonna meet us over there," he said and walked away.

Miko followed after Zyir and Enika robotically. Silently they rode to Miko's parents' home. Silently Miko watched Enika hug her mother as if they shared the same parent and it gnawed at her nerves while breaking her heart. Zyir's mother Zoya sat inside of the living room beside Miko's father and the setting made Miko extremely uncomfortable. Enika stayed glued to Miko's mother as everyone looked Miko's way.

"Baby are you okay?" Zoya asked.

Miko nodded. She was ashamed. Despite being taken advantage of and having to carry that burden on her for years somehow, she still felt at fault. Miko knew that she hadn't asked for the rape but the lie, she had agreed to and now she was paying for it.

"I never meant any harm. Momma you know I love Zyir and I made sure that Enika was around," Miko said to Zoya.

Zoya nodded. She gave Miko a warm smile.

"I'm angry baby but I knew that was his child years ago. A mother knows things like this but it's my turn to apologize because I didn't say anything," she replied.

Everyone including Zyir looked at his mother in shock. Zyir stepped off the wall and frowned at the woman that had pushed him into the world.

"What you saying, momma?"

Zoya swallowed hard.

"I'm saying that about five years ago I snuck and got her tested. She'd stayed the night and I had one of your toothbrushes. I had an inkling along with your nanna and aunts. We decided to not say anything because of the age gap. We knew that it had to be something serious and I see now that it was," Zoya replied staring up at Zyir.

Zyir shook his head. Miko went over to him and he glared at her.

"Don't even come your ass over here. I see now I got a bunch of secretive ass women in my life. I can't do this right now," he spoke vehemently before walking off.

Miko's mother's front door slammed and Zoya jumped up. She rushed out of the room after her son and Miko looked at her parents. Her father watched her with pained eyes as her mother glanced her way. They looked remorseful and even that pissed her off.

"This is all your fault! I could possibly lose the only man I have ever loved, and my daughter doesn't even believe I'm her mom. I hate you two!" Miko screamed bitterly.

Miko's mother Kawai closed her eyes. When she opened them, her tears spilled over.

"That's a shame because we love you Nanmiko. We did what we thought was best and Enika this is your mother. Nanmiko is your mother baby and we're sorry we hid that from you," Kawai said.

Enika jumped up from the sofa and ran off. Miko looked at her parents with hate in her monolid eyes. She had so many things to say to them but no energy to say them. Her shoulders dropped as she rolled her eyes.

"This is on you two. You're nothing but worthless pieces of shit," she voiced angrily and as she turned around, she caught sight of Enika standing near the doorway.

Enika shook her head while crying and Miko couldn't find it in herself to console her. Things were different now. The truth had shifted the dynamic and it made Miko uneasy. She wasn't sure how to handle the situation and instead of trying to figure it out she headed for the door. With no car and no cellphone, she walked out of her parents' home.

Four

Lovin' you is easy cause you're beautiful
Makin' love with you is all I wanna do
Lovin' you is more than just a dream come true
And everything that I do is out of lovin' you

For the night, the studio had been transformed into a lounge area. Catered food sat on the table near the wall while gift bags sat on a nearby pink acrylic table. Liquor was plentiful, and the vibe was chill still the women wasn't feeling it. Not even the one that had spent her whole day setting it up.

"See what we're not gone do is play this sappy shit. I can't listen to nothing slow, turn on some trap music," Nelly quipped and rolled her eyes.

Jerzey smiled as she did as her friend requested. She turned to rap music and Rumer and Nelly nodded in agreement with the song choice.

Yeah, you can snooze if you wanna, but not on me, baby
And nah, I ain't takin' no losses, yeah, I got heat, baby
No, I don't know nothin' 'bout dozin', no, I don't sleep, baby
You niggas ain't gassin' me, nigga, yeah, I'm on E, baby
Got all designer on me, that's on me, baby, yeah

Rumer's body involuntarily bopped to the hot record. "This will do," she murmured happily referring to the Yella Beezy track as she placed juicy purple grapes on her plate. Rumer counted the grapes and took three off the plate while smiling.

Jerzey eyed her girl skeptically and sighed.

"Grab some other food too. It's a lot in here boo," she told her with a big smile.

Rumer cocked her head to the side as she stared at Jerzey.

"Jerzey now you're sounding like Kritt. Don't start, you all know I'm dealing with a lot of shit right now," she snapped and grabbed two grapes to add to her plate.

Jerzey nodded. After spending a week calling Snowden nonstop, she'd woken up with a *fuck it* attitude. She loved Snowden, was in love with him but she also wasn't going to chase him down. That just wasn't in her being to chase a man. She'd thankfully grown out of that stupid phase that some women go through and wasn't looking to take any steps back. Jerzey instead stepped out of her comfort zone and hopped in her rarely used car. She drove to the furthest mall from her home and went shopping. She then pampered herself and set up for the girl's night. Miko was missing in action but thanks to Miko's mother Jerzey and the girls knew the tea.

Jerzey ran her hands through her deep red unit that was in soft waves that cascaded down her back. Her lash extensions were longer than usual making her almond shaped eyes appear tighter and she wore a two-piece sexy outfit that she'd gotten from Allure Boutique owned by a local designer named Mickey.

Her heart was broken but her spirit wasn't. She was going to push through no matter what. Jerzey couldn't go back to the dark place that Gnash's killing placed her in.

Fuck that she refused to.

"Miko isn't here but that doesn't mean this talk can't happen. Also, I have some news to share with you all," Jerzey announced.

Nelly stretched out on Jerzey's blue suede sofa as Rumer sat down on the pink loveseat Jerzey had in the studio. Jerzey grabbed her glass of lemonade that she'd mixed with D'usse and looked at her friends. There were so many things concerning her night with Snowden that she wanted to discuss with them, but she couldn't. Jerzey was scared to reveal everything only for them especially Nelly to possibly run off and tell it to Nero. She couldn't have that and wouldn't betray Snowden, so she chose to keep her pretty lips sealed on that matter.

"First we need to talk about Miko. Have you all spoken with her?" Jerzey asked copping a squat on her plush, fluffy teal rug.

Nelly pulled a joint out of her Judith Leiber Couture clutch bag and blew air through her nose.

"No, we haven't and honestly I'm so shocked by everything that's happening I don't know what to say. It's like we pissed off a witch and the hoe put a hex on us or some shit," she replied.

Rumer snorted. She laughed and leaned over to snatch the joint from Nelly. Nelly's freshly groomed brows pulled together as she glared at her girl.

"It's only a diminutive amount of weed," she whined.

Rumer and Jerzey snickered at her pout she'd created.

"Diminutive, girl bye. Don't try to talk educated now with your pregnant weed smoking ass. I thought you was trying to get your man back? Not give his baby some damn issue," Jerzey told her.

Nelly rolled her eyes and glanced up towards the ceiling. In her skinny jeans that she'd paired with a coral deep plunge bodysuit and black pumps, she looked gorgeous like always but the usual sparkle she carried in her eyes was missing that night.

Nelly ran her hands through her wild and curly shoulder-length fro and sighed.

"I just need an escape from my life right now. I already can't drink. I checked and saw a little weed won't harm the baby. It's not laced, its natural, from the earth," she continued to whine.

Jerzey shook her head while Rumer waved Nelly off.

"But instead of escaping your problems you need to be trying to fix it before you lose your husband," Jerzey replied.

"*And* he has Jasir, Nelly. Why the hell did you let him keep our baby?" Rumer asked angrily.

Nelly looked at Jerzey and they both shook their heads.

"I begged Nelly to just let it go Rumer. She had already knocked out Taya for talking shit. I honestly thought she was going to catch a charge out there. We was in another city on some hot shit and honestly, we all know Jasir is good. Nero is his father," Jerzey said looking Rumer's way.

Nelly's body slumped over as she stared down at her small round belly. She looked at her finger that was ringless and her eyes watered.

"But he's my son and I want him back. Nero won't even take my calls right now Jerzey. I should have just called the cops and made him bring him outside. I can't lose Nero, but I refuse to lose my son too. Fuck that, I'll kill that nigga before I allow that to happen," Nelly vented.

Nelly looked up and saw that Jerzey and Rumer were staring at her strangely. She shrugged while frowning.

"What?"

Jerzey cracked a smile wanting to ease the tension.

"Look now that we know what you're capable of please don't say things like *kill* him. Shit, we know your ass just might. Nelly, we love you and we only want the best for you. You need to get some help. Maybe even confront your mom so that you can heal and win your family back," she replied.

Nelly fell back on the sofa and closed her eyes.

"Why? I told him I was sorry," she mumbled.

Rumer ate another grape, her third one of the night.

"And you need to put action behind your words. Sorry doesn't mean shit if you're still messing up. He needs to see that you're willing to change. Nelly that's a good ass man. Don't lose him over this bullshit," Rumer scolded her.

Jerzey glanced over at Rumer. Her girl was on her shit like usual. Rumer wore a distressed tee with diamond bangles and ripped black jeans. On her feet were a pair of saucy ass Christian Louboutin's and on her lips, she wore matte red lipstick. Rumer was smaller with the hollows of her cheeks showing along with her collarbone that was exposed by the tee-shirt.

Details like that made Jerzey nervous.

"And why did you have a heart attack again, Rumer?"

Rumer swallowed her fourth grape. Her lashes fluttered as she looked up at Jerzey.

"Huh?"

It was Nelly's turn to snicker.

"You heard her. You wanna Iyanla me while you're over there keeping secrets," Nelly mumbled.

Rumer groaned and sat her plate down. She grabbed her own glass of D'usse and sighed. After taking two sips she was able to look back at her friends.

"Kritt has a possible baby on the way and the news made me nearly die," she replied casually.

Nelly frowned as Jerzey stared at Rumer.

"And it wouldn't be because of your health? I mean we've all experienced heartache, but it wasn't to the point where we suffered a heart attack. Shit I never had dick nor love that good, have you?" Jerzey asked Nelly.

Nelly smiled but didn't respond. Jerzey looked back at Rumer and watched her guzzle down her drink.

"Say what the fuck you have to say Jerzey," Rumer said glaring at her.

Jerzey swallowed hard.

"I think you have an eating disorder Rumer and I'm sorry."

Rumer's top lip curled up as her leg began to bounce. Anger radiated off her frame.

"Sorry for what?"

"Sorry for just now saying something. Sorry for ignoring the signs because that wasn't real of me. I was so wrapped up in my own life that I ignored what my friend was going through. Friends are supposed to hold each other down, no matter what. We love you and no matter what size you're gorgeous to us Rumer. If only you could see what we see. You're the fucking bomb," Jerzey replied teary-eyed.

Nelly nodded in agreement.

"You really are though Rumer. You inspire me with your tenacity and thirst for success," Nelly revealed.

Rumer closed her eyes.

"I don't have low self-esteem," she said angrily.

"You don't?" Jerzey asked not willing to let it go.

Rumer's eyes shot open and she sat the glass on the table before her.

"I *said* I fucking don't. Just because you got you some dick in your life and started walking more than one block away from your crib doesn't give you the right to do this. Bitch I'm not your patient or case study. I gotta go," Rumer replied and stood up.

"Rumer calm down," Nelly said sitting up.

Rumer shook her head. She rushed to grab her purse and car keys.

"Nah, I can't sit here with this new acting bitch. My fucking father just died and you wanna ask me about what I'm eating like that's an issue. I'm not eating shit because I'm in mourning! Fuck you Jerzey and that new dick you're hopping on that has you acting like this. I'm gone," she ranted and within minutes she'd left the studio.

Nelly's widened eyes looked to Jerzey and she shook her head.

"Um wow, and damn you're right she looks skinny as shit. She even has that thigh gap when she's never had that before. I never paid much attention to it but you're right her ass never eats. She'll make a plate then I'll look up and its clean but like I never actually watched her eat it. This is crazy for real," Nelly said and exhaled.

Jerzey swallowed hard. It wasn't her intentions to make Rumer angry. She was only trying to be there for her friend.

"Yeah, I noticed it too and I was tired of running around the issue. Let's be clear Snowden doesn't have me acting like anything. We're all dealing with heavy stuff and I feel it's because it is a turning point in our life. We can either make the right choices and walk towards our future or stay stagnant and remain miserable as fuck. I know for me I wanna be happy. I want us all to be happy. We deserve it and I can't be happy and watch my girls suffer so yes, I called the meeting. Something needs to be done. We need to hit up church. Have somebody pray over us, hell take a bath in the holy water just do something. We need to get our life together. The only way for us to get better is for us to be better. Nelly if you really want your man and baby back heal your heart. Can't you see how much it held you back?" Jerzey asked.

Nelly rubbed her baby bump. Her chest heaved up and down as she stared down at her stomach.

"I do but I'm scared. If I were to see my mom Jerzey I would probably kill her. I'm terrified of seeing that woman again. The feelings she evokes out of me aren't healthy, but I

Broken *Little* Rich *Girls* 2

do want my man. I've never loved anyone the way that I love him. I mean I love him so much it's insane," Nelly replied.

Jerzey looked at her friend and gave her a cheeky grin. She laughed lightly as a tear slipped from her eye.

"Nelly, I've never heard you say that about him before. I mean we all knew it, but you've never said Nero and love in the same sentence. Your favorite line was "*he knows how I feel about him*". Girl, you better stop playing and get that man. Have you heard anything else about the case?"

Nelly shrugged with her eyes ascending to the ceiling.

"No, apparently Jeremiah has dipped off. Nero text me the other day and said they were looking for him along with the Feds. The lawyer said that he was looking to get our charges tossed out now that he was on the run," she replied.

Jerzey's body grew cold at Nelly's words. She took a deep breath and sighed.

"I'll be right back," she said and rushed out of the room. Jerzey went into her downstairs bathroom and pulled out her cell. She closed her eyes as she called Snowden.

"Hi Jerzey, this Taya. He's gone with Nero and he left this phone by accident. I'll have him call you back and please send up some prayers for us. We can't find Jeremiah," Taya replied and ended the call.

72 | P a g e

Jerzey sat her phone on the counter and swallowed hard. She stared at herself in the mirror and her beautiful face saddened.

"Why is this happening to me?" she asked quietly.

Jerzey picked up her phone and decided to send Snowden a text message. One that she prayed he read once he had his device back in his possession.

At night when all of the outside noise dims and its just you in your home alone, do you think of me? I know I think of you. I miss you and I'm in love with you Snowden. Let me know if I'm in this alone....

Jerzey sent the text and kissed the screen of her phone. Although she wasn't chasing him it didn't mean her soul wasn't yearning for his. Jerzey wanted her Snow back in her life.

The narrow hallway was decorated with white panels and scone lamps. Fancy as fuck with its plush brown carpet and art deco photos on the walls. Jerzey stopped at door 304 and she snickered.

"This broad," she mumbled.

Jerzey knocked loudly and placed her hand over the peephole.

"Zyir it's too early for this," Miko grumbled snatching the door open.

Jerzey looked at her friend dressed in nothing, but a short ivory colored one-piece Brash pajamas outfit and she smiled. Miko looked well rested with her wavy hair piled on top of her head in a banana clip while fluffy UGG house shoes sat on her feet. Jerzey pulled Miko into her arms and hugged her tightly.

"Jerzey I keep telling you I don't want your old hairy wolf coochie. Let me go," Miko grumbled.

Jerzey smiled as she eased up on the hug. Jerzey went into Miko's suite with her friend following after her. Miko grabbed a bottle of white Remy and took a swig from the bottle as she led her over to the bedroom that she occupied in the suite. Jerzey took note of the disheveled suite and shook her head. Papers scattered the coffee table while liquor bottles covered the floor in the seating area.

Miko cleared her throat and Jerzey glanced her way.

"Who told you I was here?"

Jerzey stepped out of her Flashtrek sneakers and licked her lips. Today she wore a black one-piece with a half grey hoodie tossed over it. She felt like shit honestly but refused to let it show. Snowden hadn't called, and that fact left her moody and in her feelings.

Like a motherfucka.

"Who else? Your baby daddy did," she quipped and rolled her eyes.

It wasn't Miko's fault Snowden was dodging her but Miko running from her responsibility was making Jerzey upset.

"He also said you're not taking his calls and you stopped going over your mom's house. What's going on Nanmiko?"

Miko shrugged. She rubbed at her red rimmed eyes while gazing Jerzey's way.

"Shit you came in this bitch on your Wendy Williams shit, so you tell me."

Jerzey smiled.

"Whatever hoe. I'm serious we're all going through it, but I've always got time for my friend. Talk to me," Jerzey replied.

Miko took another swig of the bottle and sighed.

"She doesn't want me as her mom, so I let her ass stay home. I'm focusing on opening up my new location. You wanna see the pics?"

Miko whipped out her phone and passed it over to Jerzey. Jerzey shook her head and Miko frowned.

"I don't wanna see no damn building. What are you doing Nanmiko?"

Miko smiled.

"What men do. I'm focusing on my money. I'll deal with the rest later. Regardless of the fact I'ma always take care of her but I can't make her choose me Jerzey. I *won't* make her choose me. You know Rumer warned me that you was on some funny style brand-new type shit and I'm seeing what she was saying now. I figured Snow had some good dick, but his shit must be life-changing. He got you thinking you a psychiatrist instead of an artist. I'ma be fine Jerzey. I've always bounced back," Miko replied.

Jerzey took a seat on the bed beside her friend and closed her eyes. Her heartbeat increased as she envisioned the second worst day of her life.

"Miko, I'm moving. I decided to get a place in New York. I was offered a gig with Neiman Marcus but after checking out my work more closely I was given two new contracts. Business will pick up for me there, I'm sure of it. I feel like it could be a new beginning for me," Jerzey said telling Miko what she didn't get a chance to tell Rumer and Nelly.

Miko's eyes widened. Her jaw fell slack as her body relaxed.

"What? I mean damn Congrat's but how did this come about? How you gone stay in a big ass city by yourself, Jerzey? Is Snowden moving with you? Was this his idea? Is that nigga trying to take you away from us?" Miko asked getting angry.

Jerzey opened her eyes and smiled.

"I wish it was that simple but no I'm moving alone. Snowden and I are no longer friends, shit he won't even take my calls."

Miko grabbed Jerzey's hand. They'd been close for as long as they could remember, and their bond was shown in the way they responded to one another.

"Jerzey I'm sorry for talking all that shit. I'm just hurting right now. I never thought my secret would come out, but you know I appreciate you coming over here. I know we're all types of fucked up right now, but you can't leave. We need you here with us. What happened with you and Snowden?"

Jerzey squeezed her friend's hand and stared into her sad eyes.

"Miko this can never be repeated. Not even to Rumer and Nelly. *No one* can know about it." Jerzey said sternly.

Miko nodded.

"I swear. You know the only time I open my mouth is to suck Zyir's dick. Well, used to shit done changed now," Miko replied and they both snickered. Miko smiled at Jerzey. "Seriously though you my girl. I would never repeat what we discuss. What happened?"

Jerzey took a deep breath and exhaled.

"When I was in Philly with Snowden and Nelly, we had sex. Everything was so perfect Miko, but we woke up to Jeremiah beating on his door. When Snowden left out of the room with his gun I got scared. After losing Gnash I refused to lose him too. I went downstairs, and I found him arguing with his brother. Jeremiah began to talk, and it was like I was taken back to the night I was shot. Miko..." Jerzey's body shuddered. "It was him. That bitch ass nigga shot us," she said quietly.

Miko's monolid eyes widened in alarm.

"Shut the fuck up," she whispered.

Jerzey nodded.

"I'm serious. I almost passed out. I ran upstairs and found Snowden's gun. He walked into the room as I was getting ready to leave out and we started arguing. I saw a shadow in the hallway and freaked out Miko, so I shot his gun. Jeremiah stepped into the room after I stopped shooting and he started talking shit. He even pointed his gun my way with intentions to kill me."

"He what! Oh, that nigga bold," Miko grumbled.

Jerzey nodded.

"Who you telling, and I was scared as hell. I kept seeing Gnash and envisioning the shooting. I was in shock Miko then...then..." Jerzey swallowed hard and her eyes watered. Miko pulled her into a tight embrace and rubbed her arm. Jerzey closed her eyes as her heartbeat increased. "Then Snowden shot him. He killed his brother for me, Miko. He killed him," Jerzey said and tears fell from her lids.

Miko rocked her back and forth while shaking her head.

"And now he doesn't want shit to do with you? Huh?"

Jerzey nodded.

"And you saying fuck him, right?" Miko asked again.

Jerzey nodded making a smile fall onto Miko's face.

"Then I say let's go apartment shopping in NY. I would rather you move forward then on some depressed shit like before. You didn't make him have a snake ass brother. All of this is on Jeremiah's bitch ass. It's not your fault any of this happened and he'll come around."

Jerzey cried harder at the thought of being without the man she now loved.

"And what if he doesn't?"

Miko sighed.

"Then an even better man will step in his place," Miko assured her.

Jerzey returned to her place hours later. Slightly tipsy from the bottle of wine she tossed back with Miko she struggled to unlock her building door. The strong smell of an enchanting cologne mixed with a warm body caused her to jump. Jerzey grabbed her chest as she glanced behind her.

Who she assumed was Snowden was a blast from her past. Time in prison had been good to him. He looked to be in the best shape of his life as he wore up to date designer threads. His mocha brown skin was still nice as ever only now it was heavily tattooed. His hair was in low waves with a neat line up while simple jewelry completed his look.

Jerzey was used to him being flashy and larger than life so to see the man before her wear only one chain with minimal diamonds made her smile. Maybe *just* maybe he'd finally grown up.

She figured prison would do that to you.

"No hug for me?" he asked and licked his full lips.

"J-Bo?"

Jaleed shook his head. His slanted hazel eyes roamed over Jerzey's thick frame in a lusty manner.

"Just Jaleed. I don't go by that dumb shit anymore," he announced quietly.

Jerzey nodded. She leaned against her door as she gazed up at him. To see him standing before her was mind boggling. A huge part of Jerzey thought that she would never see him again.

"How long have you been out?"

Jaleed shrugged. His tongue swiped at his bottom lip as he stared down at her. He cleared his throat before speaking.

"Here a month. I was in a halfway house for three months. Once I got to the "D" I wanted to enjoy my kids and family. Check on my businesses and shit. Check on you," he replied.

Jerzey dropped her head and Jaleed walked up on her. His hands went to her waist and he pulled her into his arms. Jerzey closed her eyes as he hugged her tightly. At once she was flooded with memories of the tumultuous relationship they shared. The fighting, the lies, even the cheating. He'd done her very fucking wrong and time apart hadn't changed that. She pushed him back gently and he nodded.

He understood and if he didn't, she didn't give a damn.

"You should leave. My boyfriend could pop up at any minute," she replied wishing her statement was true.

Jaleed tugged on his chin hairs.

"Word? Who you fucking with now? Nigga must be something special. He kept you from missing me," he replied.

Jerzey spun around and successfully unlocked her building door. Jaleed represented her past and the old her. She was no longer that person and she no longer loved him. As sexy as he was standing behind her, she didn't miss it. The pain she could always do without.

"Please stay away from me," she tossed over her shoulder.

Before Jaleed could reply she closed the door and set her alarm. Jerzey checked her phone when it began to vibrate in her hand and saw she had a text from Snowden. It was only a few words, but it was enough to bring her comfort.

I'm fucked up right now but youse still special to me. I just need time ma...

Jerzey put her phone away and sighed. With her past at her doorstep and Snowden on her mind she closed her eyes. She was terrified to move to a new city, but it felt right. A change of scenery was what she needed to get her mind right.

Five

—•••〈♡〉•••—

The Reggio Bergamot notes in his cologne made sitting next to him almost unbearable. The black moto jeans that he'd paired with a crisp white V-neck, fresh butter Timberlands and a diamond Cuban link chain showed off his effortless sexy style. From the part in his low-cut fade to the way his mustache lined his mouth drove her insides wild with passion. Nelly's mouth watered as she pretended to look straight ahead while staring at him from the corner of her eye.

Her stomach growled loudly as the lawyer stepped into the office and Nero glanced over at her before turning his attention back to the man they'd both come to see.

"Have you spoken with your brother?" the stubby well-dressed lawyer asked taking his seat.

Jannero shook his head.

"Nah, he still off the map. Why?"

The lawyer cleared his throat. He went into his file cabinet and pulled out a manila folder. He slid it over to Jannero and Jannero quickly opened it. Nelly watched him as he scanned over the papers.

"Aye, what the fuck does this shit mean? I'm confused."

Mr. Shaw swallowed hard. His tawny colored skin reddened under Nelly and Jannero's penetrating stares.

"By law, I had a right to know if someone turned state's evidence against you because this is a federal case. In your situation I was finally sent over the papers and was quite shocked to learn that your brother Jeremiah revealed that you did, in fact, clean his drug money so that he could get a lesser sentence," the lawyer replied.

Nelly's eyes widened, and she looked at Jannero. He stared angrily down at the paper with his fist balled up.

"Me and Arnelle?" he asked in an low angry tone.

Arnelle? The use of her first name so easily slipping from his lips worried her. She swallowed down her worry with the state of her relationship and looked at the lawyer.

"Actually yes. He also claimed that you two were using her bakery as well to clean out his money. He's facing ten years in prison but if the courts were to charge you two that would be cut in half. I would advise you all to keep your distance from him. No disrespect but he is to not be trusted," the lawyer advised them.

Jannero nodded. He read over the papers again before passing them back to the lawyer.

"Got it. So what else they saying?"

"Honestly, it's all up to his testimony but what works in your favor is that you and your fiancé is law abiding citizens. No criminal records, not even a speeding ticket. I won't let them give you two a day in jail let alone three years. That's fucking absurd. You have nothing to worry about," the lawyer assured them.

Relief flooded Nelly's body as she rubbed her belly.

"Cool, then hit me up when you hear something," Jannero said standing up.

Nelly followed suit and together they exited the room. Nelly walked nervously beside Jannero as they walked out of the office building. The last time she'd seen him he'd taken her ring and left in his wake her shattered heart. She wanted hugs and kisses from him. The cold shoulder he was giving her was hard for Nelly to accept. She was only used to receiving love from Jannero.

Jannero began to head towards his vehicle and Nelly nervously grabbed his arm.

"Where is Jasir?"

Jannero stared straight ahead. The sadness covering his handsome face tore Nelly down. She'd always had a bad feeling about Jeremiah but to learn he was willing to toss them under the bus to save his own ass only proved what she'd been telling Jannero for years. His brother was a snake.

"Back at the house with Taya. You can follow me," he replied in a bland tone.

Nelly let his arm go and frowned. The way he spoke of her seeing her son didn't sit well with her.

"I won't need or ask for permission to see my child. What happened between us has nothing to do with my love for him. I'm his mother and nothing and no one will take that away from me. Don't you ever forget that Nero," she said before walking away.

Nelly hopped in her truck and sped off. She made it to the home she shared with Jannero before he did and attempted to use her key. As the gold key refused to slide into the lock, she felt her blood pressure rising. Nelly closed her eyes and took a deep breath.

"The locks got changed when we was still in Philly. Watch out," Jannero said walking up.

Nelly reluctantly moved to the side and ignored the anger coursing through her body. She was tempted to slap the shit out of Jannero. This was *her* home, a place she'd picked out and also poured some of her money into. There was no way in hell she was going to allow for Jannero to shut her out of her life.

It simply wasn't happening.

"Do you hate me now? Is that what it is?" Nelly asked on the verge of crying.

Jannero glanced back at her with his chestnut peepers narrowing in on her. Irritation sat on his face as he licked his lips.

"I love you more than you love yourself. Don't ask me no dumb shit like that again. Stop making yourself the fucking victim," he replied before walking into the home.

Nelly swallowed hard and walked into her place. She slipped off her mules and glanced around her hallway. Her home still smelled the same and just being in the space that she had nothing but good memories in brought her so much comfort. She walked towards the living room and heard the sound of a female's laughter. Nelly quickened her steps and found Taya sitting in the family room with Jasir. Nelly ignored the frown marring Taya's face and ran over to her baby boy. She picked him up and he giggled uncontrollably as she kissed all over his handsome face.

"I missed you so much, baby! Mommy loves you," Nelly gushed and kissed his fat cheeks once more.

"We need to pack up Jasir and head back to Philly. Jeremiah is still out of touch," his sister said as Nelly sat on the suede sectional with her son.

Jannero sat beside Nelly with a drink in his hand.

"Nah, I'm good here but you can head back if you want to," he replied.

Taya smacked her lips and glared over at Nelly.

"Did she suck your dick in the car or something? Nero, what the fuck our brother is missing and this crazy hoe doesn't deserve your loyalty. Did you forget she nearly killed you!"

Nelly's widened eyes looked Taya's way and she sat Jasir to the side. Jannero placed his hand on her leg and she looked over at him.

"Chill out. Take Jasir and get him dressed. I wanna take y'all somewhere," he told her.

Nelly looked back at Taya not sure if she could continue to let the disrespect slide and Taya looked her way with furrowed brows.

"You was always like a sister to me Nelly but that mess you pulled was out of line. You know my brothers are all I have," Taya said, and her eyes teared up.

Nelly nodded. Instead of anger, she felt embarrassment at the things she'd done.

"And again, I'm sorry. Nero didn't deserve any of that and you're right they're all you have but guess what these two are all I have as well. I get you wanna defend your brother but calling me out of my name is not gonna make things better. Its only gone make me wanna beat the shit out of you. *Again.* I won't keep repeating myself Taya please watch what you say to me. Regardless of what happened, this is my home that I built with your brother and I'm not going anywhere," Nelly told her.

Taya nodded and cleared her throat.

"I'll always be there for him whether you stick around or not. Nero do you and I'll head back to Philly my damn self to see what's up with Jeremiah. I see now that you and Snowden really don't give a fuck about him," Taya quipped angrily and stood up.

Nelly bounced her son on her leg as Taya grabbed her bag and her phone. Taya shot Jannero one last glare before leaving out of the home. The door shut and Jannero quietly finished his drink. There were so many things Nelly wanted to say but she wasn't sure where to start.

"Get him dressed so we can go take a ride," Jannero said breaking the silence.

Nelly nodded and took Jasir upstairs. She quickly changed him into presentable street clothes and they found Jannero in the kitchen texting on his phone. Nelly sat Jasir down and looked at her man.

"Is that her?"

Jannero put his phone away and grabbed his fob. "Who?"

Nelly closed her eyes. She wanted to calmly talk with him about his ex-girlfriend and was trying her best to keep her cool. She opened her eyes and exhaled.

"Nero please let's not play anymore games. The bitch that I caught grabbing on your dick, is that her?"

Jannero leaned against the island and stared at Nelly. The tension in the room grew thick as he glared at her.

"Nelly I've never cheated on you. Yes, when we got together, I was with her, but you killed all that shit. Like I told you before it was always you, ma. I never felt the shit for her that I do for you. I apologize for letting her be in a niggas face like that. I was out of line and would have fucked some shit up too if that was you, but I swear on my unborn baby's life I'm not fucking with her. I'm not fucking around period on you. You know me," he replied.

Nelly shifted from one foot to the other. As she stared up at Jannero her heart beat increased. She knew him very well but to see him flirt so casually with his ex-girlfriend did something to her. It placed thoughts in her head and made her doubt him. Even question his loyalty to her.

"But that's bullshit Nero and you know it. I was wrong for acting the way I did but you was on some trifling shit. You leave your pregnant fiancé and son at home to hang with your ex-girlfriend on the block. I don't get it," she fussed.

Jannero walked over to Nelly and grabbed her face. His fingers massaged her neck tenderly as he forced her to stare up at him.

"And I apologize for that. I went on the block to fuck with my people and she was out there. She still hang heavy with them niggas. I didn't go see her and I haven't been going to see her."

Nelly thought of the photo's she'd seen while being detained and shook her head.

"Did you forget I saw those pictures of you two together? The cops had them when they arrested us. This is not some one-time thing Jannero. You can sit and try to put this shit all on me but if I hadn't seen that then it would have never been in my mind to track your moves," she told him.

Jannero let her face go and grabbed Jasir. He looked down at Nelly and sighed.

"Look she sometimes moved shit for Jeremiah, so I would have to take him over there or I would make a stop to grab some shit from her. I kept that from you because I knew you wouldn't like it, but I swear on my life it stopped there. I know I'm wrong and again I apologize but I didn't fuck that girl Nelly. I made some mistakes but don't put that shit on me. Come on," he replied and headed for the garage door.

"I don't know what to believe," Nelly mumbled.

"Believe what the fuck I'm telling you," Jannero tossed over his shoulder.

Nelly rolled her eyes and went to the front door for her shoes. When she made it to the garage Jannero stood near the passenger door of his Wrath. Nelly stared up into his eyes and exhaled.

"We're a family. A happy family Nero. I'm sorry for what I did. From the bottom of my heart I'm truly sorry," she apologized in her most sincerest way.

Jannero nodded. His chestnut colored orbs softened as they gazed down at her.

"I know you are, but what I don't know is if you strong enough to not do that shit again. Come on Nelly."

Nelly got into the car and placed her seatbelt on. She glanced in the back seat at her son and he smiled at her.

"Hi, momma's baby! I missed you so much, did you miss me?" she asked.

Jasir grinned at Nelly without responding and her smile faltered. In two months, he would be four and he hadn't spoken one word or even attempted to. That frightened Nelly and with so much going on she was uncertain with if she could take anything else happening to her family.

"He'll be four soon," Nelly said as Jannero backed out of the garage.

Jannero nodded.

"I know, and every kid is different."

Nelly looked out of her window. She was tired as fuck from the problems in her life. She wanted a chance to scream from the mountain tops that she was fed up, but she didn't have a pause button. She had to keep it moving or else everything would fall apart.

"So, we let him become an adult then we ask what happened? He could be deaf; any fucking thing and we're ignoring it." Nelly stopped talking and she glared over at Jannero. "Are you ashamed of him? Is that why you're acting like nothing is wrong?"

Jannero glanced over at Nelly and shook his head.

"That must be the baby that has you talking like this. Why the fuck would I be ashamed of something I made? I love my kids more than I love my self. I just don't wanna label him. He's a happy kid, I want him to stay that way. When I was younger, they said I was dyslexic, and that shit fucked with me. I was put in different classes and even bullied on. Until I started playing ball wasn't nobody fucking with me like that. I don't want that for him. He's good now leave it alone," Jannero replied.

Nelly was stunned by his revelation. She had been with him for years and had no idea he was dyslexic.

"Wow, I never knew that," she mumbled.

Jannero nodded.

"It's a lot of shit that we don't know about each other," he retorted before cutting on the radio.

The rest of the car ride was quiet and before Nelly could fall asleep Jannero was pulling up to a bricked building in Oak Park on Nine Mile Road.

Nelly licked her lips as she stared at the place out of her window.

"What's this?" she asked with her voice low.

"*Save A Woman, Save A Life,*" Jannero replied in an even tone and exited the car.

As Jannero grabbed Jasir, Nelly exited the car and stared at the building. The name of the business stuck out to her as she began to breathe harder. *Save A Woman, Save A Life.* She mulled over what it could be as she followed her men into the building. At the entrance was an armed security guard with a body type similar to the actor Dwayne Johnson. He wore a warm smile as he stared their way.

"License please," he said and glanced back at the small monitor sitting on his white desk.

Jannero and Nelly handed over their ID. The security guard copied their identification as a beautiful woman with fair skin, freckles, and sleek short hairstyle smiled at them. It was strange because while Nelly didn't know her, they resembled one another.

"Jannero?" the woman asked smiling.

Jannero grinned down at her and Nelly found herself frowning.

"Yeah, Jessenia?" he asked.

She smiled and walked up on him. She gave Jannero half a hug before pulling Nelly into a warm embrace.

"I'm so glad you all could come!" Jessenia said cheerfully. She let go of Nelly and glanced down at Jasir. "And who are you? So handsome," she gushed.

Jasir grinned up at her.

"He-ll-o!" he yelled making Jannero and Nelly stare down at him in amazement.

Nelly bent down and kissed his cheek.

"Jasir, baby," she said and hugged him making him laugh.

"You all have a handsome son. We can actually go upstairs into my office," Jessenia said and walked away.

Nelly and her boys followed after her and they took the steps to the second floor. Jessenia led them to a large corner office that was littered with photos of her family along with a few politicians. As Jannero sat down Nelly took a few peeks at the photos and realized that Jessenia was married to Mauri the NBA all-star player that had given Detroit over three championship rings.

Nelly sat down beside Jannero and smiled at Jessenia.

"My fiancé loves your husband girl," she said and laughed.

Jessenia smiled and waved her off.

"The feeling is mutual. They have this man crush thing going on which is how I was able to connect with you. I first have to say congratulations on the baby."

Nelly smiled and rubbed her belly.

"Thank you."

Jess nodded.

"And I also have to know is it okay to speak in front of the little one?" she asked.

Nelly's arched brows pulled together.

"I'm not following you."

Jannero cleared his throat.

"This is a domestic violence shelter, ma."

Nelly sat back in her seat with her thoughts running wild. She crossed her legs and glanced down at her designer sneakers that housed a sock silhouette to them and licked her lips.

"I'm not getting beat on Jannero."

Jannero glanced over at Nelly. His eyes bored into her intently as he gazed her way.

"You used to and now you're beating on me."

His words made Nelly shift uncomfortably in the seat.

"I am not beating on you. How can a woman beat on a man? That's fucking ridiculous and who told you I used to get beat on? Was it Miko?"

Jannero shook his head. Disappointment covered his face as he stared at Nelly.

"Does it matter? Nelly you done spazzed out on me twice. If I hit you once I'd be a woman beater, but I can't say the same bout you?"

Nelly waved him off while frowning. He was pissing her the fuck off with his outlandish accusations.

"Nero just stop it. You're being so extra right now. We both know I'm not beating on you. I can't believe you brought me up here for this mess. This is embarrassing," she expressed ashamed to look Jessenia's way.

Nelly stood up and Jessenia looked up at her.

"Did you give him a concussion?" she asked Nelly.

Nelly grabbed her phone and frowned at Jessenia.

"If he wouldn't have been smiling in his ex's face none of it would have happened. I didn't mean to take it that far, but I lost control."

Jessenia nodded. She touched her stomach and a sad smile graced her beautiful face.

"On my stomach are faint marks of gunshot wounds. My daughter's father said much of those same things Nelly. And every time he hit me it was because *I'd* done something wrong. Now from what Jannero has told me your nothing like Deon but abuse is abuse. Regardless of the situation violence should never be the solution. Would you want that for Jasir?"

Nelly swallowed hard. Her heart was pumping so fast that she could feel it beating in her chest. Thoughts of her childhood and the hell she lived in replayed in her mind. She couldn't do it, she wasn't ready.

"I don't have time for this," she grumbled and attempted to walk away.

Jannero caught her arm and stared up at her.

"If you want this family to work then you do. This shit not a game. I'm not gone sit around and wait for you to jump on me again. I do believe you wouldn't hurt Jasir but you gotta get your shit together Nelly," he said firmly.

Nelly swallowed hard at his words. She wanted her family, that was without a doubt, but she wasn't ready. She needed time to speak about the hell that was her childhood and it would be on her own terms. Not Jannero's and definitely not some bitch she'd just met.

"I gotta go," she grumbled and walked out of the office.

Nelly quickly exited the building and waited for Jannero by the car. He walked up twenty minutes later with her son. A fierce scowl covered his handsome mug as he advanced on her.

"Baby—"

Jannero shook his head making her clamp her lips shut.

"Nah, let's get some shit clear real fucking quick. I let a lot of shit slide Nelly. A lot of your bullshit because I know I'm not perfect. That case shit and your bakery closing down was all me and you stayed by my side. You've always been by my side. That shit with my ex is nothing. I apologize again for flirting. I'ma keep shit a hundred. I have let her get too comfortable with that and that's my fault but it's nothing there. I don't want her, the minute I saw you years ago she was gone from my psyche." Jannero stopped talking and cleared his throat.

Nelly's eyes watered because she was dispirited. She was hurt, and some things were better left in the past. She didn't wanna focus on her childhood instead she wanted to fix her present issues while preparing for her future.

"Baby I'm sorry," she apologized.

Jannero nodded. He licked his full lips and cleared his throat again. His slanted peepers glossed over, and Nelly grabbed his hand.

"I can't do this by myself. Don't you get that? I can't ignore the crazy shit you keep doing, and I can't fix it. This some shit you gotta wanna change yourself. You gotta wanna be better and a funky ass I'm sorry not gone make it right. I love the fuck out of you and it's not even in my character to leave you. I love you too much to do that but you pushing me away. Got me thinking shit I never thought before. I can't marry or even lay next to you like this. I don't trust you to remain calm and I don't trust myself enough not to slap the shit out of you if you try to hit me again so I gotta bounce. This shit with Jeremiah caught me off guard now me and you beefing. I'm sick as fuck and on the verge of losing my damn mind."

Jannero leaned down and kissed Nelly's tear-stained cheek. Nelly closed her eyes and his strong arms pulled her into a hug.

"I love you so fucking much Arnelle, now I need you to start loving yourself. If you can't then what can you really offer me baby?"

Jannero let Nelly go and placed their son in his car seat. He then slid into his car and as if they were strangers instead of lover's he drove away. She watched the expensive car drive down the street and she was immediately pulled to a soft, warm side. Jessenia rubbed her arm as Nelly began to cry.

"Come with me Nelly. Let's go pray and seek guidance from the Lord. He can make any situation better," Jess said before pulling her away.

Six

Repulsive smells emanated from the clear plastic bins. The shelving was the fullest it had ever been. Brown, green gooey puke sat in the containers.

Rumer sat in the center of the room on the floor. Her weave was gone. Eyelash extensions had been yanked out while her naked body was on display. The small razor sat in her hand heavy as a knife. For hours she'd sat in contemplation.

Could she do it?

More importantly, would she?

Her heart was heavy. Her mind was tired, and her body was merely a vessel. A thinning, hunger deprived one at that. She closed her eyes and took a deep breath. Rumer wanted peace in her life. Real joy from being alive and she didn't think she would get it still she struggled with ending it all.

"I try to be a good person God. I only lie when I have to. I treat people good even when they've wronged me, and this is my life. What about the people that kill and screw people over? Why do they get to be happy?"

"Because they just do. We are to never question God baby. He's the judge and the jury. It's not up to you to wonder why the bad people get to be happy. In the end, we will all pay for our sins honey. When we get to those gates, we will all have to answer for the things we've done. Do you really wanna die?" Rachel asked from the doorway.

Rumer opened her eyes. She stared at her mother and slowly shook her head.

"I don't but living has gotten too hard. It's a struggle for me to even get out of the bed in the morning. I don't know what to do," Rumer admitted baring her soul.

Naked, depressed and on the verge of giving up, she allowed for her mother to truly see her for what she was.

A broken woman.

"I just wish I could be happy. I wish dad was still alive. Hell, I wish I could be satisfied with myself. I can't keep it together anymore. I can't keep pretending that I have it all figured out," she cried.

Rachel nodded.

"None of us do baby. You live, and you learn. We all fall and its best to get back up and keep it moving. If you're tired of running, then now is the time. Get help while you're open to it. I have some mission work I'm doing out of the country. I would like for you to come with me,

Rumer. Step away from it all and I have a therapist that can travel with us," her mom replied.

Rumer mulled over her mother's words.

"And how much are they charging?" she asked.

Her mother smiled, she walked over to Rumer and sat down with her on the floor. She grabbed the blade and winked at her daughter.

"Does it matter? You're rich now," she semi-joked.

Rumer laughed and damn it felt good. She shook her head and Rachel pulled her into her arms.

"He gives power to the faint and those who have no might he increases their strength," she whispered while hugging her tightly.

Rumer relaxed in her mother's arms hoping it was true because at the moment she had no strength to pull from. Her well had run dry and she was far from a saint, but she believed in God. And she believed in her heart that if anybody could save her it was him.

The following day Rumer sat nervously inside of the biker club. Liquor bottles along with trash littered the floor and sat on the round tables decorating the upper level of the club. Rumer watched the prospects slowly clean the space with tired, hungover dispositions. She crossed her legs and glanced down at her natural nails. Without the acrylic on them they looked bare. Plain even but she wanted to be free on her trip. Void of the things she did to *make-up* herself. Nails included. Instead she wore a manicure with a blush nude polish. Her mid-back length hair was styled in loose spiral curls with a deep side part while she wore frayed skinny jeans with a white top and Celine pointed mules.

Rumer was so famished she'd been forced to eat a spinach omelet. She didn't wanna think of the calories or weight gain from her early morning eating however it still rested on her mind to the point that it was all she could think about.

"God, I don't wanna purge. Please Lord give me strength," she said lowly.

Strong hands clamping down ontop of her shoulders made her smile. She closed her eyes as his enticing cologne wafted over the space she was sitting in. Next came his thick lips to her soft neck.

"I missed you ma," he whispered before sitting down.

Rumer smiled tightly at him as he sat beside her. Kritt who was dressed in off grey Balmain jeans with no shirt only his diamond chain and sexy face stared her way. He grabbed her hand and tenderly kissed the back of it as his eyes ventured to the left of the room. Rumer followed his line of sight and frowned.

"Looking for your club hoe?"

Kritt waved her off and smirked at her.

"You look tired ma. What's up?" he asked.

Rumer fidgeted with her nails before staring up at Kritt. She took a deep breath and sighed.

"I'm not in a good space right now Kritt. To be honest I haven't been for a while now. From my unhealthy eating habits to my father passing. I'm all over the place. I've decided to take some time off work and take a trip. My mom is doing mission work in Africa and I'm going to take her," she revealed.

Kritt slowly nodded. Rumer stared into his grey hued eyes and smiled sadly at him.

"I need this, Kritt. Last night I was..." Rumer closed her eyes and Kritt pulled her into his arms. He hugged her tightly as her heart raced. "I wanted to kill myself," she admitted.

Rumer's words made Kritt's body stiffen. He briskly stood up and pulled Rumer up with him. Kritt took Rumer back to his room and closed the door. He then discarded her clothes and slid off his jeans and boxers. Kritt led Rumer over to his bed and quietly they slid in the bed and under his thick covers. Rumer closed her eyes as he hugged her from the back. Her body was overcome with emotions as he held her tightly.

"Rumer what you said just broke my fucking heart ma. You gotta bury me, not the other way around. If leaving and healing yourself is what you need then I can't do shit but pray it helps you out because this not working. You can't keep going on like this, can you?" he asked.

Rumer shook her head. Kritt kissed her neck as his member pressed into her bottom.

"Good because I hate seeing you in pain. Go get yourself right baby. I'ma be here when you get home. Know that I love you and I'm not going no fucking where," he promised lowly.

Rumer exhaled as his member slowly slid between her silky folds. She moaned and licked her lips.

"I know baby and I love you too," she replied before he pumped harder into her.

Hey, guys it's me. I'm heading out of the country for a while. I need to get my life together before I lose it. I'm

with my mom and she's on a church mission but I'm just trying to heal Rumer.

I love each and every one of you and if you absolutely have to talk to me call my mom and she'll relay the message. I'm not sure when I'll be back just know I'm trying to get better and I pray you all are as well. You are only as strong as the people beside you so while I'm getting my shit together, I need for y'all to be doing the same damn thing. ;)

Can't have any faulty bitches in our circle. I love you chicks, talk to you all soon and check your Cash App. I know you all are good on money but let's not get it twisted. If I'm sitting pretty, then you better believe my girls will be too.

Goodbye for now.

Rumer sat her phone down and gazed out of the window. Being on her father's jet without him was *weird*. She felt out of place but was trying to ignore the sadness that so desperately wanted to creep into her body.

"Rumer now is a good time to get acquainted with one another," Melanie said sitting beside her.

Melanie was the traveling therapist that signed on to stay with Rumer for as long as she needed. Melanie had her master's degree in psychotherapy and had high accolades.

She was in her mid-forties and possessed a youthful look to her small frame.

Rumer turned to her and sighed. Now that she was actually with the therapist, she was second guessing it.

"But I ate today," she said defensively.

Melanie nodded.

"Yes, you ate a salad with leaves, no dressing, and no meat. You weigh 150 pounds, Rumer. That can hardly fill you up dear," she replied.

Rumer's mother pretended to be asleep in the front of the jet with her two church sisters that she'd brought along with her.

"I would like for you to write in your food diary daily. Explain how you feel once you eat your foods then I would like for you to read it back to yourself. I also want to start CBT therapy with you. You are what I would call a functioning purger. You purge just enough to not lose yourself in it but that's not healthy either. You suffered from a heart attack, right?"

Rumer nodded with her body heating up.

"I did," she mumbled.

Melanie gave her a warm smile.

"Its fine relax. I've been doing this for twenty years, sweetie. We're going to change this behavior and get you together. With Cognitive Behavior Therapy, you take a hands-on approach to finding out just why people do the things that they do in terms of purging, etc. It's usually twenty sessions but since I'm traveling with you, we will do it until you feel you're ready for me to leave. How do you honestly feel knowing that you ate that salad an hour ago?" Melanie asked.

Rumer took a deep breath and sighed.

"Honestly?"

Melanie nodded.

"Always. This is a judgment free zone and make no mistakes about it Rumer. No one walking this earth is perfect. Everyone has something that they could improve about themselves," Melanie replied.

Rumer sat her hands in her lap and glanced down at her manicured nails.

"I feel hungry and worried," she admitted meekly.

Melanie gazed her way.

"Why those two things?"

Rumer licked her lips as she sighed.

"Hungry because that's all I've eaten today and worried because even though it's a salad I'm wondering if I'll get fat from it? I'm wondering where will the weight go? My butt or my gut. It's a lot and it makes me feel anxious. Like I need to vomit or take a laxative. Something to just get the shit out of my body," she replied truthfully.

Rumer closed her eyes after speaking. Rumer had never spoken so candidly about her eating disorder before. It was scary yet very real and it was happening even if she didn't want to admit it.

"Rumer, how did this come about?"

Rumer opened her eyes and looked out of the window at the clouds.

"I have always been known as the pretty *fat* girl. The pretty but *fat* friend. If I met a boy, we would be cool, and he would even try to have sex with me, but it was never in public. I was always friend zoned even with Takim."

Melanie pulled out her Ipad and made a few notes.

"And who is that?"

Rumer swallowed hard. He'd sent cards, flowers and had even come to her father's funeral but he was the past. Rumer had way too much shit going on to focus on the nigga that couldn't do her right when he had the chance. Her father passing away showed her to live in the now. Don't focus on the past because it will surely hold you back.

"He's a high school crush that I later went on to be with secretly," Rumer replied and glanced across the jet at her mom.

Melanie made a few more notes.

"And how did that end?"

Rumer thought of Takim's fiancé turned wife and shook her head.

"He had a baby on me. He chose what he felt was the better woman. This skinny girl with the pretty smile and all of that and I gracefully bowed out," she replied and rolled her eyes.

"Rumer do you want to be skinny?"

Rumer immediately shook her head.

"No. I'm black and our culture doesn't care about being skinny. I just wanna be the best Rumer that I can be. The Rumer with no stomach, no stretch marks, no fat in any of the places that it shouldn't be. If I can make a bank account go from $500.00 to $500,000 on my own without my daddies help why can't I have the perfect body?"

Melanie looked at Rumer.

"Name some things that you hate to eat and do," Melanie told her.

Rumer chewed on her bottom lip before sighing.

"I hate fatty foods. I hate scary movies and I fucking hate country and western music," she replied.

Melanie smiled. She passed Rumer her Ipad.

"I want you to play some country and western music. Two songs then cut on a scary movie off Netflix," she told her.

Rumer looked at her like she was crazy.

"Why would I do that?"

Melanie shrugged.

"Why not?"

Rumer passed her back the Ipad.

"Because I hate those things and I choose to not watch or listen to that mess."

Melanie nodded while making a few notes on her device.

"But you hate your body also Rumer. Something you have control over and you're choosing to keep on hating it."

Rumer's face tightened.

"And how am I choosing to keep hating it? You think I wanna feel like this?"

Melanie sat back in her seat.

"Rumer nothing in life happens without change. You're choosing to do things that place your life in danger. I know this is a disease, but life is about choices. No matter how hard they are we have to decide what's right and wrong for us. Your happiness is right on the other side of fear.

What is the one thing that you would change about your life if you could?" she asked.

Rumer smiled.

"I'd have my father back alive," she said without having to think of the answer.

Melanie's smiled mirrored her's.

"And yet you didn't mention your weight. It's all superficial. As long as you know who you are, and you love yourself the rest will come easy," Melanie told her.

Rumer nodded although she didn't feel like anything concerning her weight issues would be easy.

Greenish blue-hued ocean waters were surrounded by pillars that raised up out of the water. Mountains could be seen from the shore along with tall buildings. After settling into their rental home Rumer began her CBT therapy with Melanie while her mother and her church sisters began their mission work.

A week ghosted by and Rumer was on the verge of going crazy. She missed working, she missed her girls, even Kritt but most of all she missed purging. Melanie connected her with a South African health coach and she'd been on a diet since touching down. With a full belly and no vomiting, Rumer felt fat as fuck.

She huffed then pouted as she sat on the sand with an empty bottle of water in her hand. In the beginning leaving felt like the right thing to do but now she was ready to take her ass back to the states.

"Hi! Can I make a sand castle over here?" a pretty copper shaded girl asked running up with two buckets in her hand.

Rumer looked up at the child who appeared to be around nine and nodded. The young girl was gorgeous. She wore a pink short set with her silky long curly hair in two pig tails. She housed chunky cheeks, with a round belly that poked out of her shirt and a bright smile. She reminded Rumer so much of her younger self.

Rumer swallowed down her tears and cleared her throat.

"Sure," she chirped with a small smile.

The child grinned and plopped down in the spot beside Rumer.

"I'm Tennille! Who are you?" she asked pulling sand towards her.

Rumer went to speak, and a wave of cologne floated her way. The notes in the cologne awakened Rumer's body as she saw a large shadow in the sand. Seconds later a muscular frame took up space on the side of Tennille. Rumer forced herself to stare straight ahead as his scent flirted with her nostrils.

"Hey, what up? I'm Nahmir. If my daughter's bothering you, you can move," he said smoothly. Rumer soaked in his words while smiling until she realized what he said. She frowned over at him and his thick lips curved into a smile. He chuckled as he looked at her. It was deep and made his abdominal muscles clench slightly as he did it. "I'm messing with you mami. Are we interrupting your waiting to exhale moment?" he asked.

Rumer's brows pulled together, and she shook her head. Nahmir's down-turned whiskey colored eyes stared at Rumer unashamedly.

"You got your wine and your books, so I figured you was having a moment. My daughter is a people's person so she's always making new friends," he explained.

Rumer tossed her blanket over the half-empty bottle of wine and smiled. She thought of her curly tresses that sat on top of her head in a messy bun and sighed.

She was positive she looked like shit.

"No, she's good. How could I ask someone as adorable as her to leave?" she asked recognizing the handsome man that was beside her. He was a celebrity in his own right. His last name along rung bells not only in Michigan but across the states. Everyone knew who the Yaasmin's were. "Do you own the casino's over here?" she asked.

Nahmir's hooded eyes narrowed, and he sat up. He grabbed his daughter's bucket pales as he frowned.

"Come on Tennille," he demanded rising to his feet.

Tennille pouted as Rumer stared up at him.

"I like to read Forbes in my downtime. I can get nerdy like that sometimes. I'm not some reporter or anything. I'm from Detroit on a recovery vacation and how could I be from the "D" and not know who you are? I didn't mean anything by it," she rambled on with her hands on her lap.

Nahmir stared down at Rumer for a few minutes before his jaw went lax. He sat back down and handed his daughter her bucket. He then adjusted the Nick Fouquet hat on his head and peered over at Rumer. Rumer studied the handsome Nahmir taken with his looks. Anyone familiar with the Yaasmin family knew they mainly consisted of biracial people. African American and Moroccan. From what Rumer knew the Yaasmin men loved black women and she could see that Nahmir did as well. Although his daughter was a pretty copper shade, he was deep olive toned with whiskey rimmed eyes and thick full lips. He carried a neatly groomed beard along with a straight nose and chiseled jaw.

Rumer's eyes deliberately slid over his physique that was on display in his basketball shorts and with every dip and groove of his muscles, her mouth grew drier. She swallowed hard and Nahmir smirked at her.

"Thirsty?"

Rumer frowned at his question.

"Excuse me?"

Nahmir pulled out water from a bag nearby and passed Rumer the bottle. Rumer took the small water bottle and smiled sheepishly.

"Yes, thank you. I'm all over the place right now," she said and laughed to hide her nervousness.

Nahmir nodded and pulled out his cell phone. Rumer sat beside him quietly as he made various phone calls. Rumer listened to a business call concerning a venture Nahmir was pursuing when his daughter splashed a bucket of water in her face.

Nahmir and Rumer looked her way in shock as she giggled.

"Come on let's play!" she yelled and ran off.

Rumer huffed as she wiped the water from her eyes. She liked looking at the ocean, but swimming wasn't her thing. She also wasn't geeked about standing up in her swimsuit. Her stomach was bloated as fuck.

"My bad about that. Her mom passed away a few months ago and since then she gets excited whenever we around a woman. It can be the chick at the Starbucks and she's hugging her and shit. You good?" Nahmir asked.

Rumer nodded. She'd read about his daughters mother's death and had honestly forgotten about it. However, her heart went out to Nahmir and his daughter. She stood up and grabbed her things.

"I'm good and I'm sorry to hear about that," she said quietly.

Rumer began to walk away, and Nahmir grabbed her arm. She glanced back at him and peered up into his eyes.

"I ain't get your name," he said before glancing over at his daughter that was now making mud pies.

Rumer sighed.

"It's Rumer. Rumer Matigo," she replied used to giving out her full name in terms of networking.

Nahmir grinned down at her.

"Rumer Matigo, huh? Well, I'm Nahmir Yaasmin. Enjoy the rest of your day mami," he replied and let her go.

Rumer walked away without replying with a small smile on her face. She remembered that she had a meeting with her therapist and the smile immediately fell.

Three days later Rumer found herself inside a small village in Port Elizabeth. She along with her mother and the church were helping hundreds of families. Rumer found a new respect for her mom as she watched her diligently work with the villagers. It was a sparkle in her mother's eye that she'd never seen before that had Rumer feeling closer to her mom. Her mother was far from perfect but what she was doing for the less fortunate was amazing. It even made Rumer pull out her check book.

"This was really nice. To see so many places without clean water or even doors is crazy to me. I knew a lot of people lived like this but to see it firsthand is disheartening," Rumer voiced looking at her mother.

Rachel nodded as she wiped her dirty hands on her long skirt. She rubbed Rumer's arm lovingly and smiled at her.

"I know, and this is why I do this. I made so many mistakes in my past. From hiding you from your father to dropping the ball as your mother. I know this can't right my wrongs, but I want to be better. This feels right for me and

I'm thankful that you were able to give me the means to do this. I love you sweetie. How are you feeling?"

Rumer shrugged. She felt a magnitude of things but didn't want to rain on her mother's parade.

"I'm good. I'm going to head back to the house now. Will you be okay here?"

Rachel nodded as she looked towards the black SUV's that were pulling up. She cleared her throat as her hand fell from Rumer's arm.

"This charity is working with us as well. They're responsible for the newly built homes we saw earlier," she replied still staring at the luxury vehicles.

Rumer looked towards the SUV's with her mom and swallowed hard when Nahmir exited the black G-Wagon. He wore blue jeans with a crisp white t-shirt and a blue blazer. He brushed his left hand over his curly low taper and Rumer took a step back. Like before she was what she considered at her worst and immediately regretted not dressing up before she left the rental home that morning.

Rumer wore cut off jean shorts with furry slides and a loose fitting dirty pink t-shirt that hung off her shoulder.

"Ms. Matigo, we meet again," he said walking up.

Behind Nahmir was two well-dressed men that strongly resembled him. Rumer smiled as Nahmir grabbed her mother's hand. He kissed the back of it as his cologne, the same as before breezed over the space they were in.

Rumer watched her mother blush and she shook her head. *Come on ma, we both can't want to fuck him,* she thought and smiled to herself.

"Mr. Yaasmin, thank you again for all of your help. The mission president would like to speak with you," Rachel announced.

Nahmir nodded as his whiskey peepers stared down at Rumer.

"Not a problem. Could I speak with your daughter for a minute?" he asked politely.

Rachel glanced over at Rumer and nodded.

"Sure, I'll be at the table," she replied and walked away with Nahmir's cousins following her.

Nahmir walked over to Rumer and touched a piece of her curly hair. What started out as a wet and go was now a loose curly fro. He twirled the soft strand around his finger as Rumer's nerves went haywire. She noted the diamond sitting in his left ear along with his diamond bezel watch. The jewelry wasn't gaudy but nice to look at however his face was what made her panties grow wet.

Nahmir was fine as shit and Rumer could tell by the smirk on his face that he knew it.

"Me and my daughter would like to take you out before we leave. Can I make that happen?" he asked boldly.

Rumer swallowed hard. She stared down at the ground becoming overwhelmed with the man before her and Nahmir leaned down. His breath fanned her neck as he cleared his throat.

"Just say yes. I'll pick you up at eight and by the way you look beautiful," he said and before she could respond he was walking away.

Rumer smiled to herself as he headed for her mother's table that was surrounded by missionary workers.

"He doesn't even know where I'm at. What the hell," she mumbled. "But he did know that was my mom, so I see he looked me up," Rumer smiled at the thought of Nahmir checking up on her before heading to her rental. She hit the locks and glanced back at him one last time. "Well if he really wants to see me, he'll get the address," she said and got into her car.

Rumer returned to her rental home and searched the space for Melanie. She found every room to be empty and her insides churned with delight. Rumer quickly went to her bedroom and locked the door. She rushed to the bathroom and grabbed her toothbrush. Rumer padded over to the toilet bowl and dropped down to her knees. Her body grew warm and her heart raced as she turned the toothbrush around and shoved the long end into her awaiting mouth.

Rumer closed her eyes and after three seconds she shoved it down her throat. She began to gag and seconds later vomit shot up her throat and out of her mouth. Rumer tossed the toothbrush onto the ground as she expelled the contents of her stomach.

After vomiting until she couldn't anymore Rumer took a hot shower and exited the bathroom. She yelped when she noticed Melanie sitting on the edge of her bed. Melanie held a pensive look on her face as she cradled her tablet.

"Hi," Melanie spoke quietly.

Rumer tugged on the top of her towel and smiled nervously.

"Hi, when did you get a key to my room?"

Melanie broke her gaze and stood up. She walked past Rumer and went into the bathroom. Melanie emerged minutes later with the dirty toothbrush. She passed the brush to Rumer and shook her head.

"I was worried when I knocked on your door and you didn't answer. I did assume the worst, so I grabbed the spare key and used it. I then heard the shower running and my thoughts ran wild. I've been doing this for years Rumer and I've seen it all before. Again, I'm not here to judge you. I'm also not here to waste my time. This isn't about money for me. I love what I do and if you aren't willing to be better for yourself then let me know so I can find another person that is," she said and walked away.

Rumer stared down at the toothbrush with watery lenses. She dropped it onto the ground and began to get dressed. Rumer brushed her teeth with a new toothbrush before brushing her hair back into a slick bun. She then put on light makeup and forced herself into the only dress she'd brought with her. A black strapless number that she paired with strappy gold sandals and gold accessories.

Rumer spritzed on her favorite perfume before looking at herself in the mirror. Already she was gaining weight and she didn't like it. It was hard to see the fullness of her stomach and face and feel good things about it.

She closed her eyes as the guilt from purging washed over her.

"God, I'm trying. Please forgive me," she whispered.

"Rumer someone's here for you," Melanie said stepping into the bedroom.

Rumer opened her eyes and stared at her therapist.

"I won't be fixed overnight."

Melanie nodded as she gave her a once over.

"I know but change only comes to those who want it. Enjoy your night and by the way you look lovely," she told her.

Rumer watched Melanie walk away before grabbing her clutch. She wanted to grab her cell that had been powered off but opted out of taking it. It felt good to not be stressed out by the outside world and for the moment she wanted to relish in that.

Rumer found Nahmir downstairs standing in the doorway with his pretty daughter standing beside him. They both wore black attire with big smiles on their faces. While Tennille wore a black dress with ballerina slippers Nahmir wore black slacks with a collard black shirt. Rumer admired the sexy way he stood, so confident, so demanding with his presence and she swallowed hard.

"Daddy she's so pretty like me!" Tennille noted as Rumer walked up.

Rumer smiled as she advanced on them.

"I wasn't sure if you two were coming but I'm glad I got dressed anyway. Tennille you look so gorgeous," she said smiling.

Tennille waved her off and Nahmir chuckled.

"My daddy already said I looked pretty now he needs to tell you that," his daughter said loudly.

Rumer glanced up at Nahmir and he smiled at her. He stepped forward and grabbed her small hand.

"You look pretty Rumer," he spoke huskily.

Rumer swallowed the extra saliva in her mouth. She stared up into Nahmir's eyes and found herself getting drunk off his gaze.

"Thank you, so do you," she murmured.

His daughter laughed, and he shook his head.

"She said you look pretty daddy," Tennille said and Nahmir chuckled.

"She doped up on candy right now. Let's head out so she can make it to bed on time. We have an early flight out tomorrow," he announced.

Rumer nodded suddenly feeling saddened by his words. She walked hand in hand out of the home with Nahmir and his child. The driver opened the door for the trio and Nahmir allowed for the women to slide into the car before he did. Rumer looked at his daughter as the sedan slowly drove away.

"Is this your first time in Africa?" she asked.

Tennille shook her head as she pulled out a small cellular device. Rumer noticed Tennille's jewelry and smiled. The young girl was more iced out than she was.

"No, my daddy and grandpa have businesses over here. I don't really know how many times I've been. How about you?" she asked.

Rumer smiled as her eyes briefly connected with Nahmir's. He watched her closely with an intense look on his handsome face.

"It's my first time. I always wanted to come but it's because of my mom that I'm here," Rumer replied.

Tennille typed away on her phone and seconds later Nahmir's phone made a ding sound alerting every one of his text message. Tennille put her phone away and gave Rumer her attention as Nahmir checked out his alert.

"So, what do you do?" Tennille asked Rumer.

Rumer wondered briefly what the text message said before answering Tennille.

"I'm a real estate agent..." Rumer thought of her late father and her heart ached all over again. Her eyes saddened as she cleared her throat. "I actually own a real estate company," she replied.

Tennille's eyes widened.

"You sell houses?" she asked.

Rumer nodded.

"Yes, and I now employ people that do as well. My father recently passed away and he left it to me," she said and stared out of the window. Rumer's eyes grew watery and Tennille grabbed her hand. She squeezed it lightly and Rumer glanced over at her.

"I lost my mommy, so I know what it feels like. It'll get better," she told her.

Rumer smiled at the adorable girl choosing to not respond to her last statement. Rumer talked with Nahmir and his daughter until the car pulled up to the vineyard. They were shown to the outside terrace overlooking the olive grove plants and mountains. Rumer gasped at the beautiful scenery as they sat down.

"My daddy owns this too!" Tennille announced excitedly.

Rumer nodded. She could see firsthand that Tennille, like her was a daddy's girl.

"And it's one of the most beautiful restaurants I've ever been too," Rumer replied still taken with the place they were at.

Tennille nodded and read over her menu. Rumer sat still in her seat and Nahmir glanced over at her.

"You not hungry?"

Rumer quickly shook her head and Tennille smacked her lips.

"You should eat some food! Every time we come it tastes good, right daddy?"

Nahmir nodded while smiling and Rumer's face fell into a grin. She grabbed the menu and read over the salad options.

"I guess I could do a salad," she mumbled.

"No, you have to eat more. My favorite food is tuna, but you might need a steak. Daddy said you needed some meat on your bones," Tennille revealed, and Rumer's eyes darted over to Nahmir.

He held his phone with widened eyes. He relaxed in his seat and peered over at his talkative daughter. Tennille pouted under his stern gaze and shook her head.

"Sorry daddy," she mumbled.

Nahmir looked back to Rumer and licked his thick lips.

"I didn't mean shit by that. I just enjoy looking at women with some weight to them. I wasn't trying to offend you beautiful," he replied.

Rumer nodded and looked back down at the menu. After eating dinner and enjoying dessert Rumer found herself leaving the restaurant with Nahmir and his daughter. His daughter slept peacefully in the car as Nahmir stared at Rumer. All night his cellphone had been ringing off the hook, yet he hadn't stepped away from the table once. Rumer was intrigued by him and tickled pink by his outgoing, beautiful daughter.

"You can take her home first. I don't have anywhere to be," she said not ready for their time to end.

Tennille carried on the entire conversation at the restaurant and while Rumer enjoyed it immensely, she felt like she had unfinished business with Nahmir.

"You sure?" he asked.

Rumer nodded quickly and stopped when she realized how thirsty she was acting. She sat back and placed her hands on her lap.

"Yes, I'm fine with that," she replied calmly.

Nahmir nodded and instructed the driver to take them by his home first. After dropping off his daughter to the nanny that traveled with him Nahmir rode back to Rumer's rental home and walked her in. Rumer grabbed his hand and led him onto the patio. Her rental home was blessed with a beautiful view of the ocean and was relaxing to look at. She waved her hand over towards the glass table and smiled.

"A drink before you head home?"

Nahmir took a seat and unbuttoned his shirt. Rumer forced herself to not stare at his bare chest that peeked out at her.

"It's hot as shit out here and yeah, you got some dark liquor?" he asked.

"I should," she replied before walking away.

Rumer grabbed a bottle of Hennessey and took it out onto the patio along with two glasses. She placed it on the table before Nahmir and he smirked up at her. He whistled as he read over the name of the liquor.

"Hennessey Paradise, what you know about that mami?"

Rumer sat down as stars filled her eyes. *Mami.* Every time the word slipped from his lips her vaginal muscles clenched together.

"I figured I would need a good drink while being out here," she replied watching him pour them both a drink.

"And why exactly are you out here again?" he asked pushing the glass her way.

Rumer slipped her shoes off and released her hair from the tight bun it was in. She ran her hands through her tresses as she stared Nahmir's way.

"I recently buried my father and I took it hard. I also have some other issues going on," she replied.

Nahmir drunk down some of his liquor before scooting closer to Rumer. His large hand covered her thigh as he stared her way.

"Close your eyes beautiful," he demanded and like an obedient woman she immediately did as he'd instructed. Nahmir leaned towards Rumer and caressed her neck. Rumer moaned as her body relaxed in the seat. "Issues like what?" he asked continuing with his sensual massage.

Rumer sighed. She swallowed down her fears as his fingers gently pressed into her skin.

"I have an eating disorder," she revealed.

Rumer could feel the weight lift off her shoulders at her revelation. She waited for him to respond as he continued with the massage. Nahmir sat back and pulled both of her legs onto his lap. He began to massage her feet and out of fear of what he was thinking Rumer kept her eyes closed.

"I would have never guessed that Ms. Matigo. I gotta say I hate to hear that. Someone as beautiful as you should embrace yourself at any weight. How is being out here helping you?"

Rumer opened her eyes as his hands did magical things to her feet.

"I have a therapist that traveled with me."

Nahmir stared at Rumer intently as his thumb pressed into the heel of her foot.

"Tell me about your pops," he said changing the subject.

Rumer smiled like she always did when thinking of her father.

"He was a loving man. My bestfriend and I miss him so much. I suffered from a heart attack and on that day he did as well. I still don't understand why God didn't take me instead of him? Lately living hasn't been that appealing to me," she revealed.

Nahmir shook his head. He grabbed his glass and tossed back the rest of his drink. As he sat the empty glass down, he stared at Rumer.

"When my mom passed away, I was fucked up about it. At that point I felt invincible at life. Me and my cousins was living on our own terms and I did what the fuck I wanted. I'd lost a few family members even a close cousin named Marcio that hurt but to lose my mom crushed a nigga. I stopped running my businesses and gave up on life. I was out popping pills, doing whatever to numb the pain and I met this woman. She was a model and we ended up fucking," he said and smirked. Rumer shook her head while smiling and he continued. "From that one night stand my daughter was created. I always say that in the midst of my storm my biggest blessing happened. I'm not saying that you gone get pregnant or nothing like that but know that something huge is on the way. Tennille's mom passed away in her sleep from a brain bleed. For months, my baby cried nonstop until she woke up one day smiling. She said that her mom came to her in a dream and told her to be happy. She'd give anything to have her back and you're sitting over here looking like you ready to jump off in the ocean at any minute. We gotta start valuing the things we have because they can be taken away from us at any minute. Especially our life."

Rumer broke Nahmir's gaze and swallowed hard. Nahmir sat her feet down and sat up in his seat. His warm hands rubbed up and down her bare arms as she thought about the things he'd said.

"I didn't say that to be an asshole. I want you to be as strong as my daughter thinks you are. She was texting me shit all night talking about you. She done known you for two days and already she sees a bunch of good things in you."

Rumer smirked. She looked at Nahmir and licked her lips.

"And what do you see when you look at me?"

Nahmir bit down hard on his bottom lip and Rumer held her breath. Being so close to him made her body come alive.

"I see a beautiful woman that is on the verge of giving up but strong enough to keep going. Temporarily broken but at some point, we all are. Next time I see you, shit will be different. Right?"

Rumer smiled. She leaned towards Nahmir as the liquor began to heat up her insides.

"I pray it'll be very different..." Rumer stopped talking and Nahmir's fingers found their way into her hair. "No, I know things will be different," she declared and Nahmir nodded.

"That's what I like to hear mami," he said before pulling her into a mouth-watering kiss.

Seven

Tall sky rises could be seen for miles and miles away. On the block, young girls played with sidewalk chalk while a few girls hung out on the steps talking to their friends. Traffic was at a stand-still and music played from the car speakers that blared out into the open air.

The building that sat on W.115 in Harlem was nice. Completely renovated. No lie high as fuck but thanks to Rumer, her ace in the whole she was able to purchase it without batting a lash. It had been hard. Making such a drastic move but it felt right.

Jerzey knew if she were to stay in Detroit, she would have gotten lost in Snowden and possibly fallen back into a depression. It also didn't help that her ex-boyfriend was back in town. Jerzey didn't feel like leaving her girls when she felt they needed her the most, but she had to choose herself. Jerzey had to put Jerzey first and not miss the opportunity God sent her way.

"Everyone is pleased with your work Jerzey. It's so many celebrities coming in for this and they're already asking for you to do more events. Giuseppe is doing a Cancer luncheon and they've mentioned you designing a few pieces for them to auction off. New York is elated to have you," Sonique said and winked at her.

Sonique was her New York plug. The manager at Neiman's and she was Jerzey's go to girl since Jerzey was new to the city.

"That's great because I damn near went broke moving here but it's all good. He wouldn't lead me this far to let me drown. Just let me know if they need anything else from me," Jerzey replied.

Sonique nodded. She sent Jerzey air kisses before leaving out of Jerzey's studio. Like before it was on the first floor of her building while her apartment or rather apartments since her building possessed two were upstairs. Jerzey was still decorating, nowhere near done but she was content. Satisfied with the changes she'd undergone to make herself happy.

Jerzey turned on some music and as the singer, Tamia's **More** cd played softly in her studio she went over to her canvas. It was a photo of Snowden. Jerzey missed him terribly. His voice, his scent even his mean scowl. Her eyes lowered as she stared at the painting. The lyrics touched Jerzey in a way that had her eyes leaking with tears as she slid her brush across the canvas.

Still,

feels like the first time we met

That I kissed,
and I told you
I love you

Jerzey stopped the music on her device and whimpered. Her moments with Snowden were cut short before they even started. That was what hurt the most. She grabbed her phone and took a deep breath. Jerzey scrolled down to his number and decided to video-call him.

The phone rang until the voicemail picked up and Jerzey ended the call. Jerzey swallowed down her pain as another tear slid down her face. She went to their text messages and decided to send him a message.

I'm in love with you Snowden. I miss you and I know what happened is hurtful, but this hurts too. Us not being together is truly hurting me.

Jerzey sent the message and immediately it was read. She watched a bubble appear and disappear twice before if disappeared. The message sat on read and Jerzey nodded. She sat her phone down as her eyes connected with the canvas.

She'd vividly painted Snowden's handsome face. Making sure to capture those intense eyes of his. Jerzey stared into them as her heart raced. She missed him so fucking much and was slowly losing her mind without him. Everything that she was doing was to keep her afloat, but the fact still remained she was without her man. Someone she was in love with and the more time that skated by the more she began to fill like getting back with him wasn't a possibility.

Camera crews lined the left wall. Glasses of champagne was passed around like water as people chatted amongst each other. Her name sat on a display against the right wall in neon pink lights.

A huge sense of pride coursed through her veins as she stared at the retro lettering. For the event, she rocked a curly unit that reached the top of her ample behind. On her body was a black Milano Di Rouge custom outfit. The material stuck to her skin exposing her sensual curves and making her stand out in the Nieman Marcus store.

Jerzey nursed her champagne wishing it was her favorite whiskey instead as she stood in the packed room.

"This is like so fucking dope," Miko gushed standing beside her.

Jerzey grinned and glanced over at her girl. Miko was rocking all white with her hair in soft curls as black matte lipstick covered her lips. Nelly stood beside her, all smiles in her stonewashed ankle jeans that she'd paired with a black blouse and Fendi pumps.

"It is, and this is only the beginning," Nelly added.

Jerzey nodded feeling the same way. She appreciated her friends showing up despite their own hectic lives.

"I know, and I wish Rumer was here. But her health is important, so I understand her being gone. Miko where's Enika?" Jerzey asked.

Miko cleared her throat.

"Home with her parents. I'm going to get another drink," she replied before walking off.

Jerzey looked at Nelly with a raised brow.

"That's your friend. How is she?" Jerzey asked.

Nelly sighed.

"Honestly, I don't know. When we met at the airport that was the first time I'd seen her in weeks. I'm dealing with a lot of shit. Nero is back in Philly and he has Jasir. My wedding day came and went Jerzey. I'm all messed up right now. I can't even sleep at home from the anxiety my life is giving me," Nelly revealed with saddened eyes.

Jerzey walked over to her friend and pulled her into a tight embrace.

"Nelly this is crazy. You shouldn't be going through this alone. Do you wanna come out here with me?"

Nelly shook her head.

"I have to fix what I've done. I'm staying with a friend and working on the issues that I have. Please keep me in your prayers," she replied quietly.

Jerzey rubbed her back while smiling.

"Always, that goes without saying."

"Just the girl we were looking for. This is Jaleed and he was looking for some custom pieces for his new restaurant," Sonique said walking over with Jerzey's ex-boyfriend.

Jerzey let Nelly go and her eyes ventured over to Jaleed. He looked more handsome than he did the night he'd popped up on her. He donned all black with a Detroit fitted sitting low on his head still the yearning in his eyes couldn't be missed. He licked his thick lips as he stared her way.

"Damn," Nelly muttered.

He smiled, and the women were blessed with his pearly whites. His right cheek showed off his deep dimple as his eyes peered down at Jerzey lustfully.

"What up ma? I love your style and I need some shit asap," he said and clasped his hands in front of himself.

Jerzey stared up at him at a loss for words. She swallowed hard and Jaleed grabbed her hand. He pulled her close to him then into a hug.

"I'm real fucking proud of you," he murmured.

Jerzey closed her eyes as he held her body tightly. Like before she was flooded with the times they'd shared. Some good and a lot of the bad. She pulled back and gave him a tight-lipped smile.

"I'd love to sell you some pieces," she said trying to remain calm.

"Then bless me with that number," Jaleed said passing Jerzey his phone.

Jerzey held the phone for several minutes before finally putting her number in. She handed the phone back to her ex-boyfriend and Sonique grinned beside him.

"Perfect! This girl is a hot commodity so don't sleep on her," she bragged and Jaleed smirked at Jerzey. His slanted eyes looked Jerzey over once more and he shook his head.

"Nah, even a blind man would see the talent she has on her. It was good seeing you, ma. I'ma be hitting you up soon," he replied and walked away.

"Jerzey you're on it!" Sonique raved and shook her head. "I'm so glad you came out here. See you next week and don't forget corporate will be at the meeting," Sonique said and walked off.

Jerzey glanced over at a smiling Nelly and shook her head.

"Nelly that was my fucking ex-boyfriend."

Nelly's jaw fell slack.

"No shit? The big-time hustler you used to talk about that was locked up?"

Jerzey nodded and her eyes scanned the room for him. She watched him exit the store and she sighed with relief.

"I can't believe he's out either. He popped up on me right before I left, and I told him to leave me alone. I had no idea he would bring his extra ass out here Nelly," Jerzey said before shaking her head.

Nelly stared at her friend with a smile gracing her pretty face.

"And looking like he's ready to get you back. I can't lie he's fine as hell too. All tall and sexy with a deep ass voice. He even smelled good. I swear you know how to pull 'em," Nelly said and they both smiled. "But I'm not sure how your new man is gonna like that. And where is Snowden at by the way?" Nelly asked and glanced around the store.

Jerzey stopped smiling when she realized Nelly knew nothing about her split with Snowden. She shifted from one foot to the other as she pondered over a way to break the news to her friend without incriminating her baby. Jerzey trusted Nelly but didn't think her friend could know of the shooting and not relay it to her own man.

"He's...he's—"

"Oh, girl there he go right there," Nelly said and Jerzey was instantly light headed.

Jerzey followed Nelly's line of sight and spotted Snowden walking into the store. He held a beautiful arrangement of red roses with a small frown marring his handsome face. Jerzey watched Miko walk up on him and exchange words with him before heading their way.

"He's still rude as fuck," Miko grumbled making Jerzey smile.

Jerzey stood by nervously as Snowden walked towards her. With their last encounter running through her mind Jerzey gazed up at the man she loved immensely with timorous eyes. Snowden was on his bullshit like usual looking handsome as ever. He wore Fear Of God white and black joggers with black Yeezy's and a black hoodie. His diamonds sparkled under the store lighting as his high-low curly fade brought attention to the soft texture of hair sitting on his head. Then there was his neatly lined up mustache that caused you to look at his thick lips. On his face were a pair of gold wired Cartier frames and they only added to his already immaculate style.

Jerzey swallowed hard as his intense eyes gave her a deliberate once-over. It felt as if an eternity went by before Snowden walked up on her. He cleared his throat as Nelly and Miko stood protectively at Jerzey's side. He licked his lips and gave her a sly smile as he entered Jerzey's personal space.

"Look at youse. This shit nice, congrats," he said and handed Jerzey the flowers.

Jerzey nodded nervously. She took the beautiful roses and sniffed them. Their scent paled in comparison to Snowden's alluring cologne.

"Thank you," she whispered avoiding direct eye contact with him.

Miko cleared her throat while looking between Snowden and Jerzey.

"Okay, now Snowden we was taking our girl out tonight to celebrate. You coming?" she asked.

Snowden nodded with knitted brows.

"Of course," he replied and Jerzey licked her lips.

Sonique clinked her glass to get everyone's attention and Snowden pulled Jerzey to his side. Jerzey stood anxiously beside him as she looked Sonique's way.

"On behalf of Neiman Marcus, I would like to thank you all for coming out. All of the pieces that were presented today were sold-out an hour into the event and we are elated at the turnout. This night couldn't have happened without the talented Jerzey. She's now a New York resident and we're thankful to have her. Let's give this gorgeous young lady a hand!"

Everyone clapped as Jerzey blushed from the attention.

"New York resident?" Snowden mumbled quietly and Jerzey ignored him.

She did a small bow and people began to leave out of the store. After packing away her things and thanking Sonique one more time Jerzey left the store with Miko, Nelly, and Snowden.

While her friends rode in the back of his Bentayaga, Jerzey rode beside him. A million thoughts swarmed her mind as she pretended to be engulfed with the soft rap that was playing throughout the truck.

The *Mon Amour* restaurant sat between Park Avenue and Madison Avenue. It was retro chic. Bringing young urban, hip-hop culture to the pricey neighborhood. Valet was packed and as the foursome waited for the cars before them to be emptied Snowden glanced over at Jerzey.

"Youse good?"

Jerzey nodded. She stared out the window at the beautiful restaurant while smiling.

"I heard about this place online. I heard the music exec Draco opened it for his wife Hill," Jerzey said to no one in particular.

"Yes, I read that too. She's pretty and he's sexy as hell. Wouldn't mind laying between them two at night," Miko quipped.

Snowden shook his head as Nelly and Jerzey snickered inside the truck.

"I met old boy a few times through my nigga Keem. That's his people and shit. We should have a table waiting on us thanks to him," Snowden said and pulled out his ringing phone.

Jerzey nearly broke a blood vessel as she attempted to watch him out the corner of her eye.

"It's just his sister," Miko said making Snowden glare back at her. She smiled at him and Snowden's hard reverie softened.

"You still say whatever the fuck you feel like saying," he commented as he texted on his phone.

Miko nodded.

"And will forever be that way," she stated proudly.

"Yeah until Zyir gets his hands on you," Jerzey mumbled and Miko pinched her arm.

Fifteen minutes later valet walked up to the Bentayaga and everyone exited the truck. While the women walked behind them Snowden walked alongside Jerzey holding her hand.

"I'm sorry," he apologized quietly as they approached a secluded booth in the back of the restaurant.

Jerzey slid into the booth and Snowden slid in beside her. Miko and Nelly looked at the attractive pair all smiles.

"We're going to slide off into another spot. Now that your man is here, we don't wanna impose. We'll be over tomorrow boo. You two have a good night," Miko said to them.

Snowden nodded always short with his words for Miko. Jerzey frowned as she looked at her girls.

"But this was my celebratory dinner," she whined.

Nelly grinned at her.

"Look we need at least one of us to have a damn man. We can't all be out here single as fuck. People gone start to think something's wrong with us. This is New York, we'll find something to do. Talk to you later," Nelly replied before they walked away.

Snowden smirked as he glanced over at Jerzey.

"Shit something just might be wrong with y'all asses," he quipped and even Jerzey cracked a smile before shaking her head.

"Me and my girls are good. We need to be discussing us anyway."

Snowden nodded as the waiter walked over with menus and a bottle of champagne. She sat everything down before them and smiled while grabbing their champagne glasses.

"Everything is on the house. Andraco wants you all to be very comfortable. Would you like anything else to drink while you read over the menu?" the polite waitress asked.

Jerzey shook her head while Snowden cleared his throat.

"Yeah some dark liquor, Don Julio if you have it and a brownie for this beautiful ass girl right here," he replied.

The waitress nodded while smiling and walked away. Jerzey took a large sip of her champagne to ease her nerves. Here they were, what she'd been wanting since she'd left

Philly and now, she didn't know what to say to him. It was crazy to her and unsettling.

"Again, I'm proud of you. I bought some shit too," Snowden announced breaking the awkward silence.

Jerzey's lips stretched into a wide smile.

"Thank you."

Snowden shrugged still gazing her way.

"That's nothing. I'ma always be your biggest supporter."

Jerzey set her glass down and licked her lips.

"Even after all that's happened?"

Snowden's eyes saddened. He dropped his head and ran his left hand over his low-cut curls. For several minutes they sat in silence both lost in their own thoughts. The waitress returned with Snowden's bottle and they decided to order. Once the waitress walked away Snowden turned his attention to Jerzey.

"This shit not easy for me. Let's talk about you. You live here now?"

Jerzey's shoulders slumped at his words. She wanted them to discuss his brother and be done with it. She didn't want to come off insensitive but not talking about the shooting was placing them in a bad space.

One she was over being in.

"Yeah," she mumbled looking around the restaurant.

Snowden leaned over and caressed her neck tenderly. She closed her eyes as his warm breath kissed her face.

"I really did miss youse. I just need some time to get myself together. Time to deal with what the fuck I did, Jerzey. Can you give me that?" he asked and kissed the soft spot behind her ear.

Jerzey sighed. Snowden pulled back and grabbed his glass as she stared at him.

"But can you get over it? Will it always be like this?"

Snowden's brows furrowed.

"Like what?"

Jerzey snorted feeling herself become angry with her handsome beau.

"Like this! Me calling and texting you for days with no reply. In case you missed it, Snowden, life is still fucking happening. I moved, I started a life here and began to hang with new people. Stepped out of my comfort zone to be better. In hopes of being a better Jerzey. That sad, scared woman you met before no longer exists," she told him.

Snowden finished off his drink and frowned at her.

"What the fuck youse saying?" he asked with a tense jaw.

Jerzey swallowed hard and sat her hands on her lap. She looked at Snowden, soaked in his sexiness and even thought back on the nice times they shared. She was in love with him but wasn't going to force it. Either they were going to be together or they weren't. He could accept the blessing that she was in his life or miss out on it.

"I'm saying that I love you, but I won't wait forever. I can no longer be that girl. I'm a woman that's trying to be happy Snowden. *Very* fucking happy and if you aren't adding happiness to my life then there isn't a point in you being in it," she replied.

"Damn," Snowden muttered staring at her. He broke her gaze and Jerzey grabbed her glass.

Soon the food was brought out and they ate in silence. Instead of pondering over what Snowden's next move would be Jerzey basked in the glow of her success. She'd achieved something that she didn't think she could do and only saw herself going up from there. Regardless of what her relationship status was, she was good, and she didn't plan on that changing anytime soon. It was like she'd told Snowden. She was a new woman with only one objective in mind and it was happiness.

Eight

—···〈♡〉···—

The news played on the TV screen on low volume as the smell of homemade bulgogi floated throughout the vast living room. The baby grand piano sat in the corner shiny and ready to be put to use and just seeing it made a faint smile appear on her face.

As Zyir stepped into the room the smile quickly dissipated. Miko sat up straight and licked her lips. She was slightly drunk from all the wine she'd guzzled down earlier that day and prayed no-one noticed but truthfully, she didn't give a damn. Knowing that she had to be at the home she provided for her family was enough for her to want alcoholic relief.

"Nanmiko and Zyir, thank you for coming," Miko's mother said as she looked at them.

Miko's father was sitting quietly beside them in his wheelchair. Exhaustion hung heavy on his frail frame and for the first time in years, Miko felt bad about his situation.

She broke his gaze not wanting to feel a thing for him beside hate and shook her head.

"What's this about?" she asked snidely.

Zyir snatched the Dior shades from her face and sucked his teeth. Miko rolled her eyes as she glared over at him.

"I'm not your fucking child, Zyir."

Zyir's jaw tensed. He sat up and leaned towards Miko. Anger vibrated off his tall, stocky frame.

"This your parents. Calm the fuck down and show some respect, Miko. You been on that bullshit and I'm not playing no more games with your ass," he said through gritted teeth.

Miko turned to her parents and cleared her throat. Zyir always had time for the shits when she didn't. She wanted a big dick to ride on and a soft bed to sleep on. Nothing more at the moment.

"Why did you call us over here?" Miko asked in a calmer tone.

Zyir sat back with her glasses on his lap and scratched at his beard.

"Is Enika good? When I dropped her off today, she was quiet and standoffish," he commented.

Miko frowned at him.

"Why did you drop her off?"

Zyir narrowed his eyes.

"I been dropping her off since she's been back. She also spends the weekend with me and Dorian," he replied.

Miko turned her body towards Zyir and glared at him.

"Dorian can't even get you in check. How the hell is she gonna play step momma to my kid? You need to ask me before you do shit like that Zyir! I let a lot of your caveman shit ride but that's crossing the line," she said angrily.

Zyir waved her off as Miko's parents looked at her.

"Nanmiko please calm down. We called you two over here because this has to stop. The truth is out and pretending it's not has only hurt Enika. Today we received a call from her school and her teacher told us some alarming things. In a journal, she'd left in her desk was goodbye notes," Miko's mother revealed.

Zyir sat up as Miko's heart raced.

"What do you mean goodbye notes?" Miko asked.

Miko's father cleared his throat.

"Goodbye notes as if she was getting ready to kill herself Nanmiko. We searched her room and found four bottles of sleeping pills stuffed under her mattress. They were 100mg pills that would easily take her life," her father replied.

Miko's body slumped and she fell back into the cushioned sofa. She swallowed hard and hugged herself.

"Did you all talk to her?"

Miko's mom shook her head as her own eyes watered.

"We didn't."

Miko glared at her mom with her nostrils flaring.

"Why the hell not? She needs her ass whooped!"

Zyir grabbed Miko's arm.

"Maybe she needs us to stop bullshitting and be her parents Miko. Can we go talk to her?" he asked and looked at Miko's parents.

Miko's mother nodded.

"We would like for you all to take her with you. This isn't easy on us. We love her so much and she is like my baby, but the truth is she is *your* daughter. I see now that me trying to keep her has only hurt her in the end. Miko, you can put us out if you want. That's fine with us we just want the best for Enika," she replied.

Miko rolled her eyes. Her body heat rose as she stared at her parents.

"What about what was best for me? Why didn't you all make sure he was locked up?" she asked and when she blinked tears fell from her eyes.

Miko's mom licked her lips.

"We'd just learned of the baby and we were overwhelmed, Miko. That will be our greatest regret baby. I swear we're sorry it happened. We're so sorry he did that to you," she replied.

Miko shook her head.

"Whatever. Sorry doesn't change anything and I do want you all gone. Get the fuck out of here or I'll call the cops," she snapped angrily and stood up.

"Aye, y'all good," Zyir mumbled standing with her.

Miko walked off briskly and Zyir was on her heels. He caught her as she headed for the stairs and grabbed her waist. Zyir pressed himself into her back as he leaned towards the side of her face.

"I can't say how you should feel about what happened to you but that was uncalled for. You not putting your parents out Miko. Your pops is on his last damn leg and you expect him to survive being homeless? What the fuck is wrong with you?"

Miko tried to pull away from him and he held her tighter.

"I'm serious. I know you hurting but would you really do your people like that? Like they didn't raise our fucking kid for twelve damn years. What the fuck," he grumbled lowly.

Miko closed her eyes as her chest heaved up and down.

"Zyir if you don't stop, I promise you we gone be on this staircase banging it out. Let me go and don't tell me how to feel. You've really shown me that you don't have my back like I thought you did. You don't love me, you're not even riding for me," Miko cried.

Zyir's hard resolve crumbled at her words. He hugged her from the back and caressed her stomach.

"When ain't nobody fucking with you, I'm still holding you down. I can't condone you doing hateful shit Miko. What you did fucked me up. Damn don't I have a right to be angry? That shit caught me off guard but I'ma always love you. You know that," he replied and kissed her neck.

Zyir turned Miko around and wiped her tears away. Miko stared into his eyes as her heart thundered in her chest. It was too much going on and she was having a hard time processing it all.

"I need to lay down and get some rest. Please just let me go home. I don't even know how to be a mom. I'm not the mom type," she said sadly.

Worry sat on her pretty face as she looked at Zyir. Zyir sighed.

"Shit, you ain't got a choice. You want her to harm herself?" he asked.

Miko quickly shook her head. Zyir caressed her cheek and Miko relaxed immediately at his touch.

"Then we gotta step up to the plate. We'll figure it out. Come on," he said and led Miko up the stairs.

Miko showed Zyir to Enika's bedroom and they found Enika sitting up on the bed. Tears stained her cheeks as she wore pajamas with Pocahontas braids. Sadness sat in her slanted eyes and the moment Miko saw her she broke down crying. Miko ran over to Enika and hugged her tightly.

"I'm so sorry Enika. I was scared, and I was young and...and...lost. I didn't know how to be a mom," Miko blubbered while holding Enika.

Enika cried harder than Miko as she hugged her back.

"But you don't come around anymore. You stop calling and seeing me. You don't love me anymore," Enika whimpered.

Miko shook her head.

"I do, I swear I do! I was just scared. You made it clear you wanted to be here. I didn't wanna force you to be

with me. I'm going to die loving you Enika. You're my..."
Miko pulled back and looked Enika in the eyes. Her
beautiful baby girl. Her biggest blessing of all. Miko sighed
as her heart began to beat at its regular pace. "You're my
daughter," Miko declared and she could feel the weight lift
from her shoulders.

Enika nodded.

"And I wasn't a product of rape?" she asked
curiously.

"Nah, you mine," Zyir said walking up.

Enika looked up at him then Miko. She licked her
lips and sighed.

"And we're a family?"

Zyir and Miko nodded in unison.

"Always, we wanna take you with us," Zyir replied.

Miko shook off her fears and nodded in agreement
with him.

"Yes, we do," she countered quietly.

Enika smiled showing off her straight white teeth.

"Are they okay with that?" she asked and looked
towards the door.

Miko smiled.

"They are," Miko said choosing to say the polite thing instead of what she wanted to say which was *they had no fucking choice but to be okay with it.*

"Then let's go home," Enika said and stood up.

Miko gave her a small smile. She stepped back and Enika began to pack up some of her things.

"This will be nice with all of us staying together," Enika said and Miko shook her head.

Zyir grabbed Miko's hand and pulled her to his side.

"Yeah, it will be baby girl," he said and glanced down at Miko.

Miko pulled away from him and walked out of the room. Zyir followed her into the hallway and closed the door.

"Zyir what are you talking about? You don't live with me," Miko snapped.

Zyir stared down into her angry eyes.

"I know that. Enika should be with both of us for a minute. You can stay in the room you was in before and we can all bond. Plus, I need to ask you something," he replied.

Miko scowled at him.

"What?"

Zyir ran his hand over his low-cut fade and cleared his throat.

"I still need you to be my best man," he voiced quietly.

Miko stared up at him like he was crazy. Her eyes narrowed into slits as Enika opened the door. A huge smile covered her face and for the moment her happiness was all that mattered to Miko.

"I'm really excited," Enika expressed and walked past them.

Zyir glanced over at Miko and sighed.

"You good?"

Miko shook her head.

"I'm in the twilight zone Zyir, I'm nowhere close to being good. Look we need to tell Enika that we aren't going to—"

Zyir snatched Miko up and took her into Enika's room. He tossed her against the door and before she could curse him out his lips assaulted her's. He kissed her passionately as he tugged on her long strands of hair. Miko fought off the kiss for as long as she could until he sucked on her bottom lip.

"Zyir please," she begged before whimpering.

Zyir pulled back.

"This coming out has already fucked up Enika. I don't need her seeing us living on no poly type mess. She's going to be all screwed up. I can't go along with this," she told him.

Zyir let her go and grabbed up Enika's other bags.

"For twelve years you hid that she was my daughter and you can't do this one thing for me? Fuck what people think. I live by my own rules and your ass definitely do too. Enika is gonna see people that love each other be together. I'll take that over some traditional dysfunctional shit any day of the week. You coming Miko. You already know what time it is," he replied calmly.

Miko shifted from one foot to the other. She was hurt to see he was still marrying Dorian but was too prideful to bring it up.

"You're not my daddy Zyir. I already told you how I feel about this. We're not going over there."

Zyir walked towards Miko and shook his head.

"I'm not your daddy but you damn sure know when to listen to me. Enika is talking suicide, Miko. We got a lot of shit to work on and you unstable right now. You need some counseling for all that fucking hate you have towards your people. While we get shit right I'ma make sure we good. That's what a man does Nanmiko. Now let's go," he said and pulled her away.

The boutique in Royal Oak was filled with boy talk. Tuxedo's and suits hung from the racks as cognac was passed around generously. Miko sat at the end of the sofa with her phone glued to her face as she attempted to read over the high ass contractor bill that she'd just been sent.

"This shit really going down, huh?" Zyir's cousin asked as he sat beside Miko.

Zyir nodded with his eyes on Miko. He stood up in a black Tom Ford tux looking uberly handsome with a small smile on his face.

"Yeah, shit been a long time coming. Who you texting Miko?" he asked.

Miko flipped him off and a few of the men chuckled. Zyir didn't as he headed her way. He casually picked up her phone and placed it in his pocket. He then went back to the center of the room and grabbed his glass. Miko's eyes burned a hole in him as he finished his talk.

"Like I was saying it's time. Y'all niggas need to settle down too," he replied.

A few of the men waved him off while the married men nodded in agreement. Zyir's right-hand man smirked as he looked at him.

"We can't all be like you though my nigga. You living the dream and shit. Now if I had a set up like that then hell yeah, I'd walk down the aisle too," he replied.

Miko sat up and glared at Zyir's boy that she'd known for years as well.

"Me and Zyir are not together. Let me make that very fucking clear. He begged to eat my pussy last night for hours and I said no. This not some Hugh Heff, Playboy type shit. We're working on healing Enika and nothing more. He's not that fucking fly so don't gas him up. Now if you all would excuse me, I have some meetings to tend to. I'll get a tux later. This bullshit ass wedding probably won't happen any fucking way," Miko snapped and stood up.

Zyir's friends fell out in laughter as Miko walked out of the room. Zyir grabbed Miko's arm and pulled her into the women's restroom before she could successfully exit the boutique. He smirked as he stared down at her.

"Damn you ain't have to call a nigga out like that. We not fucking?" he asked and nixed her chin playfully.

Miko shook her head.

"No, and we won't be fucking ever again. You about to be a married man Zyir. Go fuck your *fiancé*."

Zyir nodded with his eyes boring into Miko.

"Yeah okay and when has that ever-changed shit between us? We'll always belong to each other and you know that shit."

Miko shook her head. She was seconds away from falling apart inside of the bathroom.

"Zyir you can't force me and Enika into this sick ass shit you're trying to do. It's not normal. I didn't mind playing this game when it was just us, but we can't do that to her."

Zyir nodded. He spun Miko around and hugged her from the back. As they stared into the mirror his member began to grow in his Tom Ford slacks. Miko whimpered because her strength was wavering by the minute as she rested in his arms.

"What the fuck is normal Miko? We have a daughter together. The pussy was mine before I even knew about her, but you have to know it really belongs to me now. I need you to stop fighting shit and just let it be. Don't I make you happy?" he asked and unzipped her jeans.

Miko closed her eyes. Her chest heaved up and down as he pulled down her pants. Zyir unzipped his own pants and they fell down his narrow waist. He kicked Miko's legs open and moved her thong to the side. His teeth sunk into the tender skin on her neck as he positioned his member at her opening.

Seconds later Miko's walls were being expanded by Zyir's massive pole. Miko whimpered and her eyes widened as Zyir went deep inside of her. No matter how many times he pleasured her body it never got old. The routine was never the same and the sex was always invigorating. Miko whined in pleasure as he began to slide in and out of her vagina.

"Look at me," he demanded and pumped into her harder.

Miko's eyes shot to the mirror and she groaned when he grabbed her throat. The rapture Zyir was placing on Miko was enough for her to flood the bathroom out with her cum. She licked her lips as her heart raced.

"Do you think I'ma let you go?" he asked breathing hard.

Zyir's handsome face was covered in lust and determination. Miko meekly shook her head and Zyir tightened his grip on her neck. He leaned towards her and his hips moved faster. With purpose, they slid his dick into Miko's tight walls. Looking for her orgasm, tracking that motherfucka down like only he could.

"Answer me, fuck you waiting on," he barked and sunk his teeth into her neck.

"Oh fuck! Baby," she whined squeezing his member. "You won't, you won't!" she yelled, and her body began to shake in his hold.

Zyir licked the mark that marred his teeth on her skin and he smirked at Miko in the mirror.

"Then stop talking that crazy shit. I don't care what the fucking circumstances is, ain't neither one of us going anywhere," he said before pumping into her harder chasing his own release.

Hours later Miko sat inside of her empty building with Enika. Enika walked around the space with a smile on her face as Miko answered emails. After talking with two contractors about the cost and settling on a better price Miko was certain this would be her biggest renovation yet. While she was happy to expand the thought of shelling out so much cash made her stomach hurt. She had savings, even the money Rumer sent her, but it was all going to Enika.

Miko's only mission was to set Enika up for the rest of her life. Miko put her phone away and stared at Enika. Enika wore her school uniform with her hair in its natural curls. She looked angelic and Miko like always was taken back at how beautiful her daughter had turned out to be.

"Enika I would like for us to attend counseling together. How do you feel about that?"

Enika stopped walking and looked at Miko.

"I don't think I need it but if you would like for me to go with you then I can. For support," she replied and began pacing the open space again while holding her phone.

Miko's brows pinched together.

"But weren't you talking about killing yourself in those letters?"

Enika nodded.

"I was but I'm over that now. I guess you would say that was a call for help Miko. We're with my dad and I'm happy being there," Enika replied.

Miko swallowed hard. Immediately Enika took to calling Zyir her dad while she was still *Miko*. Miko felt at fault and didn't want to push Enika away so she dropped the subject.

"I can just go alone. Grab your backpack so we can go," Miko said suddenly feeling down.

Enika nodded and instead of doing as she was told she turned her phone onto herself.

"In a sec!" she yelled before snapchatting.

Miko stood up and gathered her things as Enika played on her device. After twenty minutes went by Enika finally grabbed her bookbag and headed for the door. She glanced back at Miko and smiled at her.

"Could we go by the mall? I wanted to get that Balenciaga fanny pack, and also could I have my driver again? My dad is cool and all, but the kids are starting to pick on me for having him pick me up and drop me off," she said.

Miko shrugged as her weary eyes stared at her daughter. Dealing with Enika as her sister was a walk in the park. However, dealing with Enika as her daughter wasn't so easy.

"Sure," she mumbled and Enika grinned.

"Thanks, Miko!" she chirped and let the door go.

As the door came incredibly close to slamming in Miko's face, Miko watched Enika prance over to her two-door car and lean against it. She rolled her eyes and pushed the door open.

"She gone make me choke her little ass for real," she grumbled and hit the locks on the car.

After the day she'd had all she wanted was a bed to slide into. Between Zyir and Enika, Miko felt like she was losing her mind.

Nine

The building was holy. At least once upon a time it was. With its long hallways, frosted windows, and cross detailing the money that had been placed in it couldn't be missed. Members filled out the large sanctuary as the pastor stood on the stage with a mic in his hand.

As she pushed through the door's several curious eyes stared her way. Her identity unknown to them. Even that hurt because she was someone of importance. The more she walked in the Valentino wedding gown the faster her heart beat. For today her hair was popping with curls. Natural makeup decorated her face as peach lipstick stained her lips. Her freckles seemed to pop off her fair skin as the bright lights from the ceiling shined down on her.

"Miss you can't—"

Nelly raised her hand and slowly shook her head. In the front pew sitting pretty, looking like she hadn't aged a bit was her mother. A woman she hadn't seen in over ten years. Nelly's eyes watered, and her hands went to her protruding belly. Pastor Greene stopped speaking as Elizabeth slowly stood up. Recognition flashed through her eyes and she swallowed hard. She looked at Nelly and her brows pinched together.

"Arnelle Elizabeth Burges. Why are you wearing a wedding gown?"

Nelly closed her eyes. Her voice, it was the same. The controlling tone of it made Nelly shudder. Nelly opened her lids and went to the stage. She ascended the steps and Thomas stared down at her curiously.

"Arnelle, sweetie—"

Nelly grabbed the microphone from his hand and she turned to the congregation and saw her mother was still standing. A stern look of annoyance sat on her mother's beautiful face as she looked her way.

"You all don't know me but I'm her daughter. *Her* as in the first lady of this church," Nelly replied, garnering gasps from everyone in the room.

Thomas sighed as he went back to his seat.

"Today I woke up with her heavy on my mind. I even went as far as to purchase this wedding gown because I've outgrown my other one. The one that I was supposed to wear for a wedding that didn't happen. My fiancé is in another state with my son that I haven't seen in a month. He left me because..." Nelly swallowed hard and her eyes watered.

"Sweetie it's okay," the pastor's sister said remembering Nelly from when she was younger.

Nelly shook her head at the pretty woman. A deep sadness covered Nelly's face as she gazed her way.

"I wish it was. I came here because everybody says that I need help. I've always been taught that God will deliver you and I need it. I need deliverance," Nelly said and began to cry.

A few people raised their hands in the air and began to pray for her. Nelly's mother crossed her arms as she stared at Nelly angrily.

"Arnelle you will leave out of here right now!" she snapped.

"Let her speak," the pastor told Elizabeth in a stern tone.

Nelly's mothers' eyes widened, and she licked her lips. Slowly she sat down and crossed her legs. Nelly kept direct eye contact with her mother as she started to talk.

"I jumped on my fiancé not too long ago. He suffered a concussion and could have died from my angry outburst. The thing is I only did what has been done to me. From as far back as I could remember I was beat on by my mother," Nelly revealed, and her mother's face went white in mortification.

Stares and whispers started, and the pastor sat up straight in his seat. His eyes as well darted over to Nelly's mom.

Nelly cleared her throat.

"It started out as small slaps here and there. I was always never good enough for her. I was always doing something wrong, something to shame her and she would beat me for it. Her own child," Nelly said and closed her eyes. Her tears fell fast down her cheeks. She opened her bloodshot red eyes and licked her lips. The saltiness of her tears could be tasted. "All I wanted was for her to be a mom. For her to treat me how normal mothers did but she never did it. I wanted to die," Nelly admitted, and the pastor walked up to her. He pulled her to his side and tears slipped from his own slanted eyes. "I need to be healed so that I can have my family back. God, I don't wanna be like her but right now I am. I would never harm my kid, but I am capable of hurting his father. I don't like being like this God. Please help me!" Nelly cried out.

Thomas pulled Nelly into his arms and hugged her tightly.

"The God we serve is a mighty God. Seek him and you shall find a peace you've never known. Close your eyes," he instructed. Nelly's eyes closed immediately as her body went lax. The pastor called over his sister, an anointed woman with a big smile and open heart and she advanced on Nelly. "Touch her heart," he said lowly with the congregation looking on. His sister did so while smiling and Nelly's body came alive.

Nelly began to shake as a feeling washed over her that she'd never experienced before.

"Repeat after her Arnelle."

Nelly nodded, and the pastor's sister began to speak.

"God grant me the courage to change the things about myself that I can, the serenity to accept the things about myself that I cannot, and the wisdom to know the difference," sister English recited.

Nelly quickly repeated the words overcome with emotion and the pastor's sister continued speaking.

"Father, God we see your need to come into Arnelle's life. Her and this unborn baby dear Lord. Please fill her up with the Holy Spirit, Lord. Take charge of her life," sister English prayed, and Nelly's tears fell heavy down her cheeks. She repeated the words again and with an open heart and clear mind, the Holy Spirit washed over Nelly.

Never in Nelly's twenty-six years of living had she received the Holy Spirit but as she stood broken, desperate and at her worst, God stepped into her life. He loved her for who she was, who he knew she could and would be. He loved her past her flaws. Nelly's legs gave out and the pastor caught her as he began to speak in tongue along with his sister. Nelly's body shook for several minutes until she was finally able to stand.

Nelly spun around and with wide, teary eyes hugged the pastor as tightly as she possibly could.

Many churchgoers praised the Lord as Nelly thanked the pastor. He took Nelly into his office and at his desk sitting in his seat was none other than Nelly's mom. Her makeup was smeared along with her mascara. A cup of water sat before her as she stared at Nelly and her husband.

"I raised you as best as I could. If an apology is what you want, then here it is. I'm sorry. I only did what I felt was best," she claimed.

Nelly nodded. After experiencing such a peaceful life-changing blessing like the Holy Spirit her issues with her mother seemed trivial. Nelly's face curved into a smile and she nodded. She needed to forgive her mom because if she didn't the hate would continue to hold her back. She needed to fully let her go in order for her to move on.

"It's fine. You will always be who you are and I'm finally okay with that. What I just received, it...." Nelly stopped talking and shook her head. She felt rejuvenated and at peace. A feeling that she'd never felt before.

She blinked and cleared her throat.

"I came here to expose you and truthfully beat you up but what I got was so much more. I'm going to be okay. I can feel it, and I forgive you...." Nelly closed her eyes as her body relaxed at the words spilling from her lips. "I forgive you for being so hurtful and hateful towards me. I forgive you for starving and beating me. I forgive you for never showing me what real love is like. That's something I will never do to my fiancé or kids. I was on my way to being you then God happened. Goodbye," Nelly said and exited the office.

As she walked down the halls of the church happy tears cascaded down her face as she strutted in her wedding gown.

Large photos sat on easels near the door as another photo on a cloth canvas hung near the back wall. Candles sat on each roundtable along with colored glass vases and flowers. Soft cries came from a few women who claimed to own his heart while the family sat in the front of the hall at the longest table.

Snowden and Jerzey retreated early from the rental hall while Taya and Jannero hung back to stay with their family and friends. Nelly's legs felt like bricks as she walked through the room with Miko by her side.

Nelly smiled faintly at her girl, that no matter what found a way to be her rock and she appreciated her for that. Friendship was a commitment. It was a mutually beneficial contract and both parties had to come through for one another. Nelly loved how her girls even in the midst of their own troubles supported her.

Rumer had even offered to come, and Nelly declined wanting her friend to get her own shit right before coming back to the states. It was the offer that warmed Nelly's heart. It was the little things that mattered at the end of the day.

"You can do it. Go get that man girl," Miko said and gave Nelly a small push.

Nelly stumbled and frowned at Miko before looking straight ahead. At the table sat Jannero with an impassive look on his handsome face. The black suit he wore complimented his peanut butter hued brown skin. His haircut was fresh. Dapper as fuck like always while his chain sparkled whenever the light hit it. Jannero's sad eyes glanced around the room once more before finally falling onto Nelly. The black lace bodycon dress hugged Nelly's curves including her baby bump that seemed to get bigger every time she gazed down at it. Her curly hair was wild and free bouncing with every step that she took as her wine-colored lipstick bounced off her skin.

Nelly watched Jannero stand up and she smiled. She couldn't contain her happiness. She missed him terribly and wasn't afraid to be the first to cave in.

"Baby I'm so sorry," she murmured walking up.

Jannero pulled Nelly into a hug and he held her tightly. His breathing grew ragged as she rubbed his back soothingly.

"I know he wasn't perfect. I know he has his shit that came with him, but he was your brother that you loved dearly and I'm sorry he's dead. I love you and I'ma be there for you," Nelly said being his rock.

Jannero's eyes closed and he swallowed hard. Taya rushed over and grabbed Jannero's arm.

"Hey, let's take him in the back," she said with teary eyes and pulled him and Nelly away.

Nelly and Jannero stepped into the backroom and Jannero sat down. He hugged Nelly's stomach as silent tears escaped his lids. Nelly rubbed his back for several minutes as she allowed for him to mourn the loss of his brother. She'd woken up to the news days prior online of Jeremiah's remains being found close to the park near his home. His body was neatly wrapped in a blanket and no damage had been done to him outside of the bullet hole decorating his forehead. Nelly immediately got a ticket and flew down to be there for Jannero.

Jannero pulled back after a few seconds to stare up into Nelly's eyes.

"You said you loved me," he mused lowly.

Nelly smiled. She rubbed the soft waves adorning his head. She nodded and licked her lips.

"Because I do. I've been in love with you since I met you, Jannero Carter," Nelly told him earnestly.

Jannero's head dipped and he smiled.

"I'm in love with you too, Arnelle. Why don't you come give me a kiss, so I can show you how much I love you?"

Nelly's cheeks reddened. She shook her head while smiling down at Jannero.

"Not yet. I want us to go to Detroit, so I can take you out."

Jannero licked his lips. His hands tightened on her hips as he sighed.

"We gotta go to the "D" for a date?"

Nelly nodded with her heart thundering in her chest.

"Actually, we do. It's a long overdue date. A date we should have been gone on," Nelly replied.

Jannero pulled Nelly onto his lap. Her eyes connected with his and a charming smile covered his sexy face.

"Then that's where we'll go," he murmured and leaned in to kiss her tenderly on the lips.

Forty-eight hours later the white Rapide S pulled onto the quiet block in Beverly Hills, Michigan. Children played on the sidewalk as the sun began to go down. With Jasir in Philly with Taya, Nelly enjoyed being around Jannero again. Although it had only been a few months it felt as if it had been forever since she'd been in his space.

"Stop right there," Nelly said and swallowed hard.

Jannero pulled into the driveway of a two-story colonial style home. Jannero shut off the car and relaxed in his seat. He wore faded jeans with a rust colored Supreme shirt and Off-White air force sneakers. Wired Bugatti frames sat on his handsome face as he gazed Nelly's way.

"This was your home?"

Nelly nodded solemnly. Sadness swept through her body as she began to remember the pain and agony that she felt living in the beautiful home. She stared out of the window as Jannero grabbed her hand.

"Tell me about it, ma," he said lowly.

Nelly squeezed his hand tightly as she licked her lips.

"Jannero my mother beat on me. I can't remember exactly when it happened but one day it was a slap for not doing something right. She got worse over time and the slaps turned into full-blown beatings. I'd sometimes go days without eating because I wet the bed. It was then that she'd put me in the closet," Nelly stopped talking and turned to Jannero. "I learned to love the dark. I learned to embrace it. It was being with her that I couldn't handle. The beatings eventually got so bad that I began to contemplate suicide. I couldn't understand why she hated me so much, Nero. All I wanted was a mother, not some angry, abusive woman. When I wouldn't tell her that I loved her she would really beat on me. The maids would sometimes sneak me medicine but for the most part, they ignored it." Nelly cleared her throat. She stared into Jannero's eyes as she licked her lips. "I'm sorry for hitting on you. I'm sorry for keeping this away from you and I'm very sorry for not trusting you enough to tell you my past. Look what it's done to us," Nelly said and looked away from him.

Softly she cried and Jannero sat up in his seat. He leaned towards Nelly and kissed her behind the ear. Her heart raced as his breath fanned against her skin.

"I was hurt by all the shit that happened with us, so I left. Our wedding day passed and yes, a nigga got kicked from the team on that Fed's shit. I even lost my brother but know this, my love for you never changed. No matter what I love the fuck out of you Arnelle. I just needed to know that you was willing to get past this so that we could be happy again. We can leave that fighting and shit to everybody else. That's not for us," he told her.

Nelly smiled at the words that Jannero had spoken to her.

"And what's for us Jannero?"

Jannero kissed Nelly's neck before kissing her cheek.

"Love and happiness, ma. I'ma fix everything. I swear," he promised, and Nelly faced her man.

She believed him. She loved him, and she told herself that this time around she would appreciate and value the good man and good life that God had been so gracious to bestow on her.

"And we'll be a family again?" she questioned quietly.

Jannero grinned at her.

"We was *never* not a family, ma. You know I don't operate like that, now give me a kiss with your pretty ass," he replied making her giggle.

Ten

Bricked walls with gold medallion printed rugs and custom animal artwork was the décor. The ambiance was high-spirited. Live drums and beaded chandeliers only added to the restaurant's good vibe.

Rumer sat thirty pounds heavier in her seat. It was her last night in Cape Town. She had to go back. Life didn't take a break just because you needed one. She had a company to run, friends to check up on and a life to live. She couldn't hide out any longer. With the help of Melanie, she was now eating food on a regular basis. The therapy was aggravating as fuck at times, but it worked for Rumer.

She wasn't perfect so yes, she cried sometimes after eating a meal. The thought to purge would become so great that she would have to write in her journal or lean on Melanie to fight it off. However, the trip had been a blessing. For *several* reasons. Rumer learned to love the person she saw in the mirror staring back at her. She'd also learned to love her mother again. They'd grown incredibly close over their stay in Africa and Rumer was grateful for that.

"Look at you looking all thick and shit. Too beautiful for your own damn good," he noted.

The deep voice and sweet words brought a genuine smile to her face. Her eyes peered up and landed on the sexiest man she'd been alive to see. Wearing a three-piece chocolate suit with a dark peach tie and black dress shoes Nahmir grabbed her attention and held it hostage. Rumer admired his outlandish good looks as he smiled at her. Nahmir leaned down and planted juicy kisses on her pouty lips.

Africa had also brought her him.

Her *man*.

Rumer glanced down at her rose gold promise ring and her body relaxed. Everything with Nahmir was fast but in a natural way. He'd gone back to the states with his daughter and from there Rumer began to talk with him several times a day. Nahmir even made it a point to fly down to see her every other week which meant a lot to Rumer considering she was in Africa. It wasn't around the corner so his efforts to get to know her better didn't go unnoticed. They'd become friends without trying and when Nahmir asked her to not see anyone else she quickly agreed. The feelings he evoked out of her were terrifying, but she welcomed them. There was no secrets between the two and the sexual attraction brewing with them was almost as great as the mental connection they shared.

"It's still shining, you don't have to keep staring down at it mami," he joked, and Rumer smiled.

Nahmir took a seat across from Rumer and checked his ringing cell before giving her his attention.

"Tomorrow's the big day huh?"

Rumer nodded with knitted brows. She peered down at her salad plate that was still full and Nahmir glanced at the plate before looking at her.

"Nervous? Come here, come sit next to me," he said and patted the seat beside him.

Rumer quickly got up and went to his side. Nahmir stood and allowed for her to sit next to him before sitting back down. He pulled Rumer close to him and she exhaled as she rested against his warm, big body.

"Relax and don't let nothing stress you out," he murmured as she basked in the alluring scent of his Creed cologne.

"Hi, Mr. Yaasmin, welcome back. What can we get you?" the waitress asked.

Nahmir smiled placing the waitress under his spell as well. He licked his lips and kissed Rumer's forehead before replying.

"I'll take the Tanzanian fried fish with spinach sauce. I'd also like a bottle of the 2009 Grand En Gout red wine,"

Nahmir turned to Rumer and stared into her eyes. "What do you want beautiful?"

Rumer's heart skipped a beat. Was love at first sight real? Or was she bugging? Was this her way of dealing with her life spiraling out of control? Numerous questions swirled through her mind but those stayed on the forefront.

Nahmir leaned towards Rumer and pecked her lips. His long beard brushed against her skin as an energy she never felt before moved through her.

"You gone be good. Worrying will only make you sick. Buck up mami and show me that beautiful smile," he said lowly and kissed her forehead again.

Rumer exhaled at his endearing words.

This was why she was so drawn to him. She hadn't known him long, but he made her feel things she'd never felt before.

"I'll take the Moroccan Zaalook," she said sweetly.

The hostess nodded and walked away. Rumer opened her mouth to speak and Nahmir attacked her with a long passionate kiss. Rumer gasped before moaning into his mouth.

After a few minutes, Nahmir pulled back on the kiss and sucked her bottom lip before sitting back in his seat. He grabbed her left hand and kissed the back of it as he gazed her way.

"Talk to me mami."

Rumer smiled. Nahmir made her feel special and in a genuine way.

"I'm nervous about going home so I'm keeping Melanie with me for a few more months. I felt bad for asking her to come, but it was needed. I'm stronger but I feel like it wouldn't hurt to have extra help."

Nahmir nodded. His assistant Jason walked over and smiled at Rumer as he passed Nahmir a stack of papers.

"Hi, Ms. Matigo. Sorry to interrupt but these need to be signed now," he said, and Rumer smiled.

Nahmir ran several of his family businesses and did it so effortlessly that it left Rumer in awe. He stayed busy but always found time for her. He was not only an amazing father, but he was also well educated. He'd even put Rumer onto business tactics to grow her real estate company's wealth and she was ready to apply them. Nahmir made his own rules and was like no other man Rumer had met before. She loved the alpha male inside of him. He was a boss. The type of man you dreamed about, and she prayed that he was who he said he was.

"It's not a problem. Especially since he flew back just to bring me home," Rumer replied.

Nahmir looked over the documents before signing them and once he was done his attention was back on Rumer. He gave her a quick kiss before sitting back in his seat.

"All the things you're feeling is natural Rumer. You're human mami. I mean if you wanna stay in this bubble then I'll make one just to float your pretty ass in all day, but I know that's not you. I can tell you miss it all. Soon me and Tennille we'll be there with you and shit will be even better. You second guessing us?" he asked.

Rumer quickly shook her head before her shoulders slumped.

"Maybe.... *a little.* I feel like out here everything with us was so perfect because we're isolated. We don't really know each other, and I don't wanna bring you into my fucked-up life," she admitted.

Nahmir nodded as he stared at her.

"First I have to say that moving shit was happening anyway Rumer. My family is in Detroit. I love being in Jersey, but it's been time for me to go home. On the real, you just gave me the push I needed to make the shit happen sooner. Also, your favorite color is red. When you was six you broke your ankle from falling off a bike. Your favorite movie is **How To Marry A Millionaire**. Your favorite singer is Tamia. Shit, your biggest fear is being a failure and..." he peered into her eyes and cleared his throat. "You have an eating disorder. Yeah, shits been hella quick with us, but I don't allow for time to dictate my life. You asked me how I kept my businesses successful even with the economy not being in the best status and its simple. I just did it. I work hard for everything that I want, and I get it. I do me without giving a fuck how people feel about that shit. I live to make my daughter and myself happy. I wanna make you happy to mami. You just gotta let me," he replied.

Rumer closed her eyes. Her heart and mind was conflicted. She wanted to go with the flow and see where this thing with Nahmir could go still something inside of her was saying that it was too soon to be falling so fast for him. However, Rumer couldn't stay away from him either.

"I want to make you happy as well," she said opening her eyes.

Nahmir grabbed her face and gently forced her to peer up at him.

"Then give us a chance. I sent you that ring, so you could see that I'm really feeling you. We only a few months in and look at how happy we are. Just wait until we get some years under our belt mami. You won't be able to stop fucking cheesing when I'm done with you now give me another kiss," he demanded, and Rumer exhaled.

That was something she had no problem doing.

The room was at capacity as happiness permeated the air. Big smiles, warm hearts, and welcome backs were pushed her way. In the front of the room stood the president of the company.

The new boss.

Confident, healthier, and happy. It showed in her eyes. The cheeky grin she expelled to her workers wasn't lost on them. Rumer pushed strands of her hair away from her face and the promise ring decorating her finger caught several people's attention. She caught the stares but wasn't interested in telling her personal business to them. To her, it was always about professionalism.

"It feels good to be back," she said excitedly.

Everyone clapped. A few people whistled, and she dropped her head in joy. She looked up and her eyes landed on Kritt. Rumer swallowed hard and cleared her throat. Suddenly her thoughts were of him and Nahmir.

"I will be sending out emails later on in the day of the changes I've made and you all will receive a packet from HR as well. Let's make him proud. That's all that I ask is that we show him that we were able to stand on our own. Thank you again for the warm welcome," she spoke earnestly.

Slowly people began to leave out of the room. Rumer sat down and watched Kritt head her way. He looked damn good. Dark jeans with a black V-neck and Balenciaga sneakers was his fit for the day. He wore a fresh cut with a big smile and those grey enchanting eyes of his seemed to eat Rumer alive.

Her heart pumped faster with every step that he took.

"Come here ma," he said and pulled her up from the seat.

Rumer hugged Kritt tightly as the door to the conference room closed. She closed her eyes and her body relaxed in his arms.

"I missed you so fucking much. Got damn," Kritt muttered.

Rumer's eyes watered.

She'd missed him too.

"Same here," she said in a whisper.

Kritt hugged her tighter and the small, pricey cellphone that rested on the table began to vibrate.

Kiki, do you love me? Are you riding?
Say you'll never ever leave from beside me
'Cause I want ya, and I need ya
And I'm down for you always

The ringtone made Rumer draw back from Kritt and lick her lips. Nahmir and his ways. He was too much for her, but funny thing was, that was what she liked most about him. His persistence. She couldn't think of the last time she'd had a ringtone still it was funny to her that he'd done that. Cute in a sense too.

"Motherfucka's got ringtones and shit now, what's good ma?" Kritt asked and pulled her back into his arms.

Rumer hugged Kritt and before she could reply his lips was on her's. His kiss was passionate and filled with love. The love in the kiss quickly turned to lust and soon Kritt was pushing Rumer onto the desk. He pushed up her tight black skirt and slapped her ass while biting his bottom lip.

Rumer gasped and attempted to stand.

"Kritt! No—"

Kritt's kisses to the side of her neck made her gasp. He tore her stockings and moved her thongs to the side. Rumer gasped as two of his fingers pushed into her snug opening.

"Damn you got thicker, I love it," he murmured in a husky tone.

Rumer closed her eyes. She was battling between doing what was right and what felt good at the moment. She sighed and soon Kritt's thick girth was stretching her walls.

"Fuck, Rumer. I missed you so much, baby. I love you," Kritt whispered in her ear before pulling back.

With his hands planted firmly on her hips, he began to pump into her. Rumer whimpered, and her mouth hung open. Kritt quickly found her spot and began to take her to ecstasy. Rumer closed her eyes getting ready for the ride of pleasure her body was heading on and there he was.

Standing before her in one of his custom suits. It fit him perfectly like always contouring to the muscles on his tall frame. His deep olive-hued, tattooed skin seemed flawless. Whiskey downturned peepers with those enticing thick lips made her whimper. A grim look sat on his handsome face. One that was so captivating it made Rumer sit up abruptly. Kritt stumbled back with his wet penis swinging and he frowned down at her.

"What's wrong?"

Rumer quickly pulled down her skirt and the promise ring caught Kritt's attention. His jaw gritted as he put his dick away. He glared at Rumer giving her no space to move as she nervously stood before him.

"What the fuck is that on your finger?"

Rumer swallowed hard. She stared down at the ring with her heart pounding.

This is a promise of what's to come beautiful.

Rumer glanced up at Kritt and cleared her throat. She loved him. Even when she didn't want to, she did, however, something was different now. *She* was different now and her trip had brought another man into her life. She hadn't planned on it but on the road to finding herself, she'd also found Nahmir.

"Kritt please sit down," she said quietly.

The softness of her tone and sadness in her eyes made Kritt back up. He went to the closest seat with his intense gaze on her. Rumer turned to him and licked her lips. She smoothed down her skirt that she was busting out of due to the weight gain and she rubbed her not so flat belly. All of this was so fucking new to her.

Her office had only seen the fabricated Rumer. She'd felt odd walking in heavier than normal, but no one said a thing. In fact, many men gawked at her added curves and fuller face. They felt it complimented her and Rumer was relieved.

She constantly told herself that it didn't matter what people thought of her now she had to make herself believe it.

"Africa was amazing Kritt. I'm sorry that I couldn't call as much as you wanted me to, but it was like I was in a different world over there."

Kritt nodded not taking his eyes off the ring.

"And what's up with that bullshit?" he asked still frowning.

Rumer cleared her throat. She was searching for the courage to speak with him about Nahmir. On her jet ride home Nahmir had held her tightly while whispering words of encouragement in her ear. They'd set up a time to see each other in the near future and she'd shed tears when she stepped off his jet with her therapist and mother minus him.

"As you know I took a therapist with me and she's really helped me out. My eating is the closest it's been to regular in years. I don't count my calories anymore and I only purged once in Africa. I feel like I'ma be okay," she replied and blinked to keep her tears at bay.

Kritt stopped frowning at the ring to look up at Rumer.

"And you gotta know how happy I am for you. I love you Rumer and it fucked me up seeing you like that. When

you had that heart attack, I nearly lost my fucking mind..."
Kritt stopped talking and he stood up. He walked up on
Rumer and grabbed her face. Rumer's eyes watered as she
peered up at him. "It's always been us, ma. You was out
there, and you was healing. You was vulnerable, and shit
happens. Neither one of us is perfect but what we feel for
each other is real. I been waiting for you. You don't love me
anymore?" he asked.

Rumer's tears spilled down her face. She nodded. Of
course, she did. Things like that didn't go away overnight but
still, it was different now.

"You know I do," she whispered wishing she could
say exactly how she felt without breaking his heart in the
process.

Kritt sighed. He leaned down and brushed his lips
against her's.

"Then don't say what I think you about to say. Don't
push me away again," he replied and kissed her passionately.

Hours later as the sun went down passionate moans
filled the bedroom. Light fluttered into the room from the
bathroom as the large king-sized bed knocked against the
wall. Her thighs shook uncontrollably as his tongue circled
her clitoris.

Rumer's chest heaved up and down as a thin sheet of sweat covered her body. She'd cum so many times she'd lost count. Her curls had long ago fallen, her lipstick had been kissed off and her body was covered with passion marks.

Kritt slid back up her body and as he slid inside of her his bedroom door slammed open.

"Kritt the baby is sick!"

Kritt and Rumer jumped up and Kritt glared back at the beautiful intruder.

"Get the fuck out of here Alisha!"

Alisha shook her head as she stared their way.

"Kritt I know you don't want me here, but I had to rush her to the hospital. She's not breathing baby, please," she begged.

Kritt sighed and glanced down at Rumer. Rumer stared up at him with curious eyes.

"So that was your baby?"

Kritt shook his head.

"Alisha we'll be out there in a minute. Get out the fucking room," he said angrily.

Alisha stomped her foot.

"Fuck her Kritt! She left you once again. You need to be with us, we're your family and our kid is sick. Come on! What the fuck!"

Kritt slowly pulled back from Rumer and eased off the bed. He tossed on his clothes while Alisha stood in the middle of the room.

"Come on Rumer," he said with his eyes on her.

Rumer shook her head and Kritt snatched her clothes off the floor. He tossed them at Rumer as Alisha glared at him.

"This shit not up for debate you coming. Come on!"

Rumer held the clothes tightly as she slid off the bed. She too got dressed in front of Alisha and together they exited the bedroom. Rumer ignored the looks of the other bikers as she followed Alisha out of the clubhouse.

Kritt hit the locks on his truck and opened the door for Rumer. Alisha slid into his backseat and Rumer shook her head. She wasn't her girl, Miko. The three's company shit she couldn't do.

"Didn't you drive here?" Rumer asked her as Kritt backed out of the lot.

Alisha smacked her lips loudly in the backseat.

"No, I don't have a car. I caught an Uber. My mom is at the hospital with my daughter. If you must know. And to get you up to date with what's happening in my fucking life, I went into labor while on his dick in the clubhouse. I live in the home he bought me, and I have his child. I think that sums it up and we took a test, so you can't throw that out there to steal him back either. While you were away, we were happy. Then you come back and fuck it all up. Thanks a lot," Alisha piped sarcastically.

Rumer nodded while smiling. Her leg began to bounce and Kritt glanced over at her.

"Shit didn't happen like that. Alisha say something else and you gone be walking to the fucking hospital."

Alisha rolled her eyes and everyone road in silence the rest of the way. Kritt pulled up to the hospital twenty minutes later and parked. Alisha quickly exited the truck and Kritt grabbed Rumer's hand. Rumer continued to stare out of the window as he looked at her.

"I was gonna tell you ma. I swear I was. I just wanted to make sure we was good first. You the only fucking woman I ever loved. This baby changes nothing between us," he said lowly.

Rumer nodded not looking to say anything to him at the moment concerning his child or the momma connected to it. She exited the truck with Kritt behind her. He grabbed her hand and led her into the hospital. They went up to the third floor and spotted Alisha talking with a woman that looked like the older version of her. The woman looked at Rumer and Kritt with disgust before walking away.

Alisha stared up at Kritt as they advanced on her.

"She's okay baby. They said she has sleep apnea. They want to give her a machine to help her with the breathing. They believe that it will go away in the next few months," Alisha replied with relief washing over her pretty face.

Rumer walked away and found a seat in the waiting area. Her eyes connected with Alisha's mother and Alisha's mother shook her head.

"They have a newborn baby. How do you feel like it's right to be with him?" she asked in broken English.

Rumer smiled to keep from going off. She couldn't believe this was happening to her. It was her first fucking day back home.

"Please don't talk to me with your old ass," she replied and smiled at the woman.

Alisha's mother scoffed and spoke in her native tongue. Rumer pulled out her phone and noticed she had several missed calls from Nahmir. She went to her text messages and when she opened the last message that had been sent to him that wasn't from her, her heart plummeted.

It was a photo of her heading to the bathroom in Kritt's bedroom. She was naked, and the caption read. *Been mine, still mine.*

Rumer's heart rate spiked as she read Nahmir's response.

Only bitches do shit like this, but you got it. That's all you.

Rumer put her phone away as Kritt stepped into the waiting room. He sat beside her and grabbed her hand. Worry sat in his enchanting grey eyes, but Rumer couldn't find it in herself to comfort him. Once again, he'd hidden things from her. The child was his and Rumer couldn't help but wonder why did all of the men she love have kids on her?

Those pesky ass insecurities came running out of the closet. As Alisha walked into the waiting room Rumer noticed how fit she was. She had a newborn and her stomach was already flat. Rumer looked away from Alisha and began to rock her leg. She knew the busty ass dummy wasn't prettier than her and she refused to let her issues make her believe it was something different.

As Kritt kissed the back of her hand. Her thoughts were once again of Nahmir. She knew he was livid with her and he had every right to be. She too was disappointed in herself at the moment.

The room smelled like white lilies. A warm comforting feeling eased over you as you entered the space. On the TV played America's Next Top Model re-runs as an adorable brown poodle rested by the leather ottoman.

On the end table was a photo of Enika with the Eiffel Tower as her backdrop. Lit tea-lights surrounded the picture and more photos of Enika covered the wall behind the leather sofa.

"Cut it on now!" Enika yelled making Rumer jump in her seat.

Rumer looked towards the hallway and seconds later Beyoncé's **Crazy In Love** began to play. Enika strutted into the room with Miko following behind her. Behind Miko was Dorian. They smiled wide as Enika walked in a black fitted dress with six-inch Giuseppe's.

Enika blew Rumer a kiss and a playful grin before strutting out of the room. Miko sat down beside Rumer and turned off the music as Dorian followed after Enika. A stunned expression covered Rumer's face as she looked at her beautiful friend. Her underdressed, blotchy faced, beautiful friend.

"Well, this is interesting. Hello is Nanmiko here? I feel like I came to the wrong house. I'm looking for my friend that has always lived by her own rules. Not the rules of a man *or* a child."

Rumer's words made Miko's shoulder's slump. Miko sat back on the sofa and her head fell onto Rumer's shoulder.

"I don't know what to do Rumer. I'm in the twilight zone, yet I can't leave. I don't wanna make her upset with me when I've already caused her so much pain then there's him. Yes, I do crazy shit, but I know this is strange for even me," Miko replied quietly.

Rumer nodded. She rubbed Miko's hair glad to be home. Clearly, they still needed each other.

"Be you, Miko. Stop letting Enika and Zyir dictate how this is going to go. Yes, you were wrong for hiding it, but you've always been good to them. You were hurt as well in this situation. Don't let them make you out to be the bad guy just so they can get their way. You are the most fearless person I know," Rumer told her.

Miko looked up at Rumer with wet eyes and she smiled.

"Really?"

Rumer pursed her lips.

"Yes, now stop acting like a damn yes girl and get your shit together. Weakness don't look good on you," Rumer replied.

Miko snorted. She glanced down at her attire and laughed.

"It sure doesn't. I look homely as fuck right now." Miko looked at Rumer and smiled. "And you look fucking great. How was Africa? I wanna know it all. Did you get some dick?" Miko asked eagerly.

Rumer laughed at her girl's line of questioning.

"Africa was what I needed. Shit, it looks like I should have taken you with me. I'm better and I'm eating food, Miko. I'm sorry I kept that from you guys," Rumer apologized sincerely.

Miko shrugged while smiling.

"I'm just happy you're okay. We all fall but what matters is if we stay down. We're built to get back up," Miko told her.

Rumer winked at her friend.

"Yes, we are, and I did meet someone. His name is Nahmir. He's—"

Miko shrieked.

"Nahmir Yaasmin? *Bitch,* I used to hang with his cousins and no I did not fuck him. He's cool as hell and very down to earth. You know them Yaasmin's rich for real and shit. Damn, how did you meet him?" Miko asked.

"Meet who and hi, Rumer. You look good!" Dorian said stepping into the living room in her workout gear.

Rumer and Miko stopped smiling and stared at Dorian. Dorian laughed and shook her head.

"*Okay*, well Miko can you tell Zyir that I'm heading to the gym. My phone broke this morning and I won't be able to get another one until the afternoon. Thanks!"

Dorian walked away, and Rumer shook her head.

"Miko..."

Miko nodded and raised her hands in the air.

"I know, I know. Its land of the coo-coo over here."

Rumer laughed.

"For real it is though. Are you fucking him?"

Miko hid her face and Rumer clicked her tongue against the roof of her mouth.

"This is messy as fuck. Does she know?"

Miko looked at Rumer.

"He sleeps with me on most nights unless I get upset with him and kick him out of the room. We try to shield that part of our lives from Enika but trust me she knows."

Rumer sighed while shaking her head.

"Enika isn't dumb. Little Beyoncé Jr. knows just what the fuck y'all in here doing," Rumer replied.

Miko snorted before falling into a fit of laughter. Rumer laughed with her and shook her head.

"I'm serious Miko. Enika was always spoiled but I see something different on her now. She's moving through this place like she's running shit. Hell, y'all done even gave her some damn theme music like she's the female Shaft. You need to stop it now," Rumer advised.

Miko smiled and waved her off.

"She's just being Enika. All of this has been hard on her but trust me she knows to stay in a child's place. So how does Kritt feel about you seeing Nahmir?"

Rumer thought of Kritt, his issues and Nahmir blocking her, and her stomach lurched. Suddenly she felt ill.

"Another story for another day. Did you get Jannero's message?"

Miko grinned. Instantly the mood in the room changed to happiness.

"Yes! Finally, our girl is getting to it. Jerzey said she would meet us there. You coming right?" Miko asked.

Rumer nodded with raised brows.

"Of course! At least one of us is getting a husband. At least until you and Zyir tie the knot."

Enika frowned as she walked into the room.

"Tie the knot? Miko is my daddy's best man. He's still marrying Dorian. She didn't tell you Rumer?" she asked.

Rumer's jaw fell slack as Miko glared at Enika. Enika smiled at Miko and grabbed her water off the table before leaving out of the room. Miko looked at Rumer and Rumer held her hand in the air.

"Save it. Just finish this shit before your life turns into a damn meme," Rumer said and Miko shoved her arm playfully.

"I will. You know we always bounce back boo. We bent but don't break and I needed to see you. I needed for my friend to tell me what I didn't wanna accept," Miko said to her.

Rumer smiled.

"That's what friends are for. To praise you, hold you down and let you know when you're doing dumb shit. Fix your life like I'm trying to fix mine and handle that lil Diana Ross you got back there. She's doing too much," Rumer said and they both laughed.

Eleven

A large industrial fan blew from the corner of the room. The walls were covered with her moving boxes due to her hectic schedule still the vibe was right. Multicolored paint splatters covered the floor while teal blue tufted suede sofa's sat near the front of the studio along with a glass coffee table.

On her desk was her speaker. From the small device played Jay-Z's *Reasonable Doubt* cd. In boyfriend jeans with a ripped tee and Fendi slides, Jerzey sat in her element. Her eyes ventured from Jaleed to the canvas as she finished up his portrait.

He'd come to collect the photo's he'd paid for. Jerzey had never painted so fast in her life but to have him up out of her space she'd done so. Now as she neared the ending of his self-portrait she could relax. Things with Snowden was still weird. They'd attended Jeremiah's service together however they still weren't regularly talking. It was always her reaching out and it didn't sit well with her, so she'd decided to step back from the situation and allow for him to put in some work.

As Jerzey sat across from her ex-boyfriend her heart sat on alert. While he looked good as sin in his blue jeans that he'd paired with a designer Polo and Detroit fitted she knew the truth. Everything that glittered wasn't gold and every handsome man wasn't good for you. However, with loneliness creeping into her life she struggled with him being back around. A lonely heart would feed on anything and Jerzey was actively telling herself to remain strong. Just because he was there, and Snowden wasn't didn't mean he was the better man.

"I put you up on this Jigga shit," Jaleed mused and smirked at her.

He removed his cap and sat it on his lap. His cologne floated around the space Jerzey sat in. The crazy thing was he looked so fucking better than he did before and even back in the day he was attractive but now his looks were on another level.

"Whatever. I've always liked Hova. Act like you don't know. You got your swag from me," she replied.

Jaleed chuckled. He licked his lips and brushed his hand over Jerzey's thigh. The small move made her think of Snowden. She cleared her throat as she pushed his hand away.

"Remember I have a man."

Jaleed nodded. His eyes looked her over and he shook his head.

"Yeah, but where that nigga at doe? I done been out here several times now and he still ain't popped up. Let me find out he a ghost and shit," he jested.

Jerzey held in her laugh and Jaleed sat up. His large hand caressed her cheek and she closed her eyes.

"I really did miss you though. The entire time I was away I thought of you. How bad I fucked shit up and how if I had another chance to, I would make it right. Back then I was young and dumb as fuck. I thought I could do no wrong and with that I hurt you. I want you to know that I'm sorry Jerzey. I apologize for how things played out with us and I want you back. I'm willing to come out here if I have to. Anything to show you that I still love you," he said gazing at her.

Jerzey's breathing grew ragged. It all sounded so good but that was something he never lacked at. Jaleed had charm and was a good dude just not boyfriend material. Jerzey opened her eyes and peered back at him intently.

"I waited for years to hear that apology so thank you but Jaleed you have to know, I don't need it anymore," she replied.

Jaleed sat back. He scratched at his beard as he frowned at Jerzey.

"You must really love this nigga, huh?"

Jerzey nodded ignoring the anger coming from his way. He didn't care in the past when he'd cheated numerous times on her, so she didn't care to spare his feelings. She'd moved on and wouldn't be sorry about it.

"I do, and he loves me too. Let's have one last drink and say goodbye to each other," she told him.

Jaleed sighed and touched her leg. Jerzey looked at him and watched his confident resolve wash away.

"What if I'm not ready to say goodbye to you? I didn't come here to go back home single ma. You know what the fuck I want and that's you. I've always wanted you Jerzey," he revealed.

Jerzey stared into his eyes as her heart raced. She wanted someone too, but it wasn't him.

"Jaleed life doesn't work that way. You don't get to break my heart and come back years later like it never happened. Sorry. I'll wash up and change then we can find a bar to fall off into," she replied before standing up.

Jaleed nodded solemnly and watched her walk away. Jerzey went upstairs to her place and made sure to lock up. She took a quick shower then put on a vintage cut out designer mini dress that was so short she paired it with lace biker shorts. Jerzey wore Zanotti heels with her sexy look along with a dark grey bob lace unit. She chose to wear a natural face and as she put on her layered necklace her cell phone vibrated on her nightstand.

Jerzey grabbed her phone and started breathing hard when Snowden's name slid across the screen. She closed her eyes as she took the call.

"Hello."

Snowden was quiet for a moment before clearing his throat.

"What's good ma? Can't lie I miss the fuck out of youse."

Jerzey sighed. Hearing his voice made her stomach knot up.

"And I miss you too Snowden," she whispered.

"Oh yeah? Youse up painting?"

Jerzey exited her apartment and standing at the top of the stairs was Jaleed with a bouquet of roses. Jerzey stared down at him nervously when she spotted them.

"For you," he said handing them over. "Damn you look beautiful," Jaleed said and caressed her chin.

Jerzey smiled and her eyes widened. She looked at her phone and saw that Snowden had ended the call on her.

She put her phone away and quickly took the roses into her place. Jaleed then grabbed her hand and led her out of the building. Jerzey thought of Snowden as she slid into Jaleed's Bentayaga. It was standard factory. Nothing like her baby's and even that did something to her. Jaleed was a lot of things but in comparison to Snowden he would always fall short.

"You good?" he asked pulling into traffic.

Jerzey gave him a plastic smile and nodded.

"I am," she lied and put her seat belt on.

Jaleed nodded and turned on some music. As the song began to play his hand mysteriously found its way back over to Jerzey's leg.

Some say the ex, make the sex
Spec-tacular, make me lick you from yo' neck
To yo back, then ya, shiverin', tongue deliverin'
Chills up that spine, that ass is mine
Skip the wine and the candlelight, no Cristal tonight

Jerzey ignored the slow rub he placed on her legs and the classic Biggie track he'd cut on. She forced herself to stare out of the window and soon they were in Harlem pulling up to a local bar. They found a spot and quickly went in. Jerzey ordered her favorite dark liquor as they stood at the bar.

"What's the story with you and your nigga?" Jaleed asked.

Jerzey smiled over at him.

"What's the story with you and your hella baby mama's," she retorted.

Jaleed chuckled. He stepped closer to Jerzey and placed his hand on her thigh.

"They not even on that drama shit like before. Shit they done moved on any damn way," he said and pulled money from his pocket to pay for their drinks.

Jerzey grabbed her drink and nodded. She didn't give a damn because she didn't plan on ever being around those silly hoes again. She followed Jaleed over to an empty table and they sat down. Jerzey's phone vibrated as she sat it on the table and she glanced down at the screen.

"That's him?" Jaleed asked.

Jerzey peered back up at her ex-boyfriend and slowly nodded.

"You're out of the streets now, right?"

Jaleed tossed back his drink and stared at Jerzey. He gave her a disarming grin and she shook her head.

"Old habits die hard huh?" she asked.

He chuckled. He called over a petite waitress and ordered a bottle of cognac before turning his attention to Jerzey.

"I'm as clean as I can be baby. I have a lot of businesses and shit though, so I can see it in my near future. A future I hope you'll be in," he replied.

Jerzey dropped her head regretting coming with him to the bar and he leaned her way. Jaleed kissed her neck as he massaged her juicy thigh.

"I wanna do so much shit to this sexy ass body. I know I hurt you and I'm here to make that shit right. You'll forever belong to me Jerzey," he whispered in her ear.

Jerzey's body went stiff at his words. She gently pushed him back and he caught her arm. Jaleed leaned towards Jerzey and placed a soft kiss on her lips. She closed her eyes as she waited for the sparks to fly.

They never came.

Jerzey sighed with relief. She knew she wasn't tripping. It wasn't there anymore. The hold he had on her was vacant now and she was so fucking grateful for that.

"Let's enjoy this drink," she told him as her phone rung once more.

Jerzey and Jaleed sat in the bar for the next hour talking of the past and enjoying each other's company. Jerzey was then brought back to her place so that he could collect his items. As they stood near his truck, he gazed down at her with sad eyes. Jerzey smiled at him and touched his chest.

"You're a sexy man with money. You'll have no problem finding somebody."

Jaleed nodded. He licked his lips as he gazed down at her.

"But not another you. You grew up to be everything that I knew you would be. I'm happy to see that you good, especially after that shooting shit. You didn't let life break you down and I respect that about you. You're still standing, ma," he said and Jerzey swallowed hard.

She leaned towards Jaleed and he pulled her into his arms. They hugged for a moment before she let him go.

"Just in case that nigga start acting up, you know what to do. I'ma make sure my number stays the same just for you," he told her, and she laughed.

"Okay, you do that," Jerzey replied with no intentions to ever call his womanizing ass.

Jaleed gave her one last look before walking around to the driver's side door of his truck. Jerzey turned around and headed for her door. As she grabbed the knob a strong hand rubbed against her ass. Her eyes widened in alarm as she spun around.

"You scared the shit out of me!"

Snowden stared down at her with knitted brows. Even in the dark of night she could see how handsome he was. The threads he wore only added to his appeal while his jewels sparkled under the street lights.

He glanced up and down the street before looking back at her. His infamous scowl covered his face.

"Who the fuck was that nigga?"

Jerzey stepped back. She was speechless as she stared up at the man she loved.

"Huh?" she asked shocked to see him.

Snowden's frown fell, and he chuckled.

"I was in the city when I called youse. I was trying to pull up but youse was on some bullshit. I said who the fuck was that nigga?" he asked again.

Jerzey went into her building with Snowden on her heels.

"And you painted that nigga?"

The hurt in his voice made Jerzey shake her head. Snowden was making her head spin. She was also upset to see that they'd somehow forgotten one of Jaleed's portraits. She knew he'd used that as an excuse to see her again, so she made a mental note to ship it to him right away.

"At least he wants to be in my space," she retorted heading for her staircase.

Snowden nodded while smirking.

"Straight, like that?"

Jerzey ignored him and made her way up the stairs. She took a step up and Snowden stopped her with his hands on her waist. She closed her eyes as his breathing grew labored.

"I'm not a vocal nigga Jerzey. I was never raised like that. I show my love with the shit I do. Jerzey if I felt nothing for youse my brother would still be here. Do you get what I'm sayin?"

Jerzey swallowed hard.

"But you're making me pay for something that I had no control over. He tried to kill me, Snowden. He ruined my life twice. I don't know what more you want from me. I love you but damn I can't say I'm sorry it happened. It was him or me," she said quietly.

Snowden took a deep breath and sighed. His grip tightened on Jerzey before his arms went around her waist.

"I don't regret it. It just fucked me up. I have trouble sleeping at night knowing what I did. I was angry with you and I'm sorry for how I acted. Let's start over," he said humbly.

Jerzey fought off a smile.

"How do you suppose we do that?"

Snowden bent his head and tongued her neck. The sensual swirls of his soft tongue instantly turned her on. His hands traveled down her thick body and eventually under her skirt. Jerzey's breath hitched when he bit her neck gently.

"Bend it over for me," he said huskily.

Jerzey quickly complied and Snowden leaned down. He pulled down her shorts then tugged at her panties until the thin material tore and he slapped her ass. "You so fucking sexy," he murmured before spreading her soft cheeks.

Snowden stuck his face between her legs and his tongue latched onto her clitoris. Jerzey gasped as pleasure traveled through her curvy physique. Snowden's long tongue ventured up and down her moist center before slipping into her slit. His finger worked magic on her clitoris as he licked her vaginal walls.

"Oh my god," Jerzey moaned.

Snowden worked his fingers harder and soon she was blessing him with her watery orgasm. Snowden licked her clean before turning her around. He unbuttoned his jeans and allowed for them to fall down his legs as he picked

Jerzey up. She kissed him passionately as he rubbed his mushroom head against her slick opening.

"You forgive me?" he asked staring into her eyes.

Jerzey's heart raced as she gazed back at him.

"Why should I Snowden? I'm not looking to keep getting hurt."

Snowden nodded. Slowly he pushed into her and they both groaned. He pushed Jerzey against the wall and moved her up and down onto his thick shaft. Jerzey whimpered with each stroke he delivered to her pussy.

"Because I love you and when I love people, I don't take that shit lightly. It wasn't my intentions to hurt youse and I swear on my life, that all I wanna do is make you happy." Snowden kissed Jerzey and sucked on her bottom lip as he pumped into her at a steady pace. "I gotta make you happy. If youse not happy then I'm not good. That's why," he replied and pulled back.

Snowden began to hammer away inside of Jerzey making her cry out. Jerzey held onto him tightly as her walls soaked up his penis. From their lovemaking, you could hear how wet she was.

"Oh, baby! I can't take it!" Jerzey cried out ready to throw in the towel. She'd cum twice and was ready to call it a night.

Snowden shook his head while smirking. He slowed up to raise up his shirt before pumping back into her harder.

"Jerzey all that whining shit really not for me. Relax and take this dick," he told her.

Jerzey nodded before he pulled back to fuck her harder. Her breast bounced as she stared into Snowden's eyes. His dick had been good before but tonight it was *fucking* amazing. Her eyes watered as his penis pushed against something inside of her that had never been touched before. Her hands shot to his chest in alarm.

"Baby wait! Oh, my goodness, please stop!" she begged in a shaky voice.

Snowden shook his head. Pleasure sat on his handsome face as he pumped himself into Jerzey. Snowden leaned towards her and kissed her lips before sliding his mouth over to her ear.

"Nah, I want that super nut. The one that's gone have your ass sleeping for a whole day straight. You going out with niggas, acting like somebody can replace me when we both know that no other motherfucka can make us happy like we can. You gone give me that shit. I want you to close your eyes, relax and squirt on this dick," he instructed sensually.

His tongue went to her neck and he put his back into it. Jerzey's mouth fell open as her legs shook.

"......What the fuck! Its cumming!" she yelled before a fountain of pleasure erupted from between her legs.

Snowden pulled back and continued his pumps as she wet them both up while screaming at the top of her lungs.

Brown, dark green and orange leaves blew with the wind. Gray clouds hovered in the sky as a melancholy mood sat over the cemetery. She held the flowers as he held the Don Julio Anejo and the blanket.

With big steps, they made it to the grey marble tombstone in no time. Jerzey swallowed hard as she followed him to the site. His name seemed to jump off the stone as they gazed down at it. For him, she would do this.

Only for him.

"Damn man," he grumbled in despair.

His head hung low as he stared at the headstone.

"I never wanted for shit to come to this. You did a lot of shady shit man." Snowden shook his head and chuckled. "A lot. From snitching on niggas to dropping a dime on me and Jannero. You stole and killed niggas...even tried to kill this one here," he said, and his eyes ventured over to Jerzey. Snowden took a swig of his drink and swallowed it down. He peered back down at Jeremiah's grave and cleared his throat. "It wasn't until you pointed that gun at her that I knew that no matter how hard I was fighting it she's the one for me. I couldn't let you shoot her but damn, me killing you really fucked my head up. Regardless we blood, and I know moms' is disappointed as fuck in me," Snowden said before clearing his throat.

Jerzey sat the roses down not emotional in the least. Her worry was more for the man she loved. She stood up and hugged his side. He glanced down at her and she could see his eyes were red-rimmed.

"He wasn't always like this," he said lowly.

Jerzey smirked up at him.

"I'm sure he was really sweet when he was an infant," she joked, and Snowden chuckled.

He licked his lips and pulled her closer to his body.

"On some real shit, I can only remember him being a real nigga until he was like ten. That nigga did turn sour quick as fuck. I gotta let this shit go, huh?"

Jerzey nodded.

"Yes, but regardless he's your brother and you're in mourning. Even when people do us wrong, we still love them. This doesn't make you the bad one. His actions is what placed him here Snowden. Your mom and God understands that," she replied.

Snowden gazed at her another minute before looking back to the headstone. He let Jerzey go and leaned down towards the grave.

"I'm sorry," he whispered before pouring the rest of his liquor onto the dirt.

Jerzey waited for Snowden to collect himself before walking with him back to the truck. Snowden tossed her the fob and licked his lips.

"Let's ride out sexy."

Jerzey clutched the fob tightly in her hand.

"And go where? Back to your place?"

Snowden shrugged as he opened his truck door.

"Nah, the airport. We heading to Vegas early. I wanna have some alone time with youse," he replied and Jerzey grinned at him.

"That sounds like a perfect idea," she murmured climbing into the truck.

Hours later after taking a nap and freshening up Jerzey walked with Snowden through the Bellagio Gallery of Fine Art. While he wore black Balmain jeans with a black crew neck and high-top designer kicks, she wore black as well. However, her attire was sexy. The dress clung to her thick frame and the red Giuseppe's she paired the look with sat her ass up just right. Jerzey wore her dark silver bob lace-unit with natural makeup and glossy lips. Since they'd exited the penthouse Snowden's eyes had been on her.

His hand once again found its way to her ass as they passed a portrait. The alluring cologne he wore made her panties moist.

"You making it hard for a nigga to concentrate on this shit in here. Why youse so fucking sexy?" he asked and slapped her ass.

Jerzey blushed as she glanced around. She noticed an older couple gawking at them and sighed.

"Snowden you got people staring at us baby."

Snowden frowned. He glanced back and spotted the older couple. He chuckled as he looked back down at Jerzey.

"Youse and this dress gone be the reason her old ass get some dick tonight," he replied and Jerzey snickered while shaking her head.

They bent a corner and Jerzey stopped smiling. Her neatly waxed brows pulled together as she stepped towards the artwork. It was familiar. She knew it, in fact, she'd created it and her hands found the gritty canvas as Snowden walked up behind her.

He hugged her from the back and she relaxed in his embrace.

"This is a Jerzey exclusive right here. I watched her freestyle this while mad as fuck at me and all I could think about was how talented she is. I believe in youse and soon everybody is gone see what I already do," he said sincerely.

His voice was low and filled with so much love that it made Jerzey tear up.

"I could be in here one day?" she asked in a low voice.

Snowden kissed her neck and looked at the canvas.

"You already are but you gotta work hard as fuck to make sure that you stay in here."

Jerzey nodded. She couldn't think of a time ever when she'd felt so much joy from being with a man. He believed in her. Pushed her towards her dreams instead of trying to take her away from them. Most of all he was sincere. His love for her wasn't because of his own selfish gain. It nearly tore them apart, but he'd even killed for her. It was obvious they had a love like no other. And she was happy to see him embrace it.

It's never fun to be in love alone.

"I love you," she whispered.

Snowden kissed her cheek and hugged her tighter from the back.

"I love your sexy ass too. My little artist and shit," he replied making her smile.

Twelve

The police station was hectic with chaos. The day before they're been ten shootings and the crowd was heavy with mourners and angry people.

The small girl held her baby in her arms making sure she was protectively wrapped up. She held a neutral look on her face as she sat at the small, cramped desk that was cluttered with papers. The handsome policeman regained his seat and shot her an apologetic smile. He looked at the child she was cradling, and his smile dropped from his face.

The look he gave wasn't nice and since her child had been born it had been one that she'd grown accustomed to receiving from people.

Judgment.

Disgust.

Anger.

That was what people felt when they learned of her baby. As if she was happy to be a mom at thirteen. She loathed it and was suffering from depression and still in shock by what had gone down the day of his shooting. However, she had to keep it moving. She needed to see to it that her abuser was arrested.

"*Did you find him?*" *her light voice probed.*

The hope in her eyes wasn't lost on the officer. The officer shifted his eyes and peered around the precinct. He cleared his throat as he leaned forward in his seat.

"*Nanmiko can I speak frankly?*" *he asked.*

Miko nodded.

The officer sniffled and rubbed at his pointy chin hairs.

"*You're a child with a child. Have you considered adoption or giving her to your parents? I know before you said they wanted her, have you changed your stance on that?*" *he asked changing the subject.*

Miko sat back and her thick brows pinched together. She was close to have a unibrow and didn't care. She had much more pressing matters to attend to. Like her livelihood and how she would raise a baby?

"*But this is my daughter. She wasn't a product of rape. She isn't his child,*" *Miko said defensively.*

The officer nodded.

"*I never said she was sweetie. All I'm saying is that she's a baby with needs. Same as you. Needs that you can't provide. I know you're concerned about your molester. I am too and I'm doing everything in my power to locate him but right now your focus needs to be on that precious child. Put her needs before your own. Love her more than you love yourself and she'll come out on top every time. You're a survivor Nanmiko. I can see it in your eyes. This won't break you and it won't break her as long as you put her first."*

Miko's eyes watered. She blinked and as she began to cry her baby started to cry too. She was only three months old and already Miko was tired of caring for her. It was overwhelming.

"So, I should give her away? What about me and her daddy Zyir? He doesn't even know she's his child. I can't give her to strangers. They could hurt her like I was hurt."

The officer nodded.

"Then give her to your parents. That way you could grow up with her. Use her as your motivation to make it. Don't let him win and don't worry about him. Whether it's on earth or in Heaven he will have to pay for what he's done to you. Give her a real chance at life, heck give yourself one Nanmiko," he replied.

Miko glanced down at her baby and her daughter stared up at her. Her chest ached as she stared into her eyes.

"I guess I can," she whispered with her heart racing. *"She could be free from all the things I've experienced. She could have a good life and be better than me. Live better than me,"* she said emotionally.

The officer shook his head to clear his own emotions from his handsome face.

"You all will both have a good life, sweetie. Let's call your parents," he replied and grabbed his black work phone.

With every thrust, the headboard hit the wall. It wasn't loud thankfully still the reason for the banging was obvious. The lights were out, and heavy grunts wafted through the air. As her sweaty body slid up the bed his tattooed body was right behind her.

She whimpered when he grabbed her throat and forced her head back, so his tongue could flirt with her neck.

"*Zy*... please," she begged tired of cumming.

It was fucking ridiculous but Zyir had the stamina of a lion. He could fuck for hours, *had* been fucking her for hours and she was tired.

Pussy sore, wet and overworked she was ready to toss in the towel.

Zyir grunted as he pounded into her.

"Nah, fuck that. You calling up that old nigga and shit like you single knowing that shit was gone piss me off. You asked for this," he said and tightened his grip on her neck.

Miko cried out and her body shook vigorously in his thick arms. Zyir was rewarded with her wetness still he didn't let up on the pleasurable pussy bashing. He went harder and Miko grabbed his forearm.

"Zyir no! It's so deep!" she whined as her body began to shiver.

Zyir licked his lips.

"How deep Nanmiko? Tell me where you feel this dick at?" he asked.

Miko's thighs shook uncontrollably. Her vagina clenched Zyir's dick tightly as her body vibrated again in pleasure.

"I feel it in my throat baby.... *Damn.* I don't wanna choke," she whined.

Zyir smirked before chuckling.

"Then let's make that motherfucka come out of your mouth," he said and let her neck go to grab her hips. Zyir raised Miko up to thrust into her and a soft hand sliding up his back caused him to let her go. "What the fuck?" he hissed pulling out of Miko.

Dorian rubbed her breast against his back and kissed his neck. She grabbed his soaked penis and stroked it gently.

"Zyir I've shown you that you can have us both. But don't leave me in the bedroom alone. I can join in. We can all just share a room baby," she whispered and kissed his lips lovingly.

Miko rushed to get out of the bed. Her legs felt like rubber as she held onto the nightstand. She turned on the light and watched in anger as Zyir and Dorian kissed each other passionately. Miko shook her head and with the last bit of her energy she stood up straight.

"I'm leaving Zyir. I should have never come here. I should have never agreed to any of this, but I was scared of losing you. I was ashamed of my actions and I didn't want you to completely hate me, but I can't do this anymore. This isn't me and for us to subject Enika to this is foul as fuck. I'm leaving and I'm taking my daughter with me."

Miko went over to the closet and grabbed a jogging suit. She quickly tossed on her clothes and Zyir was at her back. Dorian sat on the bed naked and quiet as Zyir turned Miko towards him. She stared up at him as her eyes watered.

"Don't you see how crazy this is? If you really love me, you'll let me go. I can't stay another night in this crazy house," she said lowly.

Zyir sighed. He pulled Miko into his arms and she hugged him tightly. She could feel his heart beating hard.

"You can't go Miko. Damn, why would I let you do that?"

Miko pulled back from Zyir and shook her head.

"I'm not asking your permission. I'm leaving and so is Enika. I'll call your momma if I have to," she threatened him.

Zyir sucked his teeth and Dorian shook her head.

"Let her go, baby. Finally, we can have our home back. We should be preparing for our wedding not dealing with this. Look at all of the shit she's done to you," she said to Zyir.

Miko grabbed a duffel bag and tossed a few things into it. Zyir quickly put on his clothes and tossed Dorian her robe.

"Dorian, give us a minute," he said looking at Miko.

Miko grabbed her purse and frowned at Zyir.

"No Zyir! Damn, I wanna leave. You're marrying Dorian. Worry about her, why can't I just leave?" she asked angrily.

Zyir glared at her with his nostrils flaring.

"Because I fucking love you! Fuck you mean why you can't just leave? You and Enika is my fucking family. I want y'all here."

Miko wiped her face.

"You can't have Dorian and us. It doesn't work like that. Goodbye Zyir," she said and walked away.

Zyir stood with clenched fists as Miko exited the room. She went upstairs to Enika's bedroom and stepped in. The scene before her made her gasp and drop her bags onto the floor. Enika sat naked on her bed with her laptop on her lap. A naked teenage boy engaging in a masturbation session sat on the expensive laptop screen.

Enika's eyes widened and she slammed the laptop shut. Miko rushed over to Enika and flipped her over. She began to spank her bare bottom hard making Enika scream out in pain. She'd never been whooped before.

"Ahh! Stop! Daddy!" Enika yelled at the top of her lungs.

Miko shook her head angrily.

"Your little sneaky ass! Why the fuck would you do this? Huh! Well, I'ma whoop the fast right up out of you!" Miko said and spanked her harder as Zyir and Dorian barged into the room.

Zyir ran over to Miko and pulled her back. Enika quickly tossed on her pajama shirt as she cried.

"Miko what the fuck you doing?" he asked bear hugging her.

Enika jumped off the bed and rushed over to Miko. She slapped her as hard as she could and glared at her.

"Don't you ever in your life whoop me! You're not my mother! You never was! Just somebody to buy me shit and take me places to cover up her own guilt. Rick loves me! I bet you don't know what that feels like. That's why you're over here trying to ruin Dorian's relationship!" Enika yelled angrily.

Zyir let Miko go and he glared at Enika.

"Why the fuck would you hit her! Aye, that shit is not acceptable and don't you ever in your fucking life talk to her like that again!"

His voice made Enika jump. She pouted as she stared up at him. Dorian stood by the door with wide eyes while Miko looked at Enika helplessly.

"Is that what you think of me? Am I really nothing to you? Do you know what I've given up so that you could live a good life? How hard I worked to take you to Paris and make sure you had a damn driver? It wasn't easy and every day I lived with the pain of my secrets. I wanted to tell both of y'all," Miko said sadly.

Enika shook her head. She began to cry, and Dorian quickly consoled her.

"But you didn't Miko and now you wanna be a mother to me but it's too late. I don't even know who I am anymore. All I know is that the person that was supposed to be my sister is my mom. You have ruined my life and I hate you! Just go! Go fuck one of your rich boyfriends and leave us alone. I wanna stay here or with my real mother. I don't know you," Enika replied bitterly.

Zyir walked over to Enika's closet and began to put her clothes inside of her bags. Once they was full, he placed the bag on the bed and looked at her.

"This the thing, you can be angry and hurt but you won't ever talk to her like that again and get away with it. Miko was wrong for hiding the truth but she was hurt baby. Your momma was your age with a fucking kid. Could you take care of a baby at your age?" he asked. Enika quickly shook her head and he nodded. "Then why do you think that she could? Your mom loves the fuck out of you and I'm talking bout your *real* momma. That's the most loving woman I know. Why you think I go so hard for her? She's not perfect but shit we not either. For the people, she loves she is though. She did what she thought was best and you gone respect her. You don't have no choice but too now tell her sorry?"

Enika slowly pulled away from Dorian and walked over to Miko. She stared at her for a few minutes before rolling her eyes.

"Sorry," she mumbled before walking off. She went into her connected bathroom and Dorian looked at Zyir. Hurt covered her face like never before. She shrugged while smiling faintly at him.

"I can't win, can I?"

Zyir cleared his throat.

"Win what?"

Dorian pointed between herself and Miko.

"This? You two! I can't fuckin win and now that she's pregnant I'm done trying to. I wanted the wedding to happen before she started showing but hell what's the point? You fuck her more than you fuck me. You love her in a way that you'll never love me. I need for all of you to go right now," she said and walked away.

Zyir turned to Miko and she dropped her head.

"How far are you?"

Miko sighed. How Dorian knew of the baby was lost on her. She'd just found out last week.

"Two months," she whispered as Enika exited the bathroom.

Zyir looked at Enika then Miko. He shook his head as sadness fell over his handsome face.

"Go to your place and I'll be over there."

Enika stared at him.

"You promise?" she asked.

Zyir nodded.

"On my life. I just need to make sure Dorian is good," he replied and hugged Enika. He then went over to Miko and hugged her tightly. He kissed her cheek and whispered in her ear. "I'm sorry for putting all of y'all through this. It was selfish as fuck of me. Please forgive me," he said and kissed her forehead before walking away.

After packing up her car with as many things as she could Miko took Enika to her home. They parked and cleaned out the car. Miko stood in the doorway to Enika's bedroom and watched her pout twenty minutes later. Miko had just taken all of her gadgets and Enika's anger with her showed on her pretty face.

"Are you having sex?" Miko asked.

Enika shook her head.

"No," she mumbled fiddling with the pink ruffled cover.

Miko sighed with relief.

"Do you wanna have sex?"

Enika shrugged. Her sad, monolid eyes shifted over to Miko.

"I don't know. I'm angry with everything that's happening in my life and it felt good to talk to him. It felt good for him to say he loved me," she admitted.

Miko stepped into the room and joined Enika on the bed.

"But *we* love you and we actually mean it. You're such a good kid. Why go down the wrong path now?"

Enika looked up at Miko and frowned.

"I don't like school, but I go. I was doing everything that was expected of me to make you proud. You was always so proud of me and now it's different. I figured I should just do what I wanted. Wasn't like it was gonna matter anyway," she replied.

Miko rubbed the back of her neck. She scooted closer towards Enika and tried to hug her but Enika pulled back.

"Please just leave me alone," Enika begged as she closed her eyes.

Miko stood up and nodded.

"No matter what I'm always going to be your biggest fan Enika. I'm sorry that this has hurt you so much and I love you. I love you more than I love anything in this world."

Enika's eyes tightened.

"What about that baby? I heard Dorian. Now is the chance for you two to get it right. You two could have the perfect life and kid. Can you just take me to my momma? Please, Miko," she begged.

Miko swallowed hard at Enika's words.

"Enika nobody could replace you. You are a part of me like this baby. I don't even know how to be a mom but I wanna try. I wanna be everything that you need me to be. I'm not going anywhere, and neither is your father."

Enika rolled her eyes and fell back onto the bed. She stared up at the ceiling and gritted her teeth.

"Well that's a shame because I really hate you," Enika said lowly.

Miko's eyes watered. She turned and quickly exited the room. She went into her bedroom that she hadn't slept in for months now and searched through her dresser drawer. She found an old blunt and shook her head.

"I know its stale as hell," she muttered shutting the drawer.

"What you bout to do with that?" Zyir asked walking into the bedroom.

He dropped a duffel bag and pushed his luggage against the wall. Miko glanced up at him and her heartbeat quickened.

"Nelly does it," she said quietly.

Zyir smirked at her.

"And? I ain't Nero and I'm sure my nigga not cool with her doing that shit. Enika good?"

Miko snickered.

"You talking about lil Damion in there? Nah, she's far from good and you let her slap me Zyir!"

Zyir shut the bedroom door.

"I didn't let her do shit. She slapped you and your ass didn't clap back so that's on you," he replied.

They both smiled and Miko shook her head. Zyir picked her up and took the old blunt from her. He dropped it onto the ground and placed Miko onto the bed. He rested beside her and touched her small belly.

"Is it mine?"

Miko frowned at his question.

"Are you really going to ask me that? I can't piss without your ass popping up out of the fucking toilet so yes, it's yours. I just don't know if a kid is what we need. We can't even control the one we have. She wants to beat my ass," Miko replied.

Zyir shook his head.

"I wouldn't let her. You know that. Why was you in there whooping her?"

Miko closed her eyes as he brushed his hairy cheek against her neck. *Could they do this?* She wondered. Because he was the only consistent male in her life, she never wanted to lose him. They'd tried before, and it didn't work. She wasn't sure if it would now and what made it worse was, they now had kids.

"She was face timing some boy naked," she replied.

Zyir's eyes widened. He sat up and Miko pulled on his wrist. She rubbed it as he glared down at her.

"What? Why didn't you say that shit before? Shit, I could have finished whooping her ass. I need to go holla at her. She's too young for that bullshit," he griped.

Miko shook her head.

"I know and that's why I lost it when I saw her doing that. We was having sex at her age though."

Zyir sucked his teeth.

"I don't care. One wrong don't make what she's doing right. Look what fucking got us. You want her to have a baby?" he asked.

Miko's brows pulled together.

"Of course not. I just don't know what else to do. She hates me Zyir and she heard Dorian talking about the baby. She thinks that we're going to love the baby over her. I don't know what to do."

Zyir fell onto his back and stared up at the ceiling.

"This too much. In one night, I ended my relationship, called off my wedding and found out I was having another kid. To know she's doing shit like that makes me feel like a failure. When I told y'all to come home with me all I wanted was my family. In my eyes the shit was legit. I had Dorian then I had y'all, but I fucked everything up being selfish. I hurt Dorian, I stressed you the fuck out then I showed Enika some real unhealthy shit. You was right. We could fuck all day when it was just us, but it is different with her around. I apologize ma because I didn't see that at first."

Miko licked her dry lips.

"And what do you see now?"

Zyir shifted on the bed and pulled her body close to his.

"I see that time is of the essence. I can't be selfish Zyir anymore. I wanna be better for you and for them. I can't do it alone though. You gotta stop running. Together we can fix this fucked up shit that we're in," he told her.

Miko smiled sweetly at him. She caressed his hairy cheek and his gaze peered into her.

"Okay," she whispered.

Zyir leaned down and kissed her sensually. His tongue slowly assaulted her lips eliciting a light moan to come from her.

"It's about fucking time. Get up out of these clothes," he demanded huskily.

Miko giggled as she rushed to get naked. As her last piece of clothing fell onto the floor Zyir picked her up and tickled her sides as they fell back onto the bed. Miko sat on his erection and stared down into his eyes. She could feel him hard, burning with need to fill her up and that made her own eagerness to feel him heighten.

"I've always loved you Zyir. Even before I knew what it meant. You was my escape from my pain and I'll never keep another secret away from you again. It scares me but I wanna be a family," she said emotionally.

Zyir licked his lips. He rubbed her soft waist and stared up at her.

"We've always been a family Nanmiko. Back then you could count on me and ain't shit changed. You will always be my girl," he stopped talking and he smiled. "*You're my lady, you're my lady yeah,*" he said making her blush.

The D'Angelo track was one of their favorites. Miko had been the only person lucky enough to hear him sing and that warmed her soul. She leaned down and kissed his thick lips.

"Life tried to tear us apart, but it didn't work. We're still standing. Real love can stand the test of time and take anything that's thrown its way," she whispered before he lifted her up and pulled her down onto his awaiting shaft.

The expensive private aircraft held up to its end of the bargain. The plush leather chairs were nice and big. The three women sat in them comfortably as the biggest pregnant one rocked her leg nervously.

"I swear I'ma hurt her. Why did she get locked up again? I was supposed to be going to church with Jannero and Jasir. With so much going on, I need to maintain my balance and peace with the Lord. I don't even think I'm supposed to be flying at this point in my pregnancy," Nelly vented.

Miko glanced over at her friend. They all wore travel attire and like always Nelly was slaying her pregnancy. Miko prayed she could be pretty as that once she gained thirty extra pounds. It had been so long since she'd been pregnant, she'd forgotten what it was like.

"She was with some hustler and they got picked up at the airport," Miko fibbed and her eyes connected with Rumer's.

Rumer snickered as she stuffed her face full of food. The sight of Rumer eating warmed Miko's heart.

"What? Didn't she fucking learn from Gnash? *My God*, we are a group of confused ass women. We gotta get our shit together! We can't be some old lost bitches. That's not cute," Nelly retorted.

Miko laughed as Rumer frowned over at Nelly.

"Speak for yourself. I might be stuck in a love triangle, but I'm not lost. At least not no more. I even sent Melanie home," she announced proudly.

Miko and Nelly smiled.

"Really? That's good and I see you in here eating. I'm so proud of you Rumer," Nelly told her. Rumer smiled while waving her off and Nelly frowned. "And what you mean a love triangle?"

Rumer sat her food down and sat back in her seat. She brushed her hand through her dark extensions and sighed.

"Kritt and Nahmir. Its clear Nahmir is the better choice."

Miko cleared her throat.

"Then why are you not with him? We all fuck with Kritt. We all know he loves you still that didn't stop him from making a baby. I know that has to hurt." Miko replied.

Rumer glanced down at her lap. She then looked up at her girls and her eyes watered.

"It does, and it isn't the first time. Years ago, I was with Takim. He was with someone and I still slept around with him. I even got pregnant by him," Rumer revealed.

Miko and Nelly looked at her in shock.

"Shut the fuck up," Nelly whispered with wide eyes.

Rumer nodded. She smiled at her girls and cleared her throat.

"He also had a whole ass fiancé that had a baby. I went to their place to tell her and when I saw the baby I froze. I knew then that I couldn't do it. I got an abortion and I never looked back. Now years later it's happening again only this girl isn't his fiancé. I don't know why I keep finding myself in this fucking situation. Its starts to fuck with you, you know? Make you feel like the problem is you. Like maybe I'm just not enough," she replied sadly.

Miko shook her head.

"No fuck that. The problem is those weak ass men. Don't ever blame yourself for some man's weakness. The same way you said fuck old boy from school you need to do that to Kritt. If he loved you like he said he does none of this would be happening. Nahmir could be what you need," Miko told her.

Nelly smiled.

"Or maybe you just need to be alone. Finish discovering who Rumer is. Who said we had to have the man to make our story complete? We can have it all and be single," Nelly said looking their way.

Miko rolled her eyes.

"Says the girl who almost did time behind her man," she joked.

Nelly and Rumer laughed, and Nelly flipped Miko off.

"Fuck you. Yes, I love Jannero but if he would have gone back to his ex, I would have let him go. I wouldn't have had a choice but to. Plus, y'all asses would have been on me so hard I would have let him go just to prove to you bitches that I could. I don't think anybody has friends as tough as mine," Nelly replied.

Rumer nodded while laughing and Miko sighed.

"But whoever said we had to have a man and kid just to be the perfect woman?" Rumer asked.

Nelly shrugged while staring at her.

"Hell, society did. Look at what society has done to you. Shit in one way or another we have all been affected by society," Nelly replied.

Miko twisted up her lip in disgust.

"Well, where is society at? I wanna fuck that bitch up," she said seriously, and her girls laughed. Miko shook her head. "But seriously we can live by our own rules. Zyir has taught me that. I have to admit that three's company shit we had going on was crazy, but he showed me that we have to live for us. Not for other people and what their perceptions of us should be."

Rumer shook her head.

"That's easier said than done. Women are judged way harder than men. Men can cheat and eventually its cool. Men can get divorced and bounce right back with a younger bitch like the shit never happened. Why is it always different for women? We gotta look and be perfect. Smart as hell, freaky as fuck and still cook like you from the south. That's too much pressure. Life is always harder for us," Rumer vented.

Miko smiled.

"Eve should have never eaten the apple. That's what shifted it for us," she said lowly.

Rumer and Nelly smiled and Miko licked her lips.

"I'm serious but none of us are perfect. I just want us all to be happy. We deserve it," Miko told her friends.

Nelly smiled while rubbing her belly.

"We do," she murmured.

Rumer grabbed her plate and stared down at the dish.

"Yes, we do," she added before grabbing her fork.

Inside the pricey boutique R&B music played softly through the speakers. On one side of the store was purses. Expensive and stylish with their unique designs and bright colors. On the other side of the store was a shoe wall. The shoe designs were one of a kind and jumped out at you. In the center of the store was purple, suede lounge chairs.

Miko's heels clinked against the ground as she held her phone up to her ear. She was battling heartburn and suffering from a migraine still she needed to pick Nelly out something to wear for her vacation. As her girl, it was her duty to pull through no matter what.

However, as a mother, it was now her duty to put her kids first. Her heart rate increased as she listened to the lady speak to her over the phone.

"Are you sure this was Enika?"

"Yes, mam I am. She left school at lunchtime with him and they were later caught on the side of the school making out. Enika was naked from the waist up and your significant other has been called. I also wanted to alert you that her grades are still perfect however her behavior has changed drastically. Enika along with the young man will be expelled," the principle informed her.

Miko's eyes watered. She was so angry she wasn't sure what to do.

"Okay. It won't happen again," she said displaying confidence that she didn't feel.

It was clear Enika did whatever the fuck she wanted to do. The sad thing was Miko didn't know what to do to stop her. It was like her mother had told her years ago. She'd created a monster with Enika.

"I hope so because if this happens again, we will be forced to end her relationship with the school. If I may I know of a great family counselor. I used it for myself. I can email over her information if you'd like," the principal added.

"Thank you," Miko whispered and winced.

She ended the call and sat on the nearest sofa. Her leg shook as she called someone that she hadn't spoken to in months. Someone that she didn't realize she missed terribly until the call connected.

"Honey," her mother said quietly into the phone.

Miko's eyes watered. She missed her. She actually missed her mom. That small fact messed her up because for so long she'd only hated her.

"I'm sorry. I was angry but that doesn't make how I treated you right. You raised me and Enika and you did a great job. You didn't deserve my hateful, disrespectful words," she whispered sincerely into the phone.

Miko's mother gasped.

"Oh, honey! It's okay, I swear it is," she replied.

Miko shook her head. Only now did she see the error in her ways.

"But it's not. I haven't respected you in years. I always talked over you. Showed you no real love and now my kid is doing the same thing to me. I've created a generational curse that I don't know how to break. I'm not a good mother, mommy," she cried.

Miko's head ached worse as tears slipped from her eyes.

"And here I am carrying another baby when I can't even take care of Enika. She's out of control," she said sadly.

"Oh, baby it will be fine. What's wrong?" her mother asked.

Miko wiped her face as a few people stared at her. One woman stared too hard and Miko frowned. She covered the phone as she glared at the woman.

"Bitch what's the problem? Have you never seen someone fucking crying? Damn nosey ass motherfucka's," she huffed before lifting the phone back to her face.

The woman quickly walked away as Miko licked her lips.

"Enika is out of control. She slapped me after I caught her talking to a boy inappropriately. Then I get a call from the school today saying she was kissing a boy outside. So, she's expelled."

Miko's mother cleared her throat.

"She's hurting Miko."

Miko shook her head with furrowed brows.

"So, I'm supposed to let her walk all over us? Allow for her to talk to me crazy because she's upset?" she asked.

"You behaved the same way Miko, yet I still love you. Nothing you could say or do changed that. Enika is really crying out for help. I couldn't figure out how to help you but let's not give up on her. Together all of us can help her so she can move past the pain," her mother replied.

Miko closed her eyes. Guilt and regret immediately washed over her.

"You would help us?" she asked lowly.

Her mother laughed.

"Why wouldn't I? You are a part of me, Miko. I'm going to always be there for you," she said, and more tears fell down Miko's face.

"I love you mom," she whispered saying words that she hadn't spoken in over ten years.

Her mother gasped before she sniffled into the phone.

"I love you too baby. I love you more than you'll ever know," she replied saying to Miko, what Miko always said to Enika.

Miko smiled. It was a cycle and now it was up to her to make the cycle healthy, remove the bad and start good traditions.

Thirteen

Anxiety hung heavy in the air as the car rode the Las Vegas strip. Traffic was particularly light as the sun beamed down. AC blew in the rental as the women peered out of the windows. In true Vegas fashion, the city was alive. Even at nine in the morning people were out. Mostly tourists and as the driver turned the corner Nelly's leg shook in irritation. She was beginning to have Braxton Hicks contractions and was fearful that she just might go into labor while looking for Jerzey. The last thing Nelly wanted to do was have her baby without her man by her side.

"It's been two days and you all still haven't heard anything from her?" she asked.

Miko and Rumer shook their heads. Nelly's tongue brushed against her teeth and she sighed.

"This is bullshit. I swear when we get to this girl I'ma beat her ass. Now, what happened with Enika?"

Miko licked her lips.

"She was kicked out of school for kissing some boy. They even caught her with her shirt down and shit. It's a mess."

Rumer's jaw fell slack as Nelly's brows pinched together. Enika had always been her princess doll. She couldn't envision her doing such a thing.

"Are you sure it was her?" she asked.

Miko smiled still you could see the pain in her monolid eyes.

"I'm sure it was her. I know that's your baby but she's also this new Enika. I didn't wanna say anything but before we came out here, she slapped me," Miko revealed.

Rumer grabbed her chest as Nelly stared at her girl in shock. Nelly's neck whipped back, and she shook her head.

"I'm sorry she what?" she asked for clarification.

Miko sighed.

"She slapped the shit out of me. I caught her video sexing that same boy and I started whooping her. Zyir pulled me off her and when he did that heifer slapped me. I was shocked too, hell I still am but after talking with my mom I feel better," Miko replied.

Nelly sat back in shock at what she'd heard while Rumer cleared her throat.

"I knew this would happen. She's upset but you've given her a good ass life. A better childhood than any of us had and this is how she repays you? You don't deserve that," Rumer told Miko.

Miko looked at her friends.

"But are you saying that because you love me? If you was to hear this story...my story and I was someone else would you still feel the same way?" she asked Rumer.

Nelly peered over at Rumer awaiting her response. Rumer looked at Miko and grabbed her small hand.

"I would feel the same way. Horrible shit happened to you, Miko. You could had left her in the trash. Hell abandoned her with no home, but you didn't. You gave her to your mom and you worked your ass off to give her the best of everything. Money doesn't fix all your problems but trust her life will be a hell of a lot easier than most people's because she doesn't have to worry about it. Enika knows that as well. She's trying to punish you and right now you're letting her," Rumer replied.

Miko nodded and looked out of the window. Nelly tore her gaze away from her friends as well and soon they were pulling up to the Wynn hotel. Immediately Nelly's face fell into a frown.

"Why the fuck are we at the hotel? We need to see about Jerzey, so we can go home," Nelly complained.

"I know but we have to meet the lawyer here. He's expensive as shit but he'll be able to get her out," Rumer said and pushed her door open.

Nelly groaned and pouted as she watched her friends exit the car. She eventually followed suit and trailed after them slowly.

"She is so lucky we love her. After this, she better only date Bryant Gumble type niggas I swear," Nelly fussed.

Rumer and Miko snickered and soon they were entering into the lavish hotel. Nelly followed her friends down the hall and when they neared the bar area the sight of Jannero in a custom two-piece black Gucci tux made her stop walking. She gasped as her eyes watered. Her baby was looking so handsome it seemed unreal.

"What is this?"

Jannero licked his lips. He pulled a ring box out of his pocket and made his way over to her. Miko and Rumer looked on with big smiles on their faces. Jerzey walked up with Snowden and Nelly knew then that she'd been duped.

"What is this baby?" she asked again. This time teary-eyed and with a rapidly beating heart.

Jannero fell down to one knee and he gazed up at Nelly. He peered up at her like he loved her immensely.

Like she was the only woman for him and the intense gaze made her swallow hard.

Nelly never knew real love until he came into her life. The kind of love that touched your soul. Tied you to a person and made you connect with them on a level far pass the physical. The kind of love that made you whole. That was the love she felt for Jannero. A love she almost lost but was grateful that she didn't. Now she knew better and would forever give him her best because that's what he deserved.

"Didn't I say I would fix everything?" he asked arrogantly. Nelly nodded, and he smirked up at her. "I always go back to the first time we met cause when I saw you, I knew that you would be my wife and the mother of my kids. All dat," he said sincerely.

Nelly's eyes spilled over with tears.

"All dat?" she asked smiling.

Jannero nodded. He blinked a few times and cleared his throat. His handsome face grew heavy with emotion. The love was so thick between the couple it was palpable. You couldn't witness them together and not see or feel it.

"Yeah, all dat, ma. We not perfect but this is real. The love we share is real and I'll never give up on us. Will you marry me today Arnelle?" he asked charmingly.

He sighed, and Nelly was blessed with his perfect white smile. She leaned down and kissed his forehead. Jannero closed his eyes as she kissed his cheek.

"Of course, I will baby," she whispered before kissing his lips.

After saying "I Do" in one of the hotels most lavish themed ceremonies they ate in the Primrose Courtyard. Nelly felt as if she'd never looked so beautiful. The white lace beaded envelope gown was absolutely breathtaking on Nelly. Baby bump and all the designer gown fit her nicely. Her hair was in a natural updo with a diamond tiara in the front of her hair. Diamond teardrop earrings hung from her ear as her new diamond pear-shaped ring sat on her dainty hand.

Nelly was happy and in a pure state of euphoria as her son who was donning his own black custom suit sat next to her. On the other side of her was Jannero who was talking animatedly with Snowden. Nelly admired how beautiful her girls looked in their red mermaid bridesmaid gowns and she closed her eyes to once again thank God. He'd been so good to her.

This was real. Her pain hadn't been in vain. She was now married to the love of her life and it was a wonderful feeling.

One so good it made her want to continuously cry.

Beyoncé and Jay-Z's **Summer Time** track came on and Jannero stopped talking. He glanced over at Nelly and smirked.

This was their shit.

"Come on big momma. Come dance with your husband," he demanded sexily.

Nelly laughed. She licked her lips and slowly stood up. Jannero grabbed her hand and the photographers began to snap photos as they made their way to the dance floor.

Jannero pulled Nelly into his arms and she hugged him as tightly as she could. His mother was deceased, her's might as well have been so it was just them. Of course, they had their family and friends, but their union was of them and their kids. They had each other's back and their front and Nelly was elated to call him her husband.

"You looking sexy as fuck. On your pregnant shit today," he said making her smile.

Nelly nodded and Jannero playfully spun her around. The dress she wore was so nice everyone couldn't help but stare at it. With every turn and movement of her body, the crystal beads would sparkle.

We never been this far from the shore
We might not ever go back anymore

"Got you all in your emotions," Nelly sung and Jannero spun her around again.

This time he hugged her from the back and she relaxed in his strong arms.

I brought my sand to the beach
Hopped out the Lam' with the sheep
Skin rugs on the floor
We hugged, made love on the seats

"We watched the sky turn peach," Jannero rapped and Nelly blushed.

So many times, he'd whisked them away, so they could simply *get away*. She was excited at the new memories they would make.

"I love you," she whispered, and he kissed her neck.

"I love youse too ma," he replied with his accent peeking through.

"I'd like to cut in," Taya said walking up to Nelly.

Nelly stopped smiling and looked at Jannero's sister. Since the words they'd exchanged at Nelly's home, Nelly had been as cordial to her as she could be, but it wasn't how it used to be. Lines had been crossed, things had been said and now their connection was tainted. That hurt Nelly, but she wasn't sure how to fix it.

"Sure, you can," Nelly said letting go of Jannero and Taya shook her head.

"No with you," she said and grabbed her hand.

Jannero smiled and a few more photos was taken of them. Nelly and Taya began to dance and the air between them grew thick. Nelly gave her a tight-lipped smile before licking her lips.

Taya cleared her throat.

"I won't ever apologize for protecting my brothers. When I got the call that he was in the hospital Nelly that gutted me. They are all I have left. I mean we don't even have Jeremiah anymore," Taya said becoming emotional.

Nelly nodded feeling for her but not giving a damn about Jeremiah's death.

"I understand that and for hitting Nero I am sorry. He knows that, and I will never do that again," Nelly replied.

Taya nodded and gave Nelly a genuine smile.

"And that's all that I ask. I'm sorry for trying to stab you. You was and still is the best sister a girl could ask for. I'm sorry," Taya said, and Nelly hugged her.

Jannero stood by with a big grin on his face.

"That's the shit I like to see," he commented making Nelly and Taya smile at each other.

Jannero Miller has been picked up by overseas basketball team and signed on for a reported 2.5 million!

The Waldorf Astoria in Dubai set the tranquil backdrop for Nelly's honeymoon. Jannero had even flown out Taya to assist them with Jasir whom he wanted to see Dubai not caring that his son's young mind would probably forget it. Soft baby cries filled up the suite making the parents smile with joy. At five pounds and sixteen ounces Anisah Grace was a perfect mixture of her mother and father. Fair freckled skin with a head of curly sandy brown hair and enchanting eyes. Like her father she was a sight to see.

Nelly couldn't stop staring at the beautiful little girl she'd pushed into the world a week prior. Anisah laid in the pink bassinet covered in a white onesie with a frown on her pretty face. Nelly gently rubbed her baby's belly and watched her daughter slowly began to doze off.

Nelly stopped gazing at her daughter after a few minutes to read over the papers to her future bakery. Everything was happening so fast, but she welcomed the change. Still, she knew once she broke the news of her upcoming move to her girls that they would be crushed. With Jerzey living in New York they were already separated but now that she was leaving too it would be hard for them. However, family came first. Her husband and kids would always be first priority.

"So, Spain?"

Jannero fell down beside Nelly and his tattooed hand landed on her bare thigh. Infront of the couple on the rug with his toys was Jasir.

"Yeah, and when that contracts up, we can come back to the states and see who's trying to sign me. I know it's far, but I had to secure that bag for us. I also miss playing. That's like my fifth love and shit," he replied.

Nelly nodded.

"And what's the first four?"

Jannero smirked at her.

"Don't ask dumb questions ma."

Nelly smiled. In her silk gown that stopped mid-thigh she felt at peace. A feeling that she was becoming used to. A feeling that she prayed lasted forever.

"Jannero I'd have to be in the states to get my new building off the ground."

Jannero sighed. He leaned his head back and his eyes peered over at Nelly.

"I know baby and just know that home is wherever me and the kids are at. Don't have your girls thinking you back for good and shit. How do you feel?"

Nelly rubbed her belly that was still swollen but going down further with each day that passed.

"Tired," she admitted. She cleared her throat as she glanced Jannero's way. "After seeing all the changes Rumer made with the help of her therapist, I'm ready to give one a shot. My childhood still haunts me and I wanna be over it. I'm tired of ignoring the pain I feel when it enters my mind."

Jannero pulled Nelly onto his lap and she stared into his eyes.

"I love hearing that. I want you to be happy too. The best fucking Nelly you can be. That's all I want for you baby," he told her. Jannero's eyes slid over to their son and he took a deep breath. He exhaled and licked his lips. Jannero swallowed hard before speaking. "I'm ready and I'm sorry for waiting so long," he said staring in her eyes.

Nelly kissed him before speaking.

"Ready for what?"

Jannero dipped his chin towards Jasir.

"Ready for him to get tested," he replied somberly. Nelly rubbed the soft hairs covering his chin and his eyes connected with her's. "No matter what he'll be okay though. I mean what the fuck is normal anyway?"

Nelly nodded.

"He has more love than a kid can handle. We'll make sure he'll be okay," she assured him.

Jannero nodded and kissed her again.

"Bet let's go lay him down so I can rub on your booty for alittle while," he replied and smiled at her.

Two weeks later after being back in the states for only two hours, Nelly sat in the packed condense room beside Jannero's agent. Taya was back at the house with the kids because Nelly didn't want them to come. Nelly watched her husband stand in front of the podium and she licked her lips. In a two-piece suit with a fresh cut and handsome face, he stared out at the crowd. Beside him was his lawyer looking dapper as well.

"The charges placed against me and my wife was dropped. We've been acquitted of all charges and ready to start this new part of our life," he said confidently.

Flashes of lights went off on him and a reporter from a local news station stepped closer to Jannero.

"Word has it you're already getting calls from NBA teams in the states looking to sign you once your Spain contract has ended. Do you regret signing with the Spain team so soon?"

Jannero quickly shook his head.

"Nah. My mom's always told me that change was good. She said to never run away from it because on the other side of change could be your happiness. I just married the love of my life. We recently had a daughter and she's perfect. My son is happy and healthy, and my family is good. I don't have any complaints with life right now. Hell, we need a break from the states anyway. Time to get back to us and shit."

More flashes went off and Nelly's heart warmed at his words. She loved this man so damn much.

"Will your wife re-open her bakery? In this whole ordeal her reputation was tarnished," another reporter said to him.

Jannero looked at Nelly and flashed her his sexy smile before kissing his ring finger. Beneath the pricey diamond was their initials tatted. They were in this thing called life *forever.*

"She's already got a new spot. Her work speaks for itself and I'll forever work to fix the things this federal charge did to us," he replied.

"And when you return to the states after your contract is up with Spain what will you say to all of the teams that reportedly want to sign you?" A female reporter asked.

Jannero looked at the closest camera to him and smirked.

"They better be ready to cut a check," he said smugly.

Nelly laughed while a few people clapped. Nelly closed her eyes as her body grew warm all over with love and in the softest voice she whispered, "Thank you, Lord. You loved me when I didn't love myself, protected my family and saw us through the pain. You are a merciful God. Amen," she whispered.

Jannero pulled her into his arms before she could open her eyes and he kissed her breath away. Nelly exhaled as her peaceful bubble wrapped protectively around them. Since receiving the Holy Spirit, Nelly had been feeling a covering over her like never before and she knew it was God. He was with her. Just like he'd promised he would be.

Yes, she could get used to that big think called happiness. It really was all that people made it out to be.

Fourteen

*Her heart thundered in her chest as she stood on the scale. **170**. Damn, she couldn't believe it. That purging shit actually worked. She sighed as she stepped down and walked over to the floor length mirror. She turned to the side and rubbed her stomach.*

Rumer's thoughts drifted to the baby she'd sadly terminated, and her chest ached. She thought of Takim's fiancé and held in her stomach. If only she was smaller, thinner, maybe then he would have chosen her.

Then she could have been preparing for the baby while being with the man she loved. Rumer went back to the sleek glass scale and stepped back onto it. Once again 170 slid onto the display and a triumphant smile graced her face.

"This purging might not be so bad after all," she murmured and shoved her fingers into her mouth.

Rumer rushed over to the toilet bowl and bent down. Vomit escaped her lips and she emptied the rest of the contents of her stomach into the toilet. She flushed the toilet before washing her hands. A sense of peace washed over her as she realized she cleansed her stomach. The food wouldn't blow her up. She wouldn't wake up days from now and be a few pounds heavier. Instead, she would get smaller and if she was careful with it and did it correctly, she could get down to her desirable weight.

Rumer could see the men lining up for her. Thoughts of her wearing belly tops with skinny jeans and being comfortable flooded her mind. The possibilities would be endless. No more would it be Rumer the big, pretty girl. Instead, it would be Rumer the beautiful ass woman. She was here for it. Craved that feeling as she stared at her pretty round face in the mirror.

"You can have it all," she whispered before walking out of the large bathroom.

"Rumer look what I can do!" Tennille yelled out excitedly.

Rumer was brought back to reality as Tennille jumped as high as she could in the trampoline park. Rumer gave her a thumbs up and Tennille shook her head. In a pink tutu that she'd paired with black leggings and a black top that read *Princess Tennille Turns 10* she looked out right adorable. Tennille personally called Rumer and invited her, and Rumer canceled her prior engagements to make the trip to New Jersey. For Tennille, she would always make the time.

"Come on let's jump!" Tennille yelled and ran up on Rumer.

Rumer sat her phone down and stood up. She tugged at her ripped skinny jeans that hugged all of the added weight with pleasure and she smiled. With her hair pulled into a sloppy bun and wearing one of Zyir's logo'd hoodie's she looked sexy, chic and all of the men in attendance had been eyeing her except the one man she couldn't stop thinking about.

"Get back guys! My Rumer is ready to play with me!" Tennille yelled and began to jump.

Rumer took a deep breath and jumped with the energetic child. Rumer closed her eyes and bounced. She flew up into the air and came down hard. The small kid she landed on cried out in pain and Rumer's face fell in shock.

"Oh my God, I'm so sorry!" she said pulling the small girl up.

Tennille along with a few other people laughed while Rumer's cheeks burned with embarrassment. She took the child to one of the long tables and her eyes connected with Nahmir's. He stood in front of her looking handsome as ever in his blue jeans that he wore a hunter green Polo style shirt with along with the matching Timberlands. Nahmir stood beside his cousin Hayward as they engaged in small talk. Both men were good looking but Nahmir just fucking stood out. The way his tall body commanded attention drove Rumer insane. It was a confidence in his stance that she'd never witnessed on any man before.

He stood like he was that nigga.

The sexy frown he wore even turned her on. His hand brushed over his low, soft waves on his head showing off the diamonds sitting on his gold Patek wrist watch and his hooded eyes peered up. They landed on Rumer and she gave him a small wave.

"Hi," she managed to squeak out.

After the Kritt incident she hadn't reached out to him and he hadn't reached out to her. They were both extremely busy people but if they wanted to, they could have put the effort in to make something happen like they'd done before. Rumer was embarrassed and ashamed of her actions. She missed Nahmir but out of fear of rejection hadn't called him to smooth things out.

"Sup," he muttered before walking off.

Rumer nodded and watched a few people's curious eyes gaze her way. She chose to sit down and seconds later Nahmir walked back to the long tables with Tennille. By their side was an attractive woman with a sick ass thick body on her. She was bigger than Rumer and she owned her beauty. It was in the way she held her head high and strutted in the room. She was gorgeous, and she knew it.

Rumer swallowed hard as she watched the woman clutch onto Nahmir's arm. He whispered something to the woman and she gave him a tight-lipped smile. She walked over to the table and plopped down beside Rumer. She pouted as Rumer finished sizing her up out of the corner of her eye.

Her weave is cute. Not as nice as mine but cute. Her heels are straight, last season as fuck but they bad. Her face is pretty though, but hell so is mine. Why the fuck did he bring her here? Rumer wondered.

She wasn't his girl, didn't know any of his people besides his daughter but she felt like he was being messy.

"I'ma make this short. We all know I'll stop the world from spinning for this one here. My heart in human form and she knows it. Daddy loves you so much. Let's sing her happy birthday real quick," Nahmir said in his smooth deep voice.

A voice Rumer felt she hadn't heard in so long.

Everyone stood, and Rumer once again tugged up her jeans. She looked up and her eyes connected with Nahmir's. She watched him give her a brief once-over and lick his lips before turning his attention to Tennille.

"Are you his cousin!" the pretty brown beauty yelled to Rumer as everyone sung happy birthday.

The Stevie Wonder version of course.

"No!" Rumer yelled back with a frown.

The beauty next to her rolled her eyes and Rumer ignored it. She belted the words out as well as a tall waitress pushed in Tennille's birthday cake on a cart. It was a castle similar to the one at Disney World. Rumer remembered Tennille telling her that her Disney World trip was the last time she'd seen her mother alive and that memory saddened Rumer. Rumer stepped closer to the birthday girl and smiled.

The connection she felt with Tennille was real and had nothing to do with her fine ass daddy. Whether he forgave Rumer or not she would try to be in Tennille's life.

"Make a wish," Nahmir told his daughter leaning down.

Tennille smiled. She looked at Rumer and grinned at her.

"Come here!" she yelled waving her over.

Nahmir stood up and folded his hands in front of him as Rumer nervously walked over. She leaned down, and Tennille leaned over towards her. She placed her hand to her ear and everyone laughed even Nahmir.

"I wish my mommy was still here. I also wish you could stay with us," she said in more of a shout.

Nahmir's eyes shifted and he cleared his throat. Tennille hugged Rumer before blowing out her candles. Everyone clapped as Rumer discreetly wiped her eyes. Tennille hugged Rumer tightly as she grinned up at her.

"Let's get a few pictures!" the photographer yelled and waved over Nahmir.

Nahmir walked over to Rumer and his daughter and Tennille grabbed his hand.

"Hug her daddy. You said you missed talking to her," she said and Nahmir chuckled.

Rumer held in her laugh as Nahmir looked at her.

"What you do to my daughter?"

Rumer shrugged.

"Nothing, she's the one that has me in the palm of her hands."

Nahmir nodded. Despite the heated glares from his friend, he pulled Rumer to his side. He then picked up Tennille and people seemed to float over to the trio as the camera went off. They all fit together so well and as Rumer's body pressed against Nahmir's she was reminded of all of the nights she'd spent talking with him in Africa.

"I'm sorry," she whispered as the camera's continued to go off.

Nahmir's smile fell.

"You really showed me that you was mami," he murmured and after another set of flashes went off, he sat Tennille down.

Tennille ran back over to the trampoline cage and began to play. Rumer went back to her seat and minutes later Nahmir's lady friend joined her. Rumer grabbed her phone and checked her email as the woman stared her way.

"Who are you? Why are you here?" she quietly asked.

Rumer's head snapped up. She turned to the lady as Nahmir walked up.

"Because I was invited. Who are you?"

The woman smiled up at Nahmir. His scent greeted the women seductively as he peered down at them.

"I'm here for him," she replied.

Nahmir held out his hand and she took it with a big smile on her face. She smirked at Rumer before standing up. Rumer watched Nahmir walk away with the woman and her chest tightened. She called Miko as she stood up.

"I thought you was in New Jersey giving some *I'm sorry big daddy head*," Miko quipped answering the phone.

Rumer rolled her eyes while smiling. She walked over to a deserted part of the building and leaned against the railing. She looked at the lower level as she frowned.

"I wish. He brought somebody with him."

Miko sighed.

"And?"

Rumer shook her head.

"I shouldn't have come. I feel and look dumb as hell now," she whispered into the phone.

Miko scoffed at Rumer's words.

"I'm sure he was looking dumber than you when he opened up that text to you naked as fuck in Kritt's bedroom. You know how men are Rumer. They don't take pain the same as us. They weak as shit in that department so he's trying to soothe his ego. I know Kritt loves you, but this is something new. Something fresh and you deserve something good. Don't you?" she asked.

Rumer closed her eyes.

"Yes, I do," she replied knowing in her heart that Nahmir was the better man for her.

"Good. Plus, you didn't come for him. You came for that little girl that calls you a million times a day. Fuck him for now. Just focus on her. It's a reason you're in her life. Let it be for something good," Miko told her.

Rumer nodded feeling better with each word her friend spoke.

"Listen to you sounding like somebodies momma and shit," Rumer joked.

Miko snickered.

"Kiss my ass. Stop being a party pooper and go play with his daughter. He'll come around," Miko assured her.

"He better come around," Rumer retorted and when she turned around Nahmir stood behind her with a drink in his hand. Her mouth fell open and Nahmir chuckled.

"You talking shit bout me in my hood? You must be crazy mami," he said with a lazy smirk on his face.

Miko clicked her tongue against the roof of her mouth.

"That's what your scary ass get. Call me back," Miko said and ended the call.

Rumer placed her phone in her back pocket and Nahmir walked up on her. He fixed her oversized diamond hoop earring and his thumb brushed against her cheek.

"You might wanna back up. Wouldn't want your woman coming over here acting crazy on you."

Nahmir smiled. He grabbed Rumer's hand and led her back over to the party area.

"I sent her home," he admitted quietly as they sat down.

Rumer fiddled with the rings on her fingers. She rubbed the pad of her thumb against the ring he'd given her, and her eyes connected with his. Rumer's chest heaved up and down as she gazed into his eyes.

"I'm really sorry. I know that we were working towards something and I ruined it with my reckless decision. I want you to know that I haven't slept with him since then and I won't again. It was never meant for me to be with him Nahmir. I know that," she said sincerely.

Nahmir pulled his lip in between his teeth. He broke his gaze with Rumer and looked out at Tennille as she bounced in the bin filled with colorful foam squares.

"I don't do that flaky shit, Rumer. You know that about me. Then Tennille likes the fuck out of you and that makes me nervous. I don't want her hopes to get high bout some shit that may never happen. She's been hurt enough," he said lowly.

Rumer leaned towards him. Now that she was back in his presence, she yearned to be closer to him. The pull they had on one another was strong. She scooted over on the bench until her leg brushed against his and his hand went to her thigh. Rumer took a deep breath and tossed her inhibitions out of the window. She leaned onto his arm and exhaled.

The comfort she got from being with Nahmir was priceless.

"I missed you. I would never hurt Tennille and I want you to know that. She means so much to me and my love for her is genuine. Whether you forgive me or not I'm going to be there for her. I mean as long as you allow it. Us meeting was serendipity. I know you're hurt and don't trust me but I'm willing to put in the work to show you that I'm serious about us," she promised him.

Nahmir cleared his throat. Rumer hugged his arm tighter and she closed her eyes. The silence was killing her.

"You make me feel like love, at first sight, is real. When I returned home, I was caught off guard still it's no excuse. I was scared of the way I feel for you and I convinced myself that it wasn't real. That it was just us being caught in the moment but now I know. I knew then, but I fucking know now that it wasn't in our head. We have a connection and I don't feel that something like that is easy to come by. Please forgive me Nahmir," she said quietly.

Nahmir licked his lips.

"I don't allow for people to hurt me more than once Rumer. Shit happens again and it's a wrap. Tennille included. Okay?"

Rumer nodded eagerly. She leaned up and he turned his head. Their eyes connected, and she could feel her heart swell with happiness.

"I missed you so much Nahmir," she whispered.

Wishing she could kiss him but not wanting to show PDA in front of Tennille which would only lead the small child on she didn't. Instead, she tugged on his chin hairs until a sexy smile covered his face.

"My time is valuable. I'm not saying this to be cocky I'm just stating facts. Tennille and my businesses is my life. If I take time out of my day and spend it with you then take that shit as a blessing. You're beautiful as fuck Rumer. Got redeeming ass qualities about you and I like that. I don't fucking like people, but I like you. You're busy too and when you invested time into a nigga, I appreciated it. I thought you did as well. Ain't nothing about a nigga like me ordinary," Nahmir said and shook his head.

His deep voice spoke his words with such conviction that Rumer held onto him tightly anticipating what he would say next.

"I don't do drama. That trivial shit is for dumb motherfuckas with too much time on they hands. For me and mine, our life is nothing but good shit. Trips, laughs, and love. Good ass memories. I thought you was trying to be on that tip too mami. You told me you was then you go back to the same shit that wasn't working before. Fucking with a nigga that wasn't man enough to keep you secure when he had you. If being happy and never having to worry about shit is something that scares you, I'm not your type then. You know what I saw in you when I gave you that ring?" he asked.

Rumer shook her head.

"No," she whispered immersed in the man that was Nahmir.

Nahmir kissed her forehead and the act made chills run down her spine.

"I saw somebody I could finally build something real with. It's hard to connect with a person on every level but we had that. What's funny is like you said the shit was quick but for me, nothing in my life takes long Rumer. I see what I want, and I go get it. I saw that drive in you as well. I know we can be happy together. Have love, all that good stuff and be rich as fuck while doing it. Billionaires and shit. Fuck the games. You only have one life to live. I don't know about you but I'm not trying to waste mine," he replied, and Rumer exhaled.

She wasn't sure what was more affected by his words. Her vagina or her heart?

"I choose happiness. I choose this Nahmir," she said tenderly.

Nahmir smiled and it showed the deep dimples he possessed.

"Then don't take shit for granted. I'm not the nigga you wanna lose mami," he said, and Rumer pulled her lip between her teeth before nodding.

Hours after the party Rumer sat with Tennille and Nahmir inside of Nahmir's New Jersey estate. The place was more like a palace. With separate wings and entire staff and enough amenities to drive the real estate girl inside of Rumer crazy she was in mansion heaven. It was without argue the largest home she'd stayed in. As the cartoon movie ended Tennille rested her head on Rumer's arm.

"Rumer this was the best birthday ever," she whispered.

Tennille had bathed and put on her princess pajamas for the night. Sleep hung heavy over her as Nahmir glanced her way.

"Better than Disney?"

Tennille shook her head.

"No! Mommy was there but this was fun too."

Nahmir chuckled with sadness encasing his eyes.

"Word I was gone say you bugging right now. What makes this one so nice?" he asked standing up.

Tennille rubbed her eyes.

"Because everyone I care about is here. You, me, mommy's angel and Rumer," she replied before he picked her up.

Rumer swallowed hard as Nahmir walked away with Tennille in tow. Rumer stretched out on the large sofa and pulled the chenille blanket up to her neck. As she clicked onto the latest episode of her favorite reality show Nahmir stepped into the room. He sat down beside her head and lit up his blunt.

"I'm tired as fuck," he complained lowly.

Rumer peered up at him. It wasn't one thing that attracted Rumer to Nahmir it was *everything*. From the way he casually smoked his blunt to the way his sexy body rested on the couch. Rumer's hand found its way onto his thigh. Nahmir smoked his blunt as she rubbed her hand up and down his leg. Her heart beat faster as she moved towards his dick. In his grey joggers she could see the massive imprint and like a siren, it was calling her name.

"When you heading back to Detroit?"

Rumer's hand gently rubbed over his imprint. She licked her lips at how well-endowed he was. Just feeling his girth had her extremely wet.

"I have some meetings tomorrow and I have three houses to show at the end of the week. I promised Tennille I would come back for her recital," she replied.

Rumer stroked him through his pants and Nahmir bit his lip. Rumer tried to stick her eager hand into his pants and Nahmir grabbed her wrist. He blew smoke out of his mouth before looking her way.

"Chill out."

Rumer frowned, and his hand massaged her wrist.

"You came out here for Tennille. Not me, relax," he said and let her wrist go.

Nahmir sat up and put his blunt out. Rumer sat up with him and stared at his side profile. She wanted him and from his hard-on and wildly beating heart she was positive he wanted her as well.

"Nahmir—"

Nahmir shook his head. He glanced over at Rumer and licked his full lips.

"Did you use a condom with that nigga?"

Rumer's shoulders slumped and Nahmir nodded. He stood up and adjusted himself in his joggers. He held out his hand to Rumer and she happily took it.

Quietly they went up the steps and down a long hallway. Nahmir opened the door to a vast bedroom and hit the light.

"You can stay in here tonight ma. Get some rest," he placed a chaste kiss to her forehead before walking away.

Rumer looked at her luggage then around the eggshell-colored guest room. Her thick brows knitted together before she rolled her eyes.

It had been months since she'd slept with Kritt and she was STD free. Her checkup from weeks ago told her so. Rumer couldn't help but feel like Nahmir was trying to punish her but her aching body refused to give up.

After taking a hot shower and slipping into a red lace La Perla body suit that was crotchless with the nipples cut out, Rumer put on her robe. She slipped out of the guest room and walked around the home.

"Where the hell is his bedroom at?" she questioned quietly.

"Down the other hall."

Rumer jumped and when she turned around Nahmir was in his workout pants with sweat sliding down his toned abdomen. Rumer swallowed hard and gave him an impish smile.

"I needed to talk to you."

Nahmir nodded. He gave her a quick once over before grabbing her hand. He sniffed the air around them and licked his lips.

"Damn you smell good as fuck, what you wearing?"

Rumer walked fast to keep up with Nahmir.

"J'adore Dior."

"Gotta say that's the best perfume I done smelled on you," Nahmir noted and seconds later they entered his bedroom.

Rumer gasped and Nahmir let her hand go. The size of it was grand. Much like the size of many peoples apartments. Nahmir retreated to his walk-in bathroom as Rumer toured his bedroom. In the front of the room was a seating area with a large plasma decorating the front wall. All of the walls in his bedroom were black while the wall his bed was against had a light grey hue to it.

Rumer hated to be nosey but couldn't stop herself from checking out his walk-in closet.

"My God," she whispered as she stepped into the largest closet she'd ever seen.

Rumer ran her fingers over his jeans. All of Nahmir's clothes were paired off by colors and clothing type. His jewelry case was stunning with its watches and chains on display as if they were inside of a jewelry store. Rumer bent the corner and came face to face with his sneaker and hat wall. She smiled as she looked over his exclusive shoes. Some still in the glass case and donning the NBA player's name that they belonged to.

"I think the Kobe's is my favorite then those Pat Ewing's. My pops fucking loves Patrick Ewing. I found them in Cali and had Pat sign them for him. His lazy ass just hasn't come to get them yet," he replied.

Nahmir's arms went around Rumer's waist and she closed her eyes.

"I'd love to meet your father," she said quietly.

Nahmir chuckled as he untied her long silk robe.

"So, you can get him to fall in love with you like you did Tennille? I ain't trying to share you with him too. You know he believe in having more than one woman. He'd be trying to add you to the team mami," he replied, and Rumer laughed lightly. Nahmir's thick mannish hands found her soft nipples that escaped her bodysuit and almost immediately Rumer could feel him harden behind her. "I'm really not trying to take shit there with you. You not ready for me," he said thumbing her pebbled nipples.

Rumer moaned.

"I promise I can handle it," she assured him.

Nahmir spun Rumer around and pushed her robe off her shoulders. His eyes deliberately slid up and down her body and he swallowed hard. Rumer gazed down at the thick, white towel adorning his waist and wondered how it still stayed on with the big tent peaking beneath it? She grabbed his erection and Nahmir licked his lips.

"Rumer fuck taking some dick. I'm talking about a man like me. Before I put this dick up in you, I need to know for sure that you done with the games. If a good nut is what you looking for then call some other nigga. I'm trying to give you that plus a lot more. I told you I don't have time to waste," he said in a serious manner.

Rumer let go of his erection and she nodded as she walked up on Nahmir. She gazed up into his almond-shaped eyes and smiled.

"I promise I'm serious about us. I'm here for everything that you wanna give me. Believe in me, Nahmir. I won't hurt you," she promised.

Nahmir stared down into her eyes for several minutes before grabbing her face. He leaned down towards

Rumer and she giggled. Their pull was tighter than ever. The connection they had couldn't be denied and Rumer refused to run from it any longer. She wanted Nahmir and everything that came with him. Especially his beautiful daughter.

"We gone see with your sexy ass. Come here," he said and led Rumer over to his floor to ceiling mirror that sat in the back of his closet. The mirror took up the whole wall and had built in lights in the ceiling.

Nahmir pulled Rumer in front of him and they faced the mirror. Rumer gazed at Nahmir through the mirror as he stared back at her intently. His hands slid up and down the outline of her body before cupping her breast. Rumer's breath hitched, and her lids grew lower in lust.

"Do you know how beautiful you are?"

Rumer nodded and Nahmir shook his head. He pinched her nipple before kissing her neck.

"I love these," he murmured and squeezed her heavy breast. He slid his hand down and it landed on her pudgy stomach. No longer did she have a flat abdomen and Rumer was learning that it was okay. Flat tummies wasn't for everyone. Her included. "And this," he said referring to her stomach. Nahmir slid his hands up and down her legs and licked his lips. "I really fucking love these, but you know what I like most about you?" he asked.

Rumer shook her head. She half expected him to turn her around and slap her on her ass that didn't know when to stop growing. Instead, Nahmir slid his hands up her body. Gently he cradled her head in his large hands. Rumer's eyes connected with his in the mirror and he gave her a sexy grin.

"I love how smart you are. How determined you are to be the best you. That's sexy as fuck to me Rumer. I could listen to you talk about work, your friends, shit anything you want all day. You're passionate about everything that you love," he said and tilted her head to the side.

Rumer moaned as he kissed her neck sensually. His left hand slid down her body and into the apex of her thighs. When his fingers brushed against her bare sex she whimpered.

"Damn she fat," he said and sucked Rumer's neck harder.

Rumer moaned and two of Nahmir's fingers dipped into her warm opening. Slowly he slid them in and out of her as he sucked on her neck.

"Hold onto the mirror," he told her and pulled his fingers out of her.

Rumer did as she was instructed and Nahmir pulled off his towel. He then grabbed a condom from out of his bedroom before walking back up on Rumer. He dropped down to his knees and stuck his face between her legs.

"Oh shit!" she cried as his tongue latched onto her clitoris.

Nahmir licked Rumer through a climax before standing up. He placed on his condom and stepped up behind Rumer. Rumer gasped when he slid his thick mushroom shaped head into her pussy.

Nahmir licked his wet lips and smirked at Rumer through the mirror.

"You was talking big shit when you wanted the dick. Relax," he said and slid halfway inside of her.

Rumer closed her eyes and he grabbed her waist. They both moaned in unison as he pumped himself the rest of the way in.

"Oh my.... fuck," Rumer gritted out as he rocked in and out of her.

Nahmir slapped her ample ass and his head fell back.

"No lie, you feel good as fuck baby. So, fucking tight," he expressed with pleasure dripping from his words.

Turned on by his declaration Rumer began to throw it back at him. She threw that pussy at him like he was that nigga because in her eyes he was. With an arch in her back and determination in her mind, she backed Nahmir down with her ass. He held onto her hips with his mouth agape.

Rumer could feel him harden up some more before he abruptly pulled out of her. His chest heaved up and down as he picked her up and carried her into the bedroom. Rumer yelped as he tossed her onto the bed.

"Put that ass up in the air for me mami," he said stroking his dick.

Rumer smiled as she got on all fours.

"You don't wanna cum daddy?" she asked.

Nahmir chuckled. He rubbed her round bottom before sticking his member inside of her. Rumer grabbed onto the sheets and he pushed her back further down.

"I want that shit to touch the bed with that ass all the way up in the air. Now open it up for me," he demanded.

Rumer let go of the bed and spread her ass open for Nahmir who was already rocking in and out of her tight walls. She moaned as she felt pressure like never before in her stomach.

"Oh fuck! It's so deep!" she whined.

Nahmir nodded while pumping into her.

"I know, now you gotta cum. You hear me? Cum on this dick with your sexy ass!" he demanded and slapped her bottom.

Nahmir pumped into Rumer at a fast, hard pace and within minutes her body fell apart for him.

Stark white walls with black desks, stale coffee, and desolated spirits was the ambience. The glare from the police officer wasn't lost on her. Neither was the lusty look his partner kept giving her.

Rumer rocked her leg as she clutched her purse tightly in her lap. She glanced down at her phone and saw she had another text from Tennille. Rumer smiled as she opened the message.

I miss you, Rumer. So, does daddy.

Rumer smiled harder as she text her back.

I miss you two so much! I'll be back soon.

"Let's go," Kritt said with a grunt.

Rumer's smile fell as she glanced up at him. She put her phone away and frowned.

"And hi to you too. Don't give me your fucking attitude," she quipped standing up.

Kritt waved her off and grabbed her hand. He led Rumer out of the jail and she pulled her hand away from his once they were outside. Kritt's eyes ventured around the lot and he frowned.

"Fuck your car at?"

Rumer swallowed hard.

"......Lately I've been using a driver. It was a gift. Come on!" she replied and walked towards the sleek white Phantom.

"A gift from who?"

Rumer got inside of the car and thanked the driver. She shot off Kritt's address and the driver slowly pulled away. Rumer turned to Kritt and his grey eyes bored into her as he glared her way. On his jaw were long ugly scratches while his bottom lip was busted. Handsome still he looked tired. Rumer rubbed his hand and his jaw relaxed.

"You been creeping behind my back and fucking with old boy huh? Never took you as the gold-digging type," he quipped.

Rumer stopped rubbing Kritt's hand and faced forward. Just months ago, he was her Kritt. Yes, she was fearful of what people would think to publicly be with him but still, she loved him. Now things were so different.

"He's good to me Kritt."

Kritt nodded. He rubbed his jaw as he frowned at her.

"Does he love you like I do? Who been there for you from the start? Damn sure hasn't been him."

Rumer's head snapped his way.

"And it damn sure hasn't been you! You've been too busy fucking and fighting your illiterate ass baby momma! Don't even pretend things are the same. You know they aren't," she replied.

Kritt's fists balled up.

"My baby momma is mad cause I don't wanna be with her. She mad because she wants me while I want you. All I ever fucking do is wait on you, Rumer. Got damn! You didn't say shit about going to Africa and finding somebody. It's either me or him. You fucking playing games now and I don't have time for this bullshit," Kritt snapped with his nose flaring.

Rumer turned to Kritt and grabbed his hands. When she stared into his grey irises, she was flooded with the good memories they shared. She loved him no matter what and prayed when it was all said and done, he still possessed some type of love for her.

"You started out my friend then my lover. We never had that brother, sister connection but maybe it's time for that. I was always so lost Kritt. I never had any real love for myself and like I told you before Africa changed me. My therapy opened my eyes. I was able to fall in love with Rumer and that had nothing to do with Nahmir. However, I did meet him there and the things I feel for him are very fucking real," Rumer stopped talking and swallowed hard. "I love you Kritt but I'm not in love with you. I'm falling in love with Nahmir and he is who I want to be with. I'm sorry," she apologized.

Kritt stared at Rumer until his eyes watered. The driver soon pulled up to his home and Kritt let Rumer's hand go. He cleared his throat as he pulled his house keys out of his pocket. He turned towards the window and Rumer watched him discreetly wipe his eyes. He nodded as his chest heaved up and down.

Kritt finally turned to Rumer and bored a glare into her that was enough to make her hold her breath.

"All my shit that's at your place just throw it out. You be good," he said and exited the car.

Rumer's eyes watered as she watched him rush up his steps. She wanted to go after him, but she didn't. That would only lead him on when she knew in her heart that she wanted to be with Nahmir.

Kritt just wasn't the man for her and Rumer now understood that it was never meant for him to be that. She appreciated the process and was trusting God's plan that he had for her life. If something didn't feel right, then it was probably because it wasn't right for you. For years she'd been battling with being with Kritt. It wasn't until that moment that she saw the truth.

He was in her life for that season and to be her brother. Nothing more and trying to force it would only hold her back in the end. Rumer was done with being unhappy. If something or someone wasn't adding good vibes to her life, then she had no room for it.

It was as simple as that.

She wiped her tears as the car pulled away. She loved Kritt, but the reality was she loved herself more. If Kritt loved her like he claimed he did then he would understand that. Rumer was finally putting herself first and was unapologetic about it.

Fifteen

Old-school feel-good music blasted from the speakers in the store. The layout was her most favorite one yet. Mannequins dressed in stylish second-hand designer threads decorated the first and second floor.

Purses and shoes lined the left wall downstairs while the dressing room and coffee station sat on the second floor. Miko had gone to college with a local coffee entrepreneur and was looking to not only give her college friend a clientele but also bring more business to her store. With the camera crews around she looked like a million bucks in her tailored designer pantsuit. A black fedora sat on her head as Saint Laurent heels covered her feet.

Miko rubbed at her upset stomach as she watched people shop around her third store. This was huge for her and even better for Enika and her new baby. Regardless of the hectic life she had her bank account was growing and that was a blessing. Miko didn't take anything for granted. She only wanted to give her kids the life she didn't have.

"Your publicist wants you to speak real quick," Zyir said walking up.

Miko looked at him and nodded. Zyir was looking sexy as shit in his logo button up that he'd paired with Balmain jeans and retro Jordan's. With a fresh haircut and neat line-up, he had Miko wanting to sneak off into the backroom with him and get one off real quick.

Miko gave him a quick kiss before walking over to the center of the room. Her eyes ventured around for Enika and she sighed when she couldn't find her. Since she'd been back from Vegas, Miko had begun counseling but was still struggling with raising Enika. Enika seemed to fight her at every turn and Miko was passed worried. She wasn't sure what she could do to get Enika back on track.

Miko's publicist held her hand in the air and smiled.

"Nanmiko we have a surprise for you. Are you ready?"

Miko smiled nervously. She was clueless as to what was going on.

"Sure," she replied, and her publicist smiled giddily.

"Enika, she's ready for you!"

Miko inhaled and her eyes connected with Zyir. He shrugged as he stood next to Miko's mother. Miko looked towards the stairs and Enika walked down like a supermodel in training. From head to toe, she wore Chanel. Chanel that Miko paid for with her hard-earned money. Enika's hair was flat ironed straight with a part down the middle. She smiled brightly as she clutched Dorian's hand.

Miko sighed and crossed her arms in front of herself. She looked to her left and saw Rumer had walked up along with Jerzey. Nelly was back out of the country with her family.

"I'm telling you she needs a fucking whooping," Rumer hissed loosening her Gucci belt.

Miko shook her head while holding a small smile on her pretty face. Enika walked up with Dorian and she smiled as they neared Miko.

"This place is really nice Miko!" she said, and everyone clapped in agreement. Enika grinned as she glanced around the space. She looked back at Miko and cleared her throat. "I also think it's important to let people know who Nanmiko *really* is. So, Dorian and I can clarify that for everyone," Enika said and let Dorian's hand go.

"Aye, let's go," Zyir said to Enika stepping up.

Enika looked at Zyir and held her hand in the air.

"In just a second. See everyone this is my father. For years I thought he was just one of the men my mom who is *Miko*, that I thought was my sister loves to fuck. See she's a little loose with it," Enika said causing for a few people to gasp.

Jerzey's jaw fell as Miko's eyes watered. Zyir went to grab Enika and Miko grabbed his arm.

"Let her talk. Clearly, this is what she needs to do, her and Dorian so let them finish," Miko told him.

Enika looked at Miko and narrowed her eyes. behind Enika's slanted eyes was pure hate. Hate Miko just couldn't understand still she took it. She was willing to take everything Enika threw her way.

"Thank you, Miko. Like I was saying this is what she's good at everyone. Opening stores and ruining lives. Like she ruined mine and Dorian. Zyir was with Dorian for years. Even wanted to marry her and what did Miko do? She got pregnant by him. Oops," Enika stopped talking and laughed. "I mean pregnant by him again. Did I mention she hid me from him as well for years? He's my daddy and I didn't learn the truth until earlier this year when I was almost taken. See this is what Miko does. She's selfish and conniving and we refuse to watch her ruin anyone else's life. This bitch needs to—ow! *Okay*, auntie Rumer, stop!" Enika yelled.

Rumer moved swiftly and with purpose. Her thin leather belt hit Enika anywhere that it could as Zyir took Dorian to the closest exit. People gasped in shock as Miko stood by idly in shock as well at what was transpiring.

"Nah, your little ass needs this shit!" Rumer yelled swinging the belt harder at Enika's legs.

Enika jumped, even ran from Rumer but Rumer made sure to stay on her ass. Swatting away at Enika's legs, butt even her back.

She didn't give a damn.

"Enough!" Miko yelled at the top of her lungs. Everyone looked her way and her tears clouded her vision. She blinked, and a few tears escaped her lids. She wiped her face and looked at everyone inside of her store. "I would like to thank everyone for coming. The store is now closed," she said as calmly as she could.

People moved quickly to exit the chaos. Miko turned around and slowly moved towards the stairs. Her stomach held a cramp in it that made her face writhe in pain. She took the top step and Enika grabbed her arm angrily. Enika snatched her back and Miko lost her footing. She fell back and Enika quickly moved out of the way. Zyir jogged over to Miko as her back collided with the hard floor. He quickly picked her up and Miko struggled to catch her breath.

She was winded and in a lot of pain.

"Zyir.... baby...," she whispered.

"If you don't sit your ass down somewhere, I swear I'ma hurt you!" Jerzey gritted out to a shaken up Enika.

Enika's eyes watered.

"She's bleeding, is she okay?" Enika asked worriedly.

Everyone looked to Miko and slowly her cream pants darkened in the center. Her dark blood stained the material rapidly and Miko sighed. She patted Zyir's arms and smiled weakly up at him.

"Take me to the hospital baby," she said and Zyir's eyes watered over.

He swallowed hard at her words.

"I'ma shoot her to the ER so we can check on the baby. Enika go with your grandma."

Rumer shook her head while glaring at Enika.

"She can come with me and Jerzey," she spoke up.

Enika cowered under Rumer's glare and rushed over to her grandmother.

"I'll just go with her," Enika said meekly and hugged her grandmother's side.

Zyir shrugged as he headed for the door.

"Aye, y'all should come with me then," he said to Rumer and Jerzey.

Jerzey and Rumer nodded and followed Zyir out of the store.

The wind blew hard as the sun beamed down onto them. The waves crashing into the shore was something she could never grow tired of hearing. Miko was working on two hours of sleep yet she smiled wide as she held the recorder. Venice beach was one of her favorite places and to see Enika love it as much as she did, did something to her.

Miko shook off her hangover and ended the recording. Enika got down from her horse and ran over to Miko. The diamond tiara still adorned her small head. She was tall for eight but hell Miko had been the same way at that age.

Miko kissed her forehead and they went over to the blanket. Miko sat with her legs crossed and the wind whipped through her hair. She stared at Enika in awe like she often did whenever she was around her.

"I love you princess Enika."

Enika blushed. She grabbed a glass of sparkling water and smiled.

"I love you too! So much and happy birthday too!"

Miko waved her off. Her birthdays didn't matter anymore. They hadn't since Enika had come into the world.

"Girl it's all about you. Can I get a hug?" she asked becoming emotional.

Enika giggled. She rushed over to Miko and Miko turned her around. Miko wrapped the blanket around them and together they gazed at the ocean. Miko's heart warmed as she rocked them from side to side. She'd taken Enika to Rodeo Drive. Had spent over $20,000 on her and it still didn't feel like it was enough. Nothing she did for Enika was ever enough. She carried the guilt of lying to her on her heart daily.

Miko thought of the sung she often sang Enika at night when she was a baby and she smiled. Her parents had done a great job at raising Enika but even as a baby Enika would only calm down for Miko. So Miko would get out of her bed and trample down the hallway to Enika. She'd rock her until she was asleep whenever her daughter caught a case of the cries.

"My sunshine, my little sunshine. You make me happy when skies are grey. You never know Enika, how much I love you, please don't take my sunshine away," she sung.

Miko's happy tears flowed down her face and Enika sniffled.

"Forever will I love you. Forever I will care, forever will I be your backbone even when I'm not near. You are my most prized possession Enika, the one good thing I have

in the world. My love, my heart, my precious baby girl,"
Miko whispered.

Enika began to lightly snore and Miko snickered.
They'd partied so hard that she was tired. Miko kissed her
soft hair and sighed.

"Happy birthday baby. Mommy loves you so much,"
she said lowly and watched the waves brush up against the
shore.

The room was exceptionally warm with a pumpkin
scent wafting through the air. The burnt orange sofas faced
one another as a coffee colored desk sat in the back of the
room. In front of Miko was her therapist. The session was
ending and today was special for Miko because it was her
mother's birthday. She hadn't bought her mother a gift in
years but today she planned on going all out. Miko was
trying with all of her might to break every chain that had
been placed on her and her family.

"How do you feel about the miscarriage?"

Miko licked her lips. Rumer was right therapy really
worked. To tell someone your fears hopes even dreams and
not have them judge you was freeing. She didn't see herself
canceling her therapy anytime soon.

Miko rubbed her abdomen and looked up at her
therapist.

"Sad but more so for Zyir. He really wanted this baby. I don't like to disappoint him," Miko admitted.

The therapist nodded.

"You can still have kids, right?"

Miko smiled.

"Yes, but to lose a kid has me scared to try again. I ended up needing a blood transfusion. I'm anemic so to lose so much blood nearly killed me."

"And what about Enika, how did all of this affect her?" she asked.

Miko fiddled with her coffee cup. Enika was surprisingly nice. Miko, however, wasn't sure if it was an act or genuine.

"She's been sweeter lately. I was worried before the loss of the baby. I had given up on raising her in a sense. I was just letting her set the rules but being in that hospital woke me up. I love that girl. I'd give my life for her and she knows that. I refuse to let her run shit else like she's the boss because she's not. That shit is dead," Miko said and shook her head.

The therapist smiled at her.

"I believe you. I would also love to see her in some of the sessions. Can you bring her next time?" she asked.

Miko sat up and smiled at her therapist.

"I definitely can do that," she replied before leaving the room.

After setting up a follow-up appointment Miko rushed to her parents' home. When she spotted Zyir's Jag truck and her cousins Mercedes in the driveway she smiled. Miko was thankful to be alive.

Miko grabbed her mother's gifts out of her trunk before going into the house. The sweet sounds of Otis Redding greeted Miko as she walked through the door. Miko sniffed the air and frowned.

"How is she gone cook on her birthday?" she asked slipping off her heels.

"Hey..." Peyton said walking up.

Miko looked at her cousin and smiled. Peyton looked good and she was actually glad to see her. Miko stepped forward and pulled her into a warm embrace.

"Hey! You look good," Miko told her.

Peyton fell into Miko's embrace and hugged her tightly. She closed her eyes and began to cry.

"I'm so sorry. I'm sorry Miko," Peyton apologized weakly. Miko rubbed her back and she continued to cry. "I didn't know he was raping you then when I found out I was scared to say something, but I eventually did. I was just a kid, but it was wrong to even wait. Please forgive me because you didn't deserve that," Peyton said into her blouse.

Miko took a deep breath and closed her eyes.

"It's fine. It took me a long time but I'm past it. Let's move on Peyton. I swear I'm getting better with each day that passes. Yes, he raped me for years, but it didn't break me. I'm still standing and I'm sorry for lashing out at you because you didn't make him do that. I love you," Miko told her.

When Miko opened her eyes Enika stood at the top of the steps. Enika gave Miko a small wave before rushing down the steps and into the dining room. Miko let go of her cousin and smiled at her.

"It's cool Peyton, you okay?"

Peyton nodded and hugged Miko again.

"I'm good and I'm sorry to hear about your baby. How are you doing?"

Miko sighed. She appreciated the comfort, but she hated when people asked her that. How was she supposed to be doing? Of course she was hurting.

"I'm okay," she replied quietly.

Miko took off her leather jacket and placed her mother's gifts in the dining room. She found her mother in the kitchen cooking alongside Zyir's mother. Both women turned to Miko and she smiled at them. For so long she'd fought to be her loud, obnoxious self. She ran from anything that made her face her past or attempted to slow her down. Including Zyir and her love for him yet it had been in her face all along. He was where she belonged. His family was her family and she was done with running.

Miko had no more time for that shit. All it had done was wasted years of her life that she could never get back.

"How are you cooking on your birthday, momma?"

Miko's mother smiled. Lately, she'd been showing all of her pretty white teeth. It was a look Miko could grow used to seeing on her.

"Zoya was actually doing the cooking. She said she learned some Japanese dishes just for me. It looks really good too!" her mother said smiling.

Miko gave both women quick hugs before looking at the food. Miko's mother rubbed her back as she gazed her way.

"How did your session go?"

Miko cleared her throat. Between planning the dinner party for her mom and working she hadn't had much time to recover from her miscarriage.

"It was cool. I really enjoy going. I'm thinking of taking Enika with me next time," she replied.

"Taking me where?" Enika asked stepping into the kitchen.

Everyone looked to Enika and Zyir's mom cocked her head to the side.

"Is that how you properly interrupt adults, young lady?" Zoya asked.

Enika straightened her back and quickly shook her head.

"I'm sorry. Excuse me but take me where?" she asked again.

Miko held in her grin as she looked at Enika. Everyone including Enika knew Zyir's mom didn't play that disrespect.

"To therapy with me."

Enika nodded. She glanced down at the ground before up at Miko.

"Can I think about it?" she asked.

Zoya shook her head.

"No, it seems like you've done enough on your own. Now it's time for you to be the child again. If your mom wants you to go then you're going. Okay?" she asked. Enika nodded promptly and Zoya sighed. "And what do you have to say to your mother for your behavior?" she asked her.

Enika swallowed hard. She opened her mouth to speak and Miko held her hand in the air.

"It's fine. Let me go make sure everyone is seated. I'm super hungry," she said and walked away.

Call it crazy but Miko didn't want another apology from Enika unless it was genuine. She wanted the bond that they once possessed and was determined to get it back.

Miko found her family and friends in the dining room chilling. She grinned when she spotted Jerzey sitting beside Peyton. Miko looked at them and laughed.

"Look don't try to steal back my best friend!" Miko said to Peyton only half joking.

Peyton laughed while waving her off.

"She was mine first heifer!"

Miko laughed harder and went over to her dad. He was in his wheelchair reading the paper. One of his favorite past times. He looked handsome and surprisingly healthier to Miko. She'd been sending over all of the help he needed and almost overnight his health had improved. His eyes widened with happiness as he stared up at her.

"Nanmiko, baby," he said sitting the paper down.

Miko smiled warmly at him and leaned down. She kissed both of his cheeks and slid him some cigars. Something he loved to do before his accident. Her father stared at the Cohiba Behike cigar box that sat discreetly on his lap.

"When *okaasan* is asleep," Miko said and winked at him.

Her father chuckled before nodding.

"Yes, when she's asleep," he murmured with humor in his baritone voice.

Miko went to her seat and Zyir glanced up at her. Her usual charming, happy Zyir had been sad lately. The baby passing away hurt him, much more than it hurt her. However, if Zyir was hurting then Miko was too. She hated for the people she loved to be in any kind of pain. Miko rubbed his back lovingly and she watched him stare at her stomach.

In her heart she knew that eventually, he would want to try again and when that time came, she prayed she could make it happen.

"Now that the birthday girl is here, I just wanted to make a speech really quick," Miko said as her mother along with Zyir's mom took a seat.

Enika sat quietly across the table from Miko with her eyes on her. Miko smiled at Enika before turning her attention to her mom.

"I went to Neiman's even Barney's when I was in New York last week picking up Jerzey and I kind of went crazy grabbing you some stuff. I mean you have the body that we all inspire to have at your age, so I played off that. But when I woke up this morning it hit me. You have always been about love and the perfect gift for you would have to come from the heart. So, I give you and papa this. Happy Birthday," Miko said and pulled a paper from her back pocket.

She walked over to her mother and unfolded it. Miko handed her mother the paper as she bent down, and her mom quickly read over it. Everyone at the table looked on with big smiles on their faces.

"It's roundtrip tickets back home. I bought you two an apartment there. I hope you like it," Miko said teary-eyed.

Miko's mother stared at the paper for a moment before looking at Miko. She grabbed her face and kissed her forehead before kissing both of her cheeks.

"Thank you so much Nanmiko. I never thought I would be able to go back," she said and pulled Miko into her arms.

Miko's mother Kawai began to cry and Miko rubbed her back. It had been the best money she'd ever spent. It had put a dent in one of her savings, but it had been worth it.

"Anything for you. I'm sorry," Miko whispered.

Miko cried into her mother's blouse and once she'd collected herself, she pulled herself together. She went back to her seat and they prayed over the food. After singing Happy Birthday and giving Kawai her gifts, the younger adults retreated to the basement while the older crowd stayed upstairs.

While Jerzey and Peyton caught up some more Miko rested against Zyir's chest. Zyir kicked it with Snowden who Miko was happy to see he got along with.

"Can I talk to you upstairs?" Enika asked walking up.

Miko looked up at her and Zyir stopped talking to gaze her way.

"You good?" he asked.

Enika nodded. She smiled and peered down at Miko.

"Yes, I just wanted to talk with my mom," she replied politely.

Miko's surprised eyes shot to Zyir. He shrugged and pulled her closer to him.

"If you need me just stomp on the floor three times," he jested.

Miko snickered and stood up. She followed Enika up the stairs and into the kitchen. Miko sat at the island as Enika stood nervously before her. Enika paced the floor quietly for a few minutes before looking at Miko.

"I remember everything. When I was seven you took me to Disney World. It was like a dream. Matter of fact I think Paris topped that but my best memories of you was when you would help me with my homework. You even took care of me when I was sick. If I got scared of a movie, you'd sleep in the bed with me and when I was asleep," Enika stopped talking and her eyes watered. "When you *thought* I was asleep you would call me your daughter. You would tell me how sorry you was and that you loved me. I was so scared that I never said anything. I didn't know what you meant but when you did it the last time, I knew. I could feel it in my heart that you was my mother...." Enika closed her eyes as her thin body shook.

Miko stood up and walked up on her. She pulled Enika into her arms and hugged her tightly.

"I'm so sorry. It's hard and I know I messed up. I made you lose the baby because I was hurting and jealous," Enika cried.

325 | P a g e

Miko shook her head.

"What's meant to be will always be Enika. Nothing can change the love I have for you. You will always be my Enika. You know that," Miko told her.

Enika nodded.

"I know, and I've been so awful. Auntie Rumer said I'm Dennis The Menace 2.0," Enika said sadly and Miko smiled at her.

"She loves you. We all do we just expect more. This isn't you but you're hurting so I understand. I just want you to be my happy Enika again," Miko replied.

Enika wiped her face and looked at Miko.

"I do too. I want us to be like we were."

Miko shook her head as she looked at Enika.

"No, we'll be better than we was," Miko promised and hugged her again.

Epilogue

Philly

Four months later

The building in the Northern Liberty part of Center City thumped with excitement. Rap music blasted from the DJ's speaker as the guests mingled with one another while sipping on their free drinks. For his baby, everything was on him. Including the catered food and celebrity DJ.

New freshly painted portraits sat on the colored bricked walls with hefty price tags under them. The woman of the hour stood beside her man looking stylish like always. Draped in a fitted grey blazer that she wore as a dress Jerzey looked sexy as ever. She'd paired the look with her shimmery silver YSL boots and her blunt cut grey lace unit that she wore parted down the middle.

Jerzey's makeup was neutral besides her extra volume lash extensions and Snowden stuck to her side like glue. He looked dapper as well in his black crew neck and black jeans that he wore black Timberlands with. Snowden's jewelry was on *got damn* as the heavy chain flooded with diamonds hung from his neck. On his eyes were a pair of

The Gold Gods shades while a diamond Rolex decorated his wrist.

Snowden licked his lips as he gazed down at Jerzey. Jerzey had to admit they always looked fly but tonight they were on another level. She grinned up at him and he shook his head.

"What?" he asked lowly.

Jerzey shrugged. Snowden just didn't know how fucking fine he was. He also wasn't ashamed to show his love for her. The Philly studio was his gift to her and she'd gladly accepted it. He was back in Philly for good and he wanted his woman there as well. Jerzey would still travel to New York for work and Detroit because that would always be home but trust wherever Snowden was at, she would be at too. They were a unit and they now knew that they were better together than they ever were apart.

"Nothing, I just love this place. It's so nice baby," she told him.

Snowden dropped his head and smiled. Jerzey loved when she made his mean ass blush. She leaned up on her toes and kissed his lips. Snowden grabbed her waist and deepened the kiss before pulling back. He took off his shades and his eyes bored into her.

"I'll do anything to see youse smile ma."

Jerzey nodded because she believed him.

"I know baby," she whispered as she was hugged from the back.

"Jerzey I love this place!" Hailo gushed hugging her.

Jerzey turned to her friend that she'd met through Snowden's boy Waikeem and she hugged her back. Hailo was Waikeem's wife and Jerzey loved her laid-back attitude.

"Thank you for coming!"

Hailo waved her off and gave Snowden a big smile. Her husband walked up and dapped up Snowden before giving Jerzey a pair of a dozen roses.

"Congrats this shit nice," Waikeem told her.

Hailo nodded in agreement with her husband.

"Yes, I'm getting two pictures," she added in and laughed.

Jerzey smiled. It felt good to be surrounded by love. Her girls were all over the world but definitely there with her in spirit and soon she'd link up with them for Rumer's birthday. Something she was looking forward to.

"I'm happy everything turned out good. This man here was like hands-on as hell and I appreciated that. And soon it'll be their big day," Jerzey said and grabbed Snowden's hand.

Snowden was looking to open up a chain of fast food spots with Waikeem while Jerzey and Hailo was looking forward to it.

"Yes, inshallah!" Hailo gushed and hugged Waikeem's side.

Jerzey smiled and Snowden chuckled.

"Y'all be hype as hell I swear. Jerzey, I gotta show youse something though," Snowden said.

Jerzey nodded.

"Excuse us guys," she said before he pulled her away.

Snowden took Jerzey into the bathroom upstairs and placed her onto the sink. She smiled as he stepped between her legs.

"Give me a kiss sexy," he demanded grabbing her face.

Jerzey giggled as she puckered up her lips. She kissed Snowden passionately and moaned when his thick finger brushed against the thin cotton clothing her vagina. Snowden moved her thongs to the side as he stared into her eyes. Snowden pulled out his dick and pulled back from the kiss as he probed it at her opening.

"Thank you for forgiving me. Shit for moving here. Youse made the right fucking choice, beautiful."

Jerzey smiled and Snowden slowly pushed himself inside of her.

"I know I did baby. Now fuck me really quick so we can sell them portraits," she demanded, and Snowden chuckled.

He thrust hard into Jerzey and licked his lips.

"I got youse," he said lowly and kissed her lips again.

Across the country in Spain...

The luxury villa housed a whopping three floors, six bedrooms, and five bathrooms. It faced the Mija's mountain and was breathtaking to look at. The happy family occupied the second floor. As Nelly rested with her baby girl Anisah Grace.

"Say, a-p-p-l-e," Jannero said slowly.

Jasir smiled. He pushed the flashcard away and looked at his father.

"A---a—a-aple," Jasir stuttered.

Jannero grinned at him like a proud father and kissed his forehead.

"I love you boy," he said and kissed his forehead again.

Jasir smiled and began to play with his toys. After being evaluated at one of the best special education centers in the states Jasir was diagnosed with high functioning autism. Jannero and Nelly were devoted to getting Jasir as far ahead in life as he could get. Autism or not they would see to it that he would reach his full potential.

"His classes is working already," Jannero said joining Nelly on the sofa.

Nelly nodded with her eyes on her son.

"Yes, I just want him to be great. I hate the way the world treats people with special needs. I swear if anybody tries to bully my baby so help me I'ma fucking make the news."

Jannero nodded. He kissed Nelly's cheek and grabbed their daughter from her arms. He gazed down at the baby and sighed.

"He gone be good Nelly. Mothers tend to overthink and I'm not ragging on you, just know he's alright. How you feeling?"

Nelly looked at her husband and smiled. In a few weeks, she'd be back in the states without her husband and that made her sad, but she had business to tend to in Detroit along with Rumer's party. Still, she wished her man could come along. However, he had work as well and so far, Jannero was the biggest NBA star Spain had ever seen.

Everyone loved him and already the state teams were fighting over who would have him next.

"I'm good. Nervous about traveling with them and not you. I don't wanna leave you, baby," she whined.

Jannero leaned forward and kissed her lips.

"Me too but you'll be back. Just call me if you need me and you know I'm dropping everything to get to you."

Nelly smiled at him. She caressed his hairy cheek and licked her lips.

"Promise?"

Jannero nodded.

"Any fucking thing for you beautiful," he replied before passionately attacking her lips again.

Back in the states in Detroit....

The auditorium was filled to capacity with people. In anticipation, everyone sat quietly with the recital programs in their lap. Soon the curtains drew back and the tall, modelesque young woman took the stage. She sat at the piano and with ease began to play.

Les Misérables (I Dreamed A Dream) began to play and Miko clutched his hand tightly. Beside Miko was her mother then Enika's other grandmother. Like a pro Enika slaughtered the classic song. She then went on to play

Beethoven "Moonlight Sonata". Once Enika was done Miko's eyes were flooded with tears. Everyone stood up and clapped hard as she rose from her seat.

Clothed in a knee-length black dress with ballet flats and a sleek ponytail to the back she looked classically beautiful.

Enika bowed before exiting the stage.

After the recital, everyone retreated to the Flemings Steak House in Livonia. Miko held Enika close to her as she smiled like a proud momma. Motherhood wasn't easy. Some days Miko would think she had it figured out then she'd wake up and realize that she had to revise another plan because shit wasn't working then by the end of the day her worries would be no more. Enika was making huge strides to show she was looking to be better and had even taken a few therapy sessions. Miko still attended not ready to let her seat on the comfy couch go just yet.

"You killed it, baby," Miko gushed.

Enika smiled and hid her face in Miko's black blouse.

"Don't be playing shy. You know you did good," Zoya told Enika.

Everyone laughed and Zyir cleared his throat. Enika sat up as Miko turned to him. Zyir was now down on one knee with a lollipop ring in his hand. Miko peered down at the half-eaten ring pop and rolled her eyes.

"Really, just like the old days huh?" she asked.

Zyir nodded. He licked his full lips and cleared his throat. His nervousness showed on his handsome face as he stared at Miko.

"This was your daughter's idea. I was gone ask you last night when you was washing the dishes," he cracked.

Miko playfully hit his arm and he shook his head.

"Nah but for real, I won't go into a long speech. I have to know though if the most beautiful woman in the world will marry me?" he asked.

Miko nodded while giving him a watery gaze.

"What you think, negro?" she asked and Enika clapped loudly.

"Yes! Daddy that means yes," she said making Zyir smile.

Miko tried to grab the ring pop and Zyir pulled a velvet box out of his left pocket. He opened it up and revealed a stunning solitaire diamond.

"It's beautiful," Miko whispered and Zyir pulled the ring out.

He placed the diamond on her ring finger and peered up into her eyes.

"Nah, it ain't got shit on you. Now give me a kiss," he said and Miko happily obliged.

A week later in Miami...

The dress code was black while the birthday girl wore a gold sequined Versace dress. The extensions she wore hung past her ample ass while her face was beat to perfection. No one could think of a time when she'd looked so good. A thick 225 pounds Rumer stood like a stallion in her six-inch-pumps. While she didn't count calories, she now worked out regularly with her trainer, so her body was toned but make no mistakes about it she wasn't a skinny girl and never would be again.

Rumer was simply Rumer.

"You look so fucking good, bitch!" Jerzey squealed running up on Rumer.

Rumer stood up and hugged her girl tightly. It meant a lot that everyone was able to drop what they were doing and show up for her. The only person not in attendance was Kritt. Sadly, after deciding to be with Nahmir, Kritt stopped fucking with Rumer. He even went as far as changing his number on her.

Rumer missed Kritt dearly but refused to give up what she now had, to have him back in her life. She wished him well but was moving on with her life. Even if that meant he was no longer in it.

"Thank you and look who's talking. You looking good too," Rumer told her.

Jerzey smiled and waved her off. Snowden gave Rumer a quick embrace before walking off. Rumer grinned at Jerzey and Jerzey rolled her eyes.

"What heifer?" Jerzey asked.

Rumer shrugged. She loved the glow that covered Jerzey's chunky face. What Rumer always loved about Jerzey was that she owned her weight. Rumer was now at that stage in life and it felt good to love the skin you were in. It felt good to be able to look in the mirror and smile at what stared back at you. So, what she wasn't thin anymore? She loved herself and that was priceless, she'd take that over being small any day of the week.

"Oh nothing. You just looking all happy and shit," Rumer quipped.

Jerzey playfully slapped Rumer's ass.

"That's because I am. This is what happiness looks like. Now smile *bitch*! Smile!" Jerzey replied and they both laughed loudly before high fiving.

"I know that's right," Rumer said as Miko and Nelly walked up both wearing black sexy dresses for the occasion.

Drake's **No New Friends** began to play lowly inside of the restaurant and Rumer along with her girls all got hype. The restaurant for the night belonged to Rumer and her entourage. Rumer and her friends began to dance playfully to the song while rapping the lyrics. On their faces showed real joy. The kind money couldn't buy. They'd been through the worst storm of their lives and had come out alive. They were grateful for Gods mercy that he'd shown on them. They knew a lot of people wasn't always so lucky to make it through.

> *No new friends, no new friends, no new friends, no, no new*
> *Still here with my day one niggas, so you hear me say*
> *No new friends, no new friends, no new friends, no, no new*
> *(Let's ride)*
> *I still ride with my day one niggas, I don't really need*

"No new friends!" Rumer yelled dancing up on Miko.

Miko hugged her from the back and the photographer began to snap photos of the foursome. Nahmir walked up in a custom grey two-piece suit. His whiskey hued eyes stared intently at Rumer as he smiled down at her.

Like always his presence demanded attention. Miko bumped Rumer and looked at Nahmir. Nahmir held out his hand and Rumer stood up straight. She smoothed out her birthday gown and walked up on him.

"Hey baby," she said giving him a goofy grin.

Nahmir chuckled. He leaned down and kissed her lips tenderly. Life had been hella good for them and Nahmir was in the process of moving back to Detroit with his daughter.

"You know how much I love you?" he asked holding onto her waist.

Rumer giggled and nodded. Nahmir made her feel like fairytales were real. Like all of the love you heard about did exist because he loved her that much plus more. He was thoughtful, attentive, and good to her. Yes, he had his moments, he worked more than she did and was demanding as hell at times, but it wasn't deal-breaker issues. He loved her flaws and all and she felt the same way.

He was her equal.

"Close your eyes for me beautiful," he instructed before pulling her away.

Rumer's heart thundered in her chest. She held on tightly to Nahmir's hand as he took her out of the restaurant. The warm Miami weather brushed against her skin and she heard everyone gasp. Rumer's heart rate spiked as she prepared herself for what the surprise could be.

"Happy birthday to the sexiest, most loving, hardest working woman I know. To nothing but good shit, and this only the first gift I got to give you," he whispered and kissed her neck.

Rumer's eyes adjusted to the bright lights that lit up Collins Ave. She looked at the white on white Lamborghini Urus truck. Rumer's knees buckled, and she squealed. She rushed over to the truck and like she was a sixteen-year-old getting her first car she pulled the door open and excitedly peered inside of it.

Miko, Jerzey, and Nelly got inside of the truck with Rumer and Rumer smiled at her girls.

"My baby did good y'all," she gushed.

Miko smacked her lips.

"Good? He did spectacular bitch!" Miko raved.

Everyone laughed and Nahmir peered his head into the truck. He looked at Rumer and she sighed. Rumer didn't know when, where or how long it would take but he would be her husband. She could see them building an empire together, something they were already working towards with their joint real-estate company in the works and it made her tear up. At the worst time in her life, she found the best thing that ever happened to her.

How insane was that?

"I love you Nahmir Yaasmin," she whispered.

Nahmir smirked at her.

"I love you too mami," he whispered before he grabbed her face and kissed her so hard, he took her breath away.

The End.

Book Discussions

1. Did part two end like you thought it would?

2. Were you happy to see Jerzey end up with Snowden?

3. Do you feel like Nero was stupid for forgiving Nelly?

4. Should Rumer have forgiven Kritt?

5. Do you think Miko deserved the way Enika treated her?

6. Which friend was your favorite?

7. Which friend do you think went through the most?

CPSIA information can be obtained
at www.ICGtesting.com
Printed in the USA
LVHW082006010219
606097LV00016B/512/P

9 781793 496881